The Tangled Skein

Baroness Emmuska Orczy

The Tangled Skein

The present edition is a reproduction of previous publication of this classic work. Minor typographical errors may have been corrected without note, however, for an authentic reading experience the spelling, punctuation, and capitalization have been retained from the original text.

ISBN: 978-1-64799-137-1

CONTENTS

PART I MIRRAB—THE WITCH

PART II THE LADY URSULA

PART III A GAME OF CHESS

PART IV HIS GRACE OF WESSEX

PART I

MIRRAB—THE WITCH

CHAPTER I

EAST MOLESEY FAIR

Even Noailles, in his letters to his royal master, admits that the weather was glorious, and that the climatic conditions left nothing to be desired.

Even Noailles! Noailles, who detested England as the land of humid atmospheres and ill-dressed women!

Renard, who was more of a diplomatist and kept his opinions on the fogs and wenches of Old England very much to himself, declared enthusiastically in his letter to the Emperor Charles V, dated October 2nd, 1553, that never had he seen the sky so blue, the sun so bright, nor the people of this barbarous island more merry than on the memorable first day of East Molesey Fair: as all who will, may read for themselves in Vol. III of the Granvelle Papers:—

"Aulcungs ne pourroient contempler ciel plus bleu soleil plus brilliant ni peuple plus joieult."

Yet what have we to do with the opinions of these noble ambassadors of great and mighty foreign monarchs?

Our own chroniclers tell us that East Molesey Fair was the maddest, merriest, happiest time the goodly folk of the Thames Valley had had within memory of the oldest inhabitant.

Was not good Queene Marye, beloved daughter of the great King Henry VIII, crowned at last? crowned in Westminster Abbey, as all her loyal subjects had desired that she should be, despite His Grace of Northumberland and his treasonable faction, whom God and the Queene's most lawful Majesty would punish all in good time?

In the meanwhile let us be joyful and make merry!

Such a motley crowd as never was seen. Here's a sheriff from London City, pompous and dignified in dark doublet and hose, with scarlet mantle and velvet cap; beside him his lady trips right merrily, her damask kirtle held well above her high-heeled shoes, her flowered paniers looped in the latest style, with just the suggestion of a farthingale beneath her robes, to give dignity to her figure and value to the slimness of her waist.

Here a couple of solemn burgesses in velvet cloaks edged with

1

fur, and richly slashed doublets, are discussing the latest political events; whilst a group of Hampton merchants, more soberly clad, appraise the wares of a cutler lately hailed from Spain.

Then the dames and maidens with puffed paniers of blue or vivid scarlet, moving swiftly from booth to booth, babbling like so many gaily-plumaged birds, squabbling with the vendors and chaffing the criers.

Here and there the gaudy uniform of one of the liveried Companies will attract the eye, anon the dark cloak and close black mask which obviously hides the Court gallant.

Men of all ranks and of all stations have come out to East Molesey to-day. Merchants, shopkeepers, workers, aldermen and servants, all with their womenkind, all with pouches more or less well filled, for who would go to Molesey Fair but to spend money, to drink, to eat, or to make merry?

Then there were the 'prentices!

They had no money to spend, save a copper or so to throw to a mountebank, but nevertheless they contrived to enjoy themselves right royally.

Such imps of mischief!

No whipping-post to-day! Full licence for all their pranks and madcap jokes. The torment of all these worthy burgesses out on a holiday.

Oh! these 'prentices!

Hundreds of them out here this afternoon. They've come down from Esher and Hampton, Kingston and Westminster and London City, like so many buzzing insects seeking whom they can annoy.

Now on the ground, suddenly tripping a pompous dame off her feet; anon in rows, some half-dozen of them, elbow to elbow, head foremost, charging the more serious crowd, and with a hoot and a yell scattering it like a number of frightened goslings. Yet again at the confect booth, to the distraction of the vendors of honey-cakes, stealing sugar-plums and damson cheese, fighting, quarrelling, screeching, their thin legs encased in hose of faded blue or grey worsted, their jerkins loose, their shirt sleeves flapping in the breeze, a cool note of white amidst the dark-coloured gowns of the older men.

Heavens above! what a to-do!

A group of women be-coiffed, apparelled in best kirtles and modish shoes, were pressing round a booth where pantoufles, embroidered pouches, kerchiefs, and velveted paniers were laid out in tempting array.

Just beyond, a number of buxom country wenches, with round red arms, showing bare to the grilling sun, and laughing eyes, aglow with ill-concealed gourmandise, were gaping at a mighty display of pullets, hares, and pigeons, sides of roebuck and haunches of wild boar, ready spiked, trussed, and skewered, fit to tempt Her Majesty's Grace's own royal palate.

2

Sprigs of sweet-scented marjoram, thyme, and wool-blade tastefully disposed, further enhanced the attractions of this succulent show. 'Twas enough to make the sweetest mouth water with anticipatory delight. A brown-eyed, apple-cheeked wench in paniers of brilliant red was unaffectedly licking her pretty lips.

"This way, mistress, this way!" shouted the vendor of these appetizing wares. A sturdy fellow, he, with ginger-coloured pate, and wielding a long narrow-bladed knife in his fleshy hand. "This way! a haunch of buck from the royal venery! a hare from Her Liege Majesty's own chase! a pullet from——"

"Nay, thou gorbellied knave!" responded a vendor of drugs and herbs close by, whose stall was somewhat deserted, and whose temper was obviously suffering—"Nay! an thou speakest the truth thou art a thief, but if not, then thou'rt a liar! In either case art fit for the hangman's rope!"

"This way, my masters! this way!" came in loud, stentorian cries from a neighbouring booth; "this way for Peter the juggler, the greatest conjurer the world has ever seen!"

"This way! I pray you, worthy sirs!" this from yet another place of entertainment, "this way for John the tumbler!"

"Peter the juggler will swallow a cross-bow of steel before your very eyes!" shouted one crier.

"John the tumbler will climb Saint Ethelburga's steeple without help of rope or ladder," called the other.

"Peter will show you how to shoe a turkey, how to put salt on a swallow's tail, and how to have your cake and eat it!"

"John will sit on two stools without coming to the ground!"

"Marry! and ye both lie faster than my mule can trot!" came in hilarious accents from one of the crowd.

"And Peter the juggler will show thee how to make thy mule trot faster than thou canst lie, friend," responded Peter's crier unabashed, "and a mighty difficult task 'twill be, I'll warrant."

Laughing, joking, ogling like some fickle jade, the crowd passed from booth to booth: now dropping a few coins in Peter the juggler's hat, now watching the antics of John the tumbler; anon looking on amazed, half terrified at the evolutions of a gigantic brown bear, led by the nose by a vigorous knave in leather jerkin and cross-gartered hose, and accompanied by a youngster who was blowing on a mighty sackbut until his cheeks looked nigh to bursting.

But adsheart! who shall tell of all the attractions which were set forth on that memorable day before the loyal subjects of good Queene Marye?

There were the trestles where one could play at ball and knuckle-bone, or chance and mumchance; another, where evens and odds and backgammon proved tempting. He who willed could tilt at Weekie, play quoits or lansquenet, at ball or at the billiards, or risk his coppers on

3

such games as one-and-thirty, or at the pass ten; he might try his skill, too, at throwing the dart, or his strength at putting the stone.

There were mountebanks and quacksalvers, lapidaries at work, and astrologers in their tents. For twopence one could have a bout with the back-sword or the Spanish tuck, could watch the situations and conjunctions of the fixed stars and the planets, could play a game of tennis or pelitrigone, or be combed and curled, perfumed and trimmed so as to please a dainty mistress's eye.

And through it all the loud bang! bang! bang! of the big drums, the criers proclaiming the qualities of their wares, the jarring notes of the sackbut and the allman flute, the screechy viol and the strident nine-hole pipe, all playing against one another, each striving to drown the other, and mingling with the laughter of the crowd, the yells of the 'prentices, the babble of the women, formed a' huge volume of ear-splitting cacophony which must have been heard from one end of the country to the other.

All was noise, merriment, and laughter, save in one spot—an out-of-the-way, half-hidden corner of the fair, where the sister streams, the Ember and the Mole, join hands for a space, meet but to part again, and whence the distant towers and cupolas of Hampton Court appeared like those of a fairy palace floating in mid-ether, perched high aloft in the shimmering haze of this hot late summer's afternoon.

CHAPTER II

THE WITCH'S TENT

There are many accounts still extant of the various doings at East Molesey Fair on this 2nd of October in the year of our Lord 1553, and several chroniclers—Renard is conspicuous among the latter—make mention of the events which very nearly turned the gay and varying comedies of that day into weird and tragic drama.

Certainly the witch's tent was a mistake.

But what would you? No doubt the worthy individual, who for purposes of mystification called himself "Abra," had tried many means of earning a livelihood before he and his associate in business took to the lucrative, yet dangerous trade of necromancy.

He was tall and gaunt, with hooked nose and deep-sunk eyes; he had cultivated a long, grey beard, and could call forth the powers of Mirrab the Witch with a remarkably solemn and guttural voice.

4

As for Mirrab herself, no one was allowed to see her. That was part of the business. She was a witch, a dealer in magic potions, charms and philters, a reader of the stars, and—softly be it spoken—a friend and companion of the devil! She only appeared enveloped in a thick veil, with divining wand held lightly in her hand, the ends of her gold tresses alone visible below the heavy covering which swathed her head.

It was the mystery of it all—cheap devices at best—which from the first had irritated the country-folk who thronged the Fair.

The tent itself was unlike any other ever seen at East Molesey. It stood high upon a raised wooden platform, to which a few rough steps gave access. On the right was a tall flagstaff, with black flag emblazoned with white skull and cross-bones, fluttering lazily in the breeze.

On the left a huge elm tree, with great heavy branches overshadowing the tent, had been utilized to support a placard bearing the words—

"Mirrab! the World-famed Necromancer!
Sale of Magic Charms and Love Philters
Horoscope Casting and Elixir of Life!"

Perched on the platform, and assisted by a humbler henchman, armed with big drum and cymbals, the worthy Abra, in high-peaked cap and flowing mantle covered with strange devices, had all day long invited customers to his booth by uttering strange, mysterious promises.

"This way, this way, my masters," he would say with imposing solemnity; "the world-famous necromancer, Mirrab, will evoke for you the spirits of Mars, of Saturn, or of the moon."

"She will show you the Grand Grimorium ... !"

Now what was the Grand Grimorium? The very sound of the words suggested some agency of the devil; no Christian man had ever heard or spoken of the Grand Grimorium.

"She will show you the use of the blasting rod and the divining wand. She will call forth the elementary spirits ...."

Some people would try to laugh. Who had ever heard of the elementary spirits? Perhaps if some of the more enlightened town worthies happened to be nigh the booth, one or two of them would begin to chaff the necromancer.

"And prithee, friend wizard," a solemn burgher would suggest, "prithee what are the elementary spirits?"

But Abra was nothing if not ready-witted.

"The elementary spirits," he would explain with imperturbable gravity, "are the green butterfly, the black pullet, the queen of the hairy flies, and the screech owl."

The weird nomenclature was enough to make any one's hair stand on end. Even the sedate burgesses would shake their heads and silently edge away, whilst their womenkind would run swiftly past the

5

booth, muttering a quick Ave to the blessed Virgin or kissing the Holy Scapulary hung beneath their kerchiefs, as their terrified glances met the cabalistic signs on the black flag.

The humbler country-folk frankly spat upon the ground three times whenever they caught sight of the flag, and that is a sure way of sending the devil about his business.

The shadows now were beginning to lengthen.

The towers and cupolas of Hampton Court Palace were studded with gold and gems by the slanting rays of the setting sun.

It had been a glorious afternoon and, except in the open space immediately in front of the witch's tent, the fun of the fair had lost none of its zest.

The witch's booth alone was solitary—weird-looking beneath the spreading branches of the overhanging elm.

The tent seemed lighted from within, for as the evening breeze stirred its hangings, gleams of brilliant red, more glowing than the sunset, appeared in zigzag streaks between its folds.

Behind, and to the right and left of it, the gentle murmur of the sister streams sounded like ghostly whisperings of evening sprites, busy spreading their grey mantles over the distant landscape.

As the afternoon wore on, the crowd in the other parts of the Fair had grown more and more dense, and now, among the plainer garb of the burgesses and townsfolk, and the jerkins and worsted hose of the yokels, could be seen quite frequently a silken doublet or velvet trunk, a masked face perhaps beneath a plumed bonnet, or the point of a sword gleaming beneath the long, dark mantle, denoting the Court gallant.

Now and then, too, hooded and closely swathed forms would flit quickly through the crowd, followed by the inquisitive glances of the humbler folk, as the dainty tip of a broidered shoe or the richly wrought hem of a silken kirtle, protruding below the cloak, betrayed the lady of rank and fashion on gay adventure bent.

Most of these veiled figures had found their way up the rough wooden steps which led to the witch's tent. The fame of Mirrab, the Soothsayer, had reached the purlieus of the palace, and Abra, the magician, had more than once seen his lean palm crossed with gold.

"This way, noble lords! this way!"

He was even now trying to draw the attention of two cloaked figures, who had just emerged in sight of the booth.

Two gentlemen of the Court evidently, for Abra's quick eye had caught a glimpse of richly chased sword-hilts, as the wind blew the heavy, dark mantles to one side.

But these gentlemen were paying little heed to the worthy magician's blandishments. They were whispering excitedly to one another, whilst eagerly scanning the crowd all round them.

"They were ladies from the Court, I feel sure," said the taller man of the two; "I swear I have seen the hem of that kirtle before."

"Carramba!" replied the other, "it promised well, but methinks we've lost track of them now."

He spoke English very fluently, yet with a strong, guttural intonation, whilst the well-known Spanish oath which he uttered betrayed his nationality.

"Pardi!" he added impatiently, "I could have sworn that the damsels were bent on consulting the witch."

"Nay, only on seeing the fun of the Fair apparently," rejoined the other; "we've lain in wait here now for nigh on half an hour."

"Mirrab the Soothsayer will evoke for you the spirits of the moon, oh noble lords!" urged Abra, with ever-increasing persuasiveness. "She will give you the complaisance of the entire female sex."

"What say you, my lord," said the Englishman after a while, "shall we give up the quest after those elusive damsels and woo these obliging spirits of the moon? They say the witch has marvellous powers."

"Bah, milor!" rejoined the Spaniard gaily, "a veiled female! Think on it! Those who have entered yon mysterious tent declare that scarce an outline of that soothsayer could they glean, beneath the folds of thick draperies which hide her from view. What is a shapeless woman? I ask you, milor. And in England, too," he added with affected gallantry which had more than a touch of sarcasm in it, "where all women are shapely."

"Mirrab, the world-famous necromancer, will bring to your arms the lady of your choice, oh most noble lords!" continued the persistent Abra, "even if she were hidden beyond the outermost corners of the earth."

"By my halidame! this decides me," quoth the Englishman merrily. "I pray you come, my lord. This adventure promises better than the other. And, who knows?" he added in his turn with thinly-veiled, pleasant irony, "you Spaniards are so persuasive—the witch, if she be young and fair, might lift her veil for you."

"Allons!" responded the other, "since 'tis your wish, milor, let us consult the spirits."

And, standing aside with the courtly grace peculiar to those of his nationality, he allowed his companion to precede him up the steps which led to Mirrab's tent.

Then he too followed, and laughing and chattering the two men disappeared behind the gaudily painted draperies.

Not, however, without tossing a couple of gold pieces into the hands of the wizard. Abra, obsequious, smiling, thoroughly contented, sat himself down to rest awhile beside his patient, hard-worked henchman.

7

CHAPTER III

MISCHIEF BREWING

At some little distance from the mysterious booth a trestle table had been erected, at which some three or four wenches in hooped paniers and short, striped kirtles, were dispensing spiced ale and sack to the thirsty village folk.

Here it was that Mirrab the witch and her attendant wizard were most freely discussed—with bated breath, and with furtive glances cast hurriedly at the black flag, which was just visible above the row of other booths and gayer attractions of the Fair.

There was no doubt that as the evening began to draw in, and the sun to sink lower and lower in the west, the superstitious terror, which had all along set these worthy country yokels against the awesome mysteries of the necromancer's tent, had gradually culminated into a hysterical frenzy.

At first sullen looks had been cast towards that distant spot, whence the sound of Abra's perpetual "This way, noble lords, this way!" came every now and then as a weird and ghostly echo; but now muttered curses and even a threatening gesture from time to time had taken the place of angry silence.

As the hard pates of these louts became heated with the foaming ale, their tempers began to rise, and the girls, with characteristic love of mischief and gossip, were ready enough to add fuel to the smouldering flames.

There was also present in the minds of these wenches an obvious feeling of jealousy against this mysterious veiled witch, who had proved so attractive to the Court gallants who visited the Fair.

Her supposed charms so carefully hidden beneath thick draperies, were reputed to be irresistible, and Mistress Dorothy, Susan, and Joan, who showed their own pretty faces unblushingly, were not sufficiently versed in mountebanks' tricks to realize that Mirrab's thick veil was, without doubt, only a means for arousing the jaded curiosity of idlers from the Court.

Be that as it may, it was an established fact that no one had seen the soothsayer's face, and that Mistress Dorothy, who was pouring out a huge tankard of sack for her own attendant swain, was exceedingly annoyed thereby.

"Bah!" she said contemptuously, as Abra and his magic devices were being discussed at the table, "he is but a lout. I tell thee, Matthew, that thou'rt a fool to take count of him. But the woman," she added under her breath, "is possessed of the devil."

Matthew, the shoemaker, took the tankard, which his sweetheart had filled for him, in both hands and took a long draught before he made any reply. Then he wiped his mouth with the back of his hand, spat upon the ground, and looked significantly at the circle of friends who were gathered round him.

"I tell you, my masters," he said at last with due solemnity, "that I saw that witch last night fly out from yonder tree astride upon a giant bat."

"A bat?"

A holy shudder went round the entire assembly. Pretty Mistress Susan crossed herself furtively, whilst Joan in her terror nearly dropped the handful of mugs which she was carrying.

Every one hung on the shoemaker's lips.

Short and somewhat tubby of body, Matthew had a round and chubby face, with pale blue, bulging eyes, and slightly elevated eyebrows, which gave him the appearance of an overgrown baby. He was for some reason, which has never transpired to this day, reputed to have wonderful wisdom. His items of news, gleaned from a nephew who was scullion in the royal kitchen, were always received with boundless respect, whilst the connection itself gave him a certain social superiority of which he was proudly conscious.

Like the true-born orator, Matthew had paused a moment in order to allow the full strength of his utterance to sink into the minds of his hearers.

"Aye!" he said after a while, "she flew out from between the branches and up towards the full moon, clad only——"

A brusque movement and a blush from Mistress Dorothy here stopped the graphic flow of his eloquence.

"Er—hem—!" he concluded more tamely, "I saw her quite plainly."

"More shame then on thee, master," retorted Dorothy, whose wrath was far from subsiding, "for thus gazing on the devil's work."

But the matter had become of far too great import to allow of feminine jealousies being taken into account.

"And I know," added an elderly matron with quaking voice, "that my sister Hannah's child caught sight of the witch outside her tent this morning, and forthwith fell into convulsions, the poor innocent lamb."

"She hath the evil eye, depend on it," quoth Dorothy decisively.

The men said nothing. They were sipping their ale in sullen silence, and looking to Matthew for further expressions of wisdom.

"Those evil spirits have oft a filthy countenance," explained the shoemaker sententiously, "and no doubt 'twas they helped to convulse Mistress Hannah's child. Some have four faces—one in the usual place, another at the back of the head, and one looking out on either side; others appear with a tall and lean body and bellow like a bull."

"Hast seen them, Matthew?" came in awed whispers from those around.

"Nay! God and the Holy Virgin forbid!" protested Matthew fervently. "God forbid that I should enter their abode of evil. I should lose my soul."

There was a long, ominous silence, broken only by quickly muttered invocations to the saints and to Our Lady.

The men looked furtively at one another. The women clung together, not daring to utter a sound. Mistress Dorothy, all the boldness gone out of her little heart, was sobbing from sheer fright.

"Friends," said Matthew at last, as if with sudden resolution, "if that woman be possessed of the devil, what's to be done?"

There was no reply, but obviously they all understood one another, for each wore a shame-faced look all of a sudden, and dared not meet his neighbour's eye. But the danger was great. The devil in their midst would mean poisoned wells, the sweating sickness, some dire calamity for sure; and it was the duty of every true-hearted countryman to protect his home and family from such terrible disasters.

Therefore when Matthew in his wisdom said, "What's to be done?" the men fully understood.

The women, too, knew that mischief was brewing. They drew closer to one another and shivered with cold beneath their kerchiefs, in spite of the warmth of this beautiful late summer's afternoon.

"Beware of her, Matthew," entreated Mistress Dorothy tearfully.

She drew a small piece of blue cloth from the bosom of her dress: it was pinked and broidered, and had the image of the Holy Virgin painted on one side of it. Quickly she slipped it under her lover's jerkin.

"Take it," she whispered, "the scapulary of Our Lady will protect thee."

This momentous conclave was here interrupted by the approach of the small detachment of the town guard which had been sent hither to ensure order amongst the holiday-makers.

Matthew and his friends began ostentatiously to talk of the weather and other such trifling matters, until after the guard had passed, then once more they put their heads together.

But this time they bade the women go. What had to be discussed now was men's work and unfit for wenches' ears.

CHAPTER IV

FRIENDS AND ENEMIES

In the meanwhile the two gallants were returning from their visit to the witch's tent.

As they came down the steps more than one voice among the passers-by inquired eagerly—

"What fortune, sirs?"

"In truth she hath strange powers," was the somewhat guarded response.

The two men strolled up to a neighbouring wine-vendor and ordered some wine. They had thrown their cloaks aside and removed their masks, for the air was close. The rich, slashed doublets, thus fully displayed, the fine lace at throat and wrist, the silken hose and chased daggers, all betokened the high quality and wealth of the wearers.

Neither of them seemed much above thirty years of age; each had the air of a man in the prime of life, and in the full enjoyment of all the good things which the world can give.

But in their actual appearance they presented a marked contrast.

The one tall and broad-shouldered, florid of complexion, and somewhat reddish about the hair and small pointed beard; the other short, slender, and alert, with keen, restless eyes, and with sensuous lips for ever curled in a smile of thinly veiled sarcasm.

Though outwardly on most familiar terms together, there was distinctly apparent between the two men an air of reserve, and even of decided, if perhaps friendly, antagonism.

"Well, milor Everingham," said the Spaniard after a while, "what say you to our adventure?"

"I say first and foremost, my lord," replied Everingham with studied gallantry, "that my prophecy proved correct—the mysterious necromancer was no proof against Spanish wiles; she unveiled at a smile from Don Miguel, Marquis de Suarez, the envoy of His Most Catholic Majesty."

"Nay," rejoined Don Miguel, affecting not to notice the slight tone of sarcasm in his friend's pleasant voice, "I scarce caught a glimpse of the wench's face. The tent was so dark and her movements so swift."

There was a moment's silence. Lord Everingham seemed lost in meditation.

"You are thoughtful, milor," remarked Don Miguel. "Have the genii of the moon conquered your own usually lively spirits?"

"Nay, I was thinking of the curious resemblance," mused Everingham.

"A resemblance?—to whom?"

"As you say, the tent was dark and the wench's movements swift, yet I could see that, though coarsely clad and ill-kempt, that witch, whom they call Mirrab, is the very physical counterpart of the new Court beauty, the Lady Ursula Glynde."

"The fiancée of the Duke of Wessex!" exclaimed the Spaniard. "Impossible!"

"Nay, my lord," rejoined Everingham pointedly, "she scarce can be called His Grace's fiancée as yet. They were children in their cradles when her father plighted their troth."

The Spaniard made no immediate reply. With an affected, effeminate gesture he was gently stroking his long, black moustache. Everingham, on the other hand, was eyeing him keenly, with a certain look of defiance and challenge, and in a moment the antagonism between the two men appeared more marked than before.

"But gossip has it," said the Marquis at last, with assumed nonchalance, "that Lady Ursula's father—the Earl of Truro, was it not?—swore upon his honour and on his deathbed that she should wed the Duke of Wessex, whenever he claimed her hand, or live her life in a convent. Nay, I but repeat the rumour which has reached me," he added lightly; "put me right if I am in error, my lord. I am but a stranger, and have not yet had the honour of meeting His Grace."

"Bah!" said Everingham impatiently, "His Grace is in no humour to wed, nor do the Earl of Truro's deathbed vows bind him in any way."

He took up his bumper, and looking long and thoughtfully into it, he said with slow emphasis—

"If the Duke of Wessex be inclined to marry, believe me, my lord Marquis, that it shall be none other than the Queen of England! Whom may God bless and protect," he added, reverently lifting his plumed hat with one hand, whilst with the other he held the bumper to his lips and tossed down the full measure of wine at one draught.

"Amen to that," responded Don Miguel with the same easy nonchalance.

He too drained his bumper to the dregs; then he said quietly—

"But that is where we differ, milor. His Eminence the Cardinal de Moreno and myself both hope that the Queen of England will wed our master King Philip of Spain."

Everingham seemed as if he would reply. But with a certain effort he checked the impatient words which had risen to his lips. Englishmen had only just begun to learn the tricks and wiles of Spanish diplomacy, the smiles which hide antagonisms, the suave words which disguise impulsive thoughts.

Lord Everingham had not wholly assimilated the lesson. He had frowned impatiently when the question of the marriage of his queen had been broached by the foreigner. It was a matter which roused the temper of every loyal Englishman just then; they would not see Mary

Tudor wedded to a stranger. England was beginning to feel her own independence; her children would not see her under another yoke.

Mary, in spite of her Spanish mother, was English to the backbone. Tudor-like, she had proved her grit and her pluck when opposing factions tried to wrest her crown from her. She was Harry's daughter. Her loyal subjects were proud of her and proud of her descent, and many of them had sworn that none but an English husband should share her throne with her.

With the same sarcastic smile still lurking round his full lips the Spaniard had watched his friend closely the while. He knew full well what was going on behind that florid countenance, knew the antagonism which the proposed Spanish marriage was rousing just then in the hearts and minds of Englishmen of all classes.

But he certainly did not care to talk over such momentous questions at a country fair, with the eyes and mouths of hundreds of yokels gaping astonishment at him.

As far as he was concerned the half-amicable discussion was closed. He and his friend had agreed to differ. According to Spanish ideas, divergence in political opinions need not interfere with pleasant camaraderie.

With a genuine desire, therefore, to change the subject of conversation, Don Miguel rose from his seat and idly scanned the passing crowd.

"Carramba!" he ejaculated suddenly.

"What is it?"

"Our two masks," whispered the Spaniard. "What say you, milor, shall we resume our interrupted adventure and abandon the tiresome field of politics for the more easy paths of gallantry?"

And without waiting for his friend's reply, eager, impetuous, fond of intrigues and mysteries, the young man darted through the crowd in the direction where his keen eyes had spied a couple of hooded figures, thickly veiled, who were obviously trying to pass unperceived.

Everingham followed closely on the young Spaniard's footsteps. But the sun had already sunk low down in the west. Outlines and silhouettes had become indistinct and elusive. By the time the Marquis de Suarez and his English friend had elbowed their way through the throng the two mysterious figures had once more disappeared.

13

CHAPTER V

LADIES AND GALLANTS

Breathless, half laughing and half crying, very merry, yet wholly frightened, those same two hooded and masked figures had paused almost immediately beneath the platform of Mirrab's tent.

They had been running very fast, and, exhausted, were now clinging to one another, cowering in the deepest shadow of the rough wooden construction.

"Oh! Margaret sweet," whispered a feminine voice from behind the silken mask, "I vow I should have died with fright!"

"Think you we have escaped them?" murmured the other feebly.

She who had first spoken, taller than her friend and obviously the leader of this mad escapade, tiptoed cautiously forward and peered out into the open space.

"Sh—sh—sh!" she whispered, as she dragged her unwilling companion after her, "do you see them? ... right over there ... they are running fast ... Oh! ho! ho! ho!" she laughed suddenly with childish glee as she clapped her hands together; "but, Margaret dear! ... did we not fool them merrily? ... Oh! I could shriek for joy! Aye, run, run, run, my fine gallants!" she added, blowing an imaginary kiss to her distant pursuers, "an you go that way you'll ne'er o'ertake us, e'en though you raced the wind ... ha! ha! ha! ..."

Her laugh sounded a little forced and hysterical, for she had had a terrible fright, and her companion was still clinging miserably, helplessly to her side.

"Nay, Ursula, how can you be so merry?" admonished Margaret in a voice almost choked with tears; "think if the Duchess of Lincoln were to hear of this adventure—or Her Majesty herself—oh! ..."

But Ursula's gay, madcap mood was proof against Margaret's tears.

"Oh! oh! oh!" she ejaculated, mimicking her friend's tones of horror. "Oh!" she added with mock seriousness, "well, then, of course, there would be trouble, Margaret mine! ... sweet Margaret! ... such a lecture! ... and oh! oh! oh! such black looks from Her Majesty! ... we should e'en—think on it!—have to look demure for at least two days, until our sins be forgiven us! ..."

She paused awhile, mischief apparent even beneath the half-transparent lace which hid her laughter-loving mouth. She drew her trembling companion closer to her, and, still laughing, she coaxed her gently.

"There, there, sweet," she murmured, "cheer up, I pray thee, cheer up.... See, we have come to the end of our journey. We have baffled those persistent gallants, and this is the witch's tent. Margaret!" she added with an impatient tap of the foot, "art a goose to go on crying so? I vow I'd have come alone had I known thou'rt such a coward."

"Ursula!" said Margaret, somewhat emboldened by her friend's assurance, "could you guess who were those two gallants?"

"Nay," replied Ursula indifferently, "one of them, methinks, was the Marquis de Suarez, for I caught sight of his black silk hose, but what do we care about these nincompoops, Margaret? Come and see the witch—we have no time to lose."

Eagerly she turned towards the booth, and somewhat awed, anxious, yet not wholly daring, she gazed up in astonishment at the gaudy draperies, the tall flagstaff, the weird black flag with its strange device. Then with sudden resolution she planted her foot upon the bottom step.

"Wilt follow me, sweet?" she asked.

Even as she spoke Abra, in tall peaked cap and flowing mantle, emerged from within the tent.

Margaret, who was screwing up her courage to follow her friend, gave a shriek of dismay.

"No! no! no! Ursula!" she said, clinging to the other girl, not daring to look up at the awesome figure of the lean magician. "I implore you, give up the thought."

"Give up the thought?" rejoined Ursula, boldly trying to smother her own superstitious fears, "when I've gone thus far?"

"I cannot think what you want with that horrid witch!" pleaded Margaret.

At sight of Abra's long white beard, his wizard's wand, and cloak covered with cabalistic signs, even Ursula's courage had begun to ebb. She had hastily retreated from the steps and followed Margaret once more within the protecting shelter of the shadows.

"I want to know my fortune, Margaret mine," she said in a voice which was not quite as firm as before, "and I hear that this witch can see into the future. 'Tis said that she has marvellous powers."

"Why should you want to know the future?" persisted timid, practical Margaret; "is not the present good enough for you?"

"His Grace of Wessex comes back to Court to-day," rejoined Ursula, "after an absence of many months."

"Well?—what of him?"

"What of him? ... Margaret, art stupid, or art not my friend? ... Is it not natural that I should wish to know whether I am to be Duchess of Wessex or abbess in a holy but uncomfortable convent?"

"Yes, 'tis natural enough," assented Margaret thoughtfully, "but-"

"His Grace has never seen me since I was so long," said Ursula with a short, impatient sigh, and stretching out a round arm decked with a sleeve of rich silk and fine lace. "I had a red face then, and pap

15

was stuffed into my mouth to keep me quiet. You see, I could not have been madly alluring then."

"And you are beautiful now, Ursula. But of what avail is it? You cannot wed His Grace of Wessex, for he'll never ask you to be his wife. He'll marry the Queen. All England wishes it."

"But I wish him to marry me," quoth Ursula with a resolute tap of her high-heeled shoe against the ground. "Yes, me! and I want that witch yonder to ask the stars if he will fall in love with me when he sees me, or if he will yield to those who want to make of him a tool for their political ambition, and marry an ugly, ill-tempered old woman who happens to be Queen of England."

"Ursula!"

Margaret's horror, amazement, and awe had rendered her almost speechless. Ursula's utterance was nearly sacrilegious, in these days when kings and queens ruled by right divine.

But the young girl continued, quite unabashed by her friend's rebuke.

"Well," she said imperturbably, "you can't deny that the Queen is old! ... and ugly! ... and ill-tempered! ..."

Margaret, however, was prepared to deny these monstrous statements with the last breath left in her delicate body. The poor little soul was frightened out of her wits.

Suppose some one had overheard!—and repeated the tale that two of the Queen's ladies-in-waiting had called Her Majesty old!—and ugly!—and ill-tempered!——

Nay, Ursula's madcap freaks were past bearing! and would lead her into serious trouble one of these days.

"Margaret," whispered the delinquent, who still seemed quite unaware of the enormity of her offence, "hast thou ever seen His Grace of Wessex?"

"No," replied Margaret curtly, for she was still very wrathful, and vaguely felt that, at this stage, all references to the Duke were somehow treasonable.

"Nor I since I was a baby," sighed Ursula; "but see here ...."

From beneath the folds of her cloak she drew a chain and locket, and holding the latter before Margaret's unwilling eyes, she said ecstatically—

"That's his picture. Isn't he handsome?"

"You've fallen in love with his picture!"

"Madly!"

"Madly indeed!" retorted Margaret.

Ursula once more hid the locket inside her robe. She had regained all her courage. Once more dragging her weaker companion by the wrist she turned towards the witch's booth.

Abra, the magician, tired out by his day's exertions, had settled himself down on a tattered piece of rug outside the tent; there he had

16

fallen peacefully asleep, his venerable head thrown back, his lean shanks hanging over the edge of the platform and snoring the snore of the just. Thus he had failed to spy the two hooded, dainty figures, who had all along kept within the shadows.

Suddenly through his pleasant slumbers he heard an eagerly whispered—

"Hey! friend!"

Whilst the toe of his shoe was violently tagged at from below.

"Friend, wake!"

"They won't listen!" added an impatient, half-tearful voice.

But already Abra was on his feet. Giving his humble henchman a violent kick to wake him up, he began to mutter mechanically, even before he was fully conscious—

"What ho, my masters! consult the world-famous necromancer-"

Bang! bang! bang! on the big drum came automatically from his henchman, who was only half awake.

"No! no! no!" entreated Ursula, "I prithee not so much noise! We wish to consult the soothsayer ... we've brought some money ... three gold pieces ... is that enough? ... But in the name of Our Lady I beg of thee not to make so much noise."

Timidly she held up a silken purse towards the astonished wizard. Three gold pieces!—why, 'twas a fortune, the like of which the worthy Abra had never beheld in one sum in his life.

To ask him not to make a noise was to demand the impossible. With one hand he pushed his henchman vigorously to one side. The latter dropped his cymbals, which rattled off the platform with an ear-splitting crash.

All the while Abra in stentorian tones, and holding back the folds of the tent, was shouting at the top of his voice—

"This way, ladies! for the great soothsayer Mirrab, the sale of love-philters and charms, and of the true elixir of life."

"The die is cast, Margaret mine," said Ursula, trying vainly to steady her voice, which was trembling, and her knees which were shaking beneath her. "Art coming?—Oh! I—I—feel a little nervous," she admitted in spite of herself, "and you—oh! how your hand trembles..."

She was frankly terrified now. The noise was so awful, and though she did not dare look to the right or left of her she was conscious that she and her friend were no longer alone on the open place. She could hear the murmur of voices, the sound of idle folk gathering in every direction.

Her instinct suggested immediate flight, and the abandonment of this mad adventure while there was yet time, but her pride urged her to proceed. She gripped Margaret's wrist with a resolute hand and made a quick rush for the steps.

Alas! she was just two seconds too late. The next instant she felt her waist seized firmly from behind, whilst a merry voice shouted—

17

"Cornered at last!"

Wrenching herself free with a sudden twist of her firm young shoulders, Ursula contrived to liberate herself momentarily. She was dimly conscious of having caught sight of Margaret in the like plight as herself.

"Not so fast, fair one," whispered an insinuating voice close to her, "a word in thy pretty ear."

Oh! the shame of this vulgar adventure! Pursued like some kitchen wench out on a spree, by a gallant, eager for an idle kiss.

She felt her cheeks tingle underneath her mask; saw and guessed the short laugh, the shrug of the shoulders of the idlers round, far too accustomed to these spectacles to take more than passing note of it.

Once more the firm grip had seized her waist. This time she felt herself powerless to struggle.

"Nay, in the name of heaven, sir," she entreated tearfully, "I pray you let me go."

"Not until I have caught a nearer sight of those bright eyes, that shine at me through that cruel mask."

The soft guttural tones revealed the identity of the speaker to Ursula. She knew Don Miguel well; knew his wild, impudent spirit, his love of idle flirtations which had already made him the terror of the prim Queen's Court. She knew that she would not be allowed to escape before this ridiculous episode had been brought to its usual conclusion.

Oh! how she longed for the Duchess of Lincoln's severe guardianship at this moment! How bitterly she repented the folly which had prompted her to drag Margaret along into this wild adventure.

Poor Margaret! she, too, was doing her best to evade the unwelcome attentions of her gallant! and that magician! and those louts! all grinning like so many apes at the spectacle.

It was maddening!

And she was helpless!

The next moment the young Spaniard's indiscreet hands had snatched the protecting mask from her face, and the daintiest and most perfect picture Nature had ever fashioned stood revealed, blushing with shame and vexation, before his delighted, slightly sarcastic gaze.

"Ah! luck favours me indeed!" he murmured with avowed admiration, "the newly-risen star—nay! the brightest sun in the firmament of beauty! the Lady Ursula Glynde!"

CHAPTER VI

THE LADY URSULA

She was only nineteen then. Not very tall, yet perfectly proportioned, and with that small, oval face of hers which delighted yet puzzled all the artists of the epoch.

The dark hood of her cloak had fallen back at the impertinent gesture of the young Spaniard; her fair hair, slightly touched with warm gold, escaped in a few unruly curls from beneath the stiff coif of brocade which encircled her pretty head.

The neck was long; the shoulders, rich, young and firm, gleamed like ivory beneath the primly folded kerchief of lace of a dead, bluish white, a striking note of harmonious contrast.

Have not all the rhymesters of the period sung the praises of her eyes? What shall the poor chronicler add to these poetical effusions, save that Ursula's eyes were as changeable in colour as were her moods, her spirits, the expression of her face, and the inflexions of her voice.

And then there was the proud little toss of the head, that contemptuous curl of the lip which rendered her more desirable than any of her more yielding companions.

Indeed, Don Miguel felt in luck. His arm was still round her waist. He felt the young figure stiffen beneath his admiring glances.

The fair one was half mad with rage, and quite adorable in her wrath.

"My lord Marquis, this is an outrage!" she said at last, "and here in England——"

"Nay, fair one," rejoined the Spaniard with a slight accent of irony, "even in England, when two ladies, masked and alone, are held prisoners at nightfall, and in a public place, by their ardent adorers, they must needs pay ransom for their release. What say you, my lord?" he added, turning gaily to where his friend held pretty Margaret a not too unwilling prisoner.

"'Tis but justice," assented Lord Everingham, "and yours the first prize, Marquis. Fair one," he said, looking down into Margaret's shyly terrified eyes, "wilt pay toll to me the while?"

"Gentlemen!" proudly protested Lady Ursula, "an there's any honour in you——"

"Nay! honour lies in snatching a kiss from those sweet lips," rejoined Don Miguel with a graceful flourish of his plumed hat.

This act of gallantry, however, almost cost him the price of his victory. Ursula Glynde, born and bred in the country, was the daughter of a sturdy Cornish nobleman. Accustomed to ride untamed foals, to have bouts at the broadsword or the poniard with the best man in the

19

county, she would not yield a kiss or own herself vanquished quite as readily as the Spaniard seemed to expect.

With a vigorous jerk of the body she had once more freed herself from the Marquis's grasp, and running up to Margaret, she snatched her by the hand and dragged her away from Lord Everingham, readjusting her hood and mask as she flew towards the booth, vaguely hoping for shelter behind the folds of the tent.

But once more fate interposed relentlessly betwixt her and her attempts at escape. Two gallants, seeing the episode, eager to have a hand in the adventure, friends no doubt too of Don Miguel and Everingham, laughingly barred the way to the steps, just as the two girls had contrived to reach them. With a cry of disappointment Ursula, still dragging Margaret after her, tried to double back. But it was too late. Don Miguel and Lord Everingham were waiting for them on the other side. They were two to one now, and all chances of escape had hopelessly vanished.

Never had Ursula Glynde felt so mortified in her life.

"Many thanks, gentlemen, for this timely interference," came in mocking accents from that odious Spaniard. "The ransom, sweet one," he added, as the chase 'twixt gallants and maids became more general, and the girls at last felt themselves quite helpless and surrounded.

Ursula's pride alone prevented her from bursting into tears.

"By my faith! here is strange sport!" said a pleasant, slightly mocking voice suddenly. "What say you, Harry Plantagenet? A lively sight ... what? ... four gallants frightening two ladies!"

Instinctively every one had turned in the direction whence the voice had come. A man was standing some dozen yards away with mantle tightly drawn round him, his tall figure stooping to pat and fondle a powerful-looking boarhound, which clung closely to his side.

He had spoken very quietly, apparently to the dog, whose great ears he was gently stroking.

Without taking any further heed of the somewhat discomfited gentlemen, he came forward towards the little group.

"Ladies, your way stands clear," he said, with that same pleasant irony still apparent in his voice, and without casting more than a cursory glance at the close hoods and dark masks, which was all that he could see of the ladies, whom he had so incontinently saved from an unpleasant position.

"Sir," murmured Ursula, under her breath and without attempting to move, for she felt as if her knees would give way under her.

"Nay, Madam," rejoined the newcomer lightly, "if my interference has angered you, I pray you forgive me and I'll withdraw, as these gentlemen here obviously desire me to do. But an you really wish to escape, my friend here will assure you that you can do so

20

unmolested.... Eh, Harry? what say you?" he added, once more turning his attention to the dog.

The boarhound, as if conscious of this appeal to his chivalry, turned a knowing eye on the two girls.

The four men had been taken so absolutely unawares that during the few seconds while this brief colloquy took place they had scarcely realised that an interfering and unknown stranger was trying to hamper them in their amusements.

They had remained quite speechless, more astonished at the newcomer's impertinence than wrathful at the interruption; and when the next instant Ursula and Margaret suddenly fled with unaffected precipitancy, no one attempted to stop them.

Harry Plantagenet's intelligent eyes followed the retreating figures until they were out of sight. Then he yawned with obtrusive incivility, and plainly showed his master that the present company no longer interested him.

"Well, Harry, old man, shall we go?" said the stranger, calmly turning on his heel.

But at this final piece of cool insolence Don Miguel de Suarez at last recovered from his astonishment. This tame ending to an unwarrantable intrusion was certainly not to his liking, and he, for one, was unaccustomed to see his whims or caprices thwarted.

In these days tempers ran high, hot blood was allowed free rein, and at a word or a smile out of place, swords and poniards were soon out of their sheaths and friendships of yesterday changed to deadly antagonism in the space of a few minutes.

"Carramba!" swore the young Spaniard, "this passes belief. What say you, gentlemen?"

4And, drawing his long, tapering sword, he barred the way threateningly to the stranger.

The silence, thus broken, seemed to restore at once to the other three gallants the full measure of their wrath. One and all following Don Miguel's example, had put their hands to their sword-hilts.

"Aye! unmask, stranger," said Lord Everingham peremptorily.

"Unmask! unmask!" came in threatening accents from all.

"Unmask, or ..."

"Or by our Lady!" rejoined the stranger lightly, "you'll all run your blades into my silken doublet and thus end pleasantly a chivalrous escapade. Eh?"

One could divine the pleasant, ironical smile lurking behind the thick curtain of the mask. The Spaniard's blood was boiling with vexation. Harry Plantagenet gave an impatient whine.

"Your name, stranger, first," commanded Don Miguel haughtily, "then your sword if you are not a coward; after that I and these gentlemen will deal with your impudence if you have any left."

There was a moment's silence; the stranger whistled to his dog.

21

"My sword is at your command," he said; "mine impudence you shall deal with as you list.... My name is Wessex!" he added with a sudden hauteur which seemed to tower above Don Miguel as the gigantic oak of the glen towers above the bustling willow beneath.

And he removed the mask from his face.

CHAPTER VII

HIS GRACE OF WESSEX

There are several portraits extant of Robert d'Esclade, fifth Duke of Wessex, notably the one by Antonio Moro in the Pitti Gallery at Florence.

But in the somewhat stiff portraiture of that epoch it is perhaps a little difficult to trace the real image, the inner individuality of one of the most interesting personalities at the Court of Mary Tudor.

There is, however, a miniature of him, attributed to Holbein, and certainly drawn by the hand of a great master, which renders with greater truth and loving accuracy the peculiar charm made up of half-indolent nonchalance, gracious condescension, and haughty reserve which characterized the Duke of Wessex.

So justly styled His Grace!

The reserve was so little apparent. The hauteur only came to the surface in response to unwelcome familiarity. But the debonair indolence was always there, the lazy droop of the lids, the nonchalant shrug of the shoulders, when grave matters were discussed, and also that obvious fastidiousness—a love of everything that was beautiful, from a fine horse, down to a piece of delicate lace—which annoyed the more sedate-minded courtiers of the Queen.

And with it all that wonderful virility and vigour, that joy of life and delight in gaiety and laughter which lent to the grave face at times a spark of almost boyish exuberance; that mad, merry, proud insouciance, which throughout his life made him meet every danger—aye! every sorrow and disgrace—with the same bright smile on his lips.

Scheyfne, in his letters to the emperor, Charles V, says of the Duke of Wessex that he was insufferably conceited—"il est tres orgueilleux de sa beauté personelle, laquelle certes est plus que médiocre."

Noailles, too, speaks of him as "moult fatueux et vaniteux de sa personne."

But it was hardly likely that these foreign delegates, each bent upon their own schemes, would look with favour upon His Grace. His only merit in their eyes was that same characteristic indolence of his, which caused a man of his great wealth and boundless influence to abstain from politics.

Certes no one could accuse him of intriguing for his own political advancement. Mary Tudor's own avowed penchant for him was so well known, that he had but to say the word and the crown of England would be his, to share with the Queen.

Yet since the death of Edward VI he had not been seen at Court. Small wonder, therefore, that at sight of the Duke all four men seemed amazed.

"His Grace of Wessex!" they ejaculated in one breath.

But already Lord Everingham had put up his sword and gone to Wessex with hands outstretched.

"Wessex!" he said with unmistakable delight. "By Our Lady, this is a joyful surprise!"

The other two Englishmen also shook the Duke warmly by the hand.

"I did not know you were in England, my lord," said the one.

"Right glad are we to welcome you back," added the other.

"Well, Harry, my friend," quoth the Duke gaily, "methinks you and I are not to be spiked after all."

Harry Plantagenet, however, was looking doubtfully at the young Spaniard, who had remained somewhat in the background, regarding the first effusions of his friends with a certain ill-concealed impatience. With almost human intelligence the dog seemed to understand that here was a person who was inimical to his master, and in his faithful eyes there came that unmistakable furtive look and blink, with which dogs invariably show their mistrust and dislike.

But Don Miguel de Suarez was above all a diplomatist. Capricious and fond of adventure, not over-scrupulous as to the choice of his pleasures, yet he never allowed his dearest whim to interfere with political necessities.

A few seconds' quick reflection soon made it clear to him that a quarrel with the Duke of Wessex would, at this juncture, greatly endanger his own popularity at the English Court, and thereby minimize his chances of carrying through the negotiations entrusted to him by King Philip of Spain.

Under the leadership of His Eminence the Cardinal de Moreno he certainly hoped to bring about the marriage of Philip with the Queen of England.

He knew perfectly well that he and his eminent colleague were opposed in this design by the entire ultra-English faction here, and also that this faction was composed of practically the whole of the nobility and chivalry of the realm.

23

The Duke of Wessex was the pride and hope of this party, for Courtenay, weak and effeminate, had lost all his partisans. What more natural than that the most distinguished, most brilliant of Queen Mary's subjects should share her throne with her?

All this and more passed swiftly through Don Miguel's active brain. Therefore, as soon as there was a lull in the joyful welcome accorded to the Duke by his friends, he too stepped forward, having with vigorous self-will curbed his unruly temper and forced his full, sensuous lips to a smile. He had realized the expediency of, at any rate, outward amiability.

"A great name, my lord," he said, bowing with grave ceremony to Wessex, "and one familiar to me already, though I have not yet been honoured by seeing you at Court."

The Duke eyed him for the space of two brief seconds, whilst just the faintest touch of superciliousness seemed to be lurking somewhere at the back of his neck. But he returned the Spaniard's bow with equal ceremony. Then he placed his hand on the head of his dog.

"Nay, sir," he said, "my friend here bears a prouder name than mine. Harry Plantagenet, make your bow to the envoy of His Most Catholic Majesty. I call him Plantagenet, sir, after our King Harry V, who drove back the French at Agincourt. Nay, your pardon; this scarce interests you. You were not born then, and Spain was not yet a kingdom."

He spoke lightly, and none but Everingham's devoted ears caught the slight tone of impertinence which underlay the bland, seemingly empty speech.

Don Miguel himself was determined to keep urbane.

"A beautiful creature, indeed," he said suavely; "but you, milor Duke, do you return to Hampton Court with us this night?"

"Oh!" replied Wessex, "among so many brilliant diplomatists from Spain there's scarce room for a mere idler like myself."

"Yet we diplomatists are hoping to pit our poor wits against Your Grace's," added Don Miguel pointedly.

"Against those of my friends perhaps, my lord," rejoined the Duke drily. "Mine own are incorrigibly idle."

Don Miguel, as was his wont, did not pursue the subject any further. He was trying to read the refined, distinctly haughty countenance, which was smiling down at him so pleasantly just now, and taking mental stock of this antagonist, whom rumour had described to him and to his chief as the only serious obstacle to the proposed Spanish alliance.

He saw before him a man in the full pride of youth and manhood, tall and well knit, and wearing with easy grace the elaborate slashes and puffs, trunks and silk hose, which present fashion had decreed.

The Spaniard's keen and critical eye took in every detail of this interesting personality: the short, light brown hair worn close to the

24

head, the fair moustache and delicately refined hands, the richness of the doublet, the priceless value of the lace at throat and wrist.

"A fop and an idler!" he murmured mentally.

Then he thought of the Queen of England. No longer young, with but little taste in ornament and dress, and certes quite unversed in all those wiles, which might have drawn this brilliant butterfly into her net.

The Spaniard longed to see these two together. The presence of this formidable adversary gave additional zest to the game he was playing on the political chess-board.

An unwilling courtier! A love-sick Queen! Carramba! it was interesting.

"When do you return to the Palace, my lord?" Everingham was asking of the Duke.

"To-night," replied the latter, "by our gracious Liege Lady's own command."

"To-night then?"

"Without fail. Harry Plantagenet and I will present our humble respects to Her Majesty."

"'Tis au revoir then, Your Grace," quoth Don Miguel. "We meet again to-night."

"At your service, my lord Marquis."

Still smiling amicably the Spaniard took his leave, soon followed by two of his companions. Lord Everingham too was about to depart, but he felt Wessex' detaining hand on his arm.

"That unpleasant-looking Spaniard? ..." queried the Duke.

"Don Miguel, Marquis de Suarez," replied Everingham, "envoy of His Majesty, the King of Spain."

"Aye, I knew all that. I was merely reflecting that if he happen to be a specimen of our Liege Lady's Court, meseems I were a fool to go back to it."

"Come back to it with me now," urged his friend earnestly.

"Not till to-night. Do not grudge me these few last hours of freedom. By Our Lady! I meant to consult the famous witch, like a sober burgher out on a holiday. But in the name of all the saints in the calendar let us forget there are such things as Spaniards at the English Court just now."

He laughed, a half weary, wholly pleasant laugh, as, followed by his dog, he led his friend in the opposite direction to that in which Don Miguel had rapidly walked away.

CHAPTER VIII

SILKEN BONDS

Wessex and Everingham had readjusted their masks and wrapped their cloaks around them, ere they once more mingled with the crowd which still thronged around the gaily decked booths.

The evening now was rapidly drawing in. Hampton Court, in the fast-gathering haze beyond, looked grey and ghostlike, with brightly illumined windows beginning to gleam here and there.

With an impatient frown, Wessex deliberately turned his back on the gorgeous pile: it represented boredom to him, politics and dullness, and he loved gaiety, sunshine, and laughter, these merry-makers here, the pretty country wenches with their bare arms and neat ankles showing beneath their brightly coloured robes.

Everingham was silent as he followed his friend through the crowd. But Wessex' laugh was always infectious, and he seemed in a merry mood to-night. Harry Plantagenet alone seemed morose; he disapproved of all these country louts, who were over free with their caresses. He kept close to his master's heel, and only gave an occasional growl, when some impudent 'prentice dared to come too nigh.

"Well, Harry, old friend," said the Duke after a while, "shall we go and consult the witch, or wait until the stars are out? Friend Everingham here is none too good company to-night, eh? In thine ear, proud Plantagenet, he hath designs on our freedom. But the soothsayer shall cast our horoscope, and look into our future, see if you are to become chief lapdog to the Queen of England, or if we are both of us to fall in bondage to the mistress plighted to us by an uncomfortable old gentleman, who had not consulted us in the matter. 'Sdeath man," he added, suddenly looking straight into Everingham's serious face, "why do you look so grave? Tell me, pending that witch's starlit lies, what's your best news?"

"By my faith!" responded Everingham simply, "the best news is Your Grace's return. 'Twas an ill wind that wafted you away from Court."

"Aye! 'twas the wind of infinite boredom wafted my Grace away," replied the Duke with a smile. "Confess, friend, that the Court cannot be alluring with the Queen telling her beads, the foreign ambassadors ruling England, the Privy Council at loggerheads, the people grumbling, and the ladies yawning. Brrr!"

He gave a mock shiver, and seemed not to notice the quick look of reproach cast at him by his friend.

"And out of sheer boredom," quoth Everingham with a sigh of deep disappointment, "you piqued the Queen of England."

26

Wessex did not reply at once. At Everingham's tone of rebuke a slight frown had contracted his forehead, and that certain look of hauteur, never wholly absent from his face, at once became more apparent.

There was more than mere camaraderie between these two men: unity of thought, similarity of tastes and education, a great and overwhelming love for their own country, together with mutual understanding and appreciation, had long ago knit the ties of friendship closely between them. It was generally admitted by every one that Lord Everingham might venture on a ground of familiarity with His Grace which no one else quite dared to tread.

This time too, after that instant's hesitation, the reserve which every now and then seemed entirely to detach the Duke of Wessex from his surroundings, quickly disappeared again. The pleasant smile returned to the proud lips, he shrugged his shoulders and said simply—

"Is the Queen of England piqued?"

"Can you ask?" rejoined the other with increased vehemence.

Then he checked himself abruptly, feeling no doubt how useless it was to discuss such matters seriously just now.

"The only woman," he added, falling in once more with his friend's lighter mood, "the only woman whose blandishments His Grace of Wessex has ever been known to resist."

"And that with difficulty," concluded the Duke gaily. "But you see, friend," he added with mock gravity, "with a Tudor you never can tell; you might lose your heart one day and your head the next."

"Mary Tudor loves you too well ..." protested Lord Everingham.

"She is the daughter of King Harry VIII, remember, and would threaten me with the block or the rack at every indiscretion."

He paused, then added quaintly—

"And I would commit so many."

"A woman who loves always forgives," urged his friend.

"A woman, my good Everingham, will forgive a grave infidelity—perhaps! but not a number of little indiscretions. Mine," he added with a light sigh, "would be the little indiscretions."

"And while you fled from Court the Queen of England has almost promised to wed the Spanish king," said Everingham bitterly.

He watched his friend keenly as he spoke and paused a moment before he added pointedly—

"'Twill be a proud day for the peers of England when they bow the knee to their Liege Lord, a foreign king."

Wessex shrugged his broad shoulders and turned to where a pretty wench, dispensing ale to a scarlet-cloaked burgher, formed a picture pleasing to his artistic eye.

Everingham, somewhat proud of his own diplomatic skill, had noted, however, a certain stiffening of His Grace's figure at the vision which had been conjured before him.

That of a Wessex bending the knee before a Spaniard.

"You were away," continued Everingham, eager to goad his friend into speech, "and my Lord Cardinal and Don Miguel know how to blow upon the flames of Mary's jealousy. Your influence can still save England, my lord," he added with great earnestness, "let not your enemies say that fear of a woman keeps you from exerting it."

"H'm! do they say that?" mused Wessex quaintly, whilst a smile, which almost might be called boyish, altered the whole expression of his serious face. "By my faith! but they are right. One's enemies usually are."

He drew his friend away from the immediate vicinity of a jabbering crowd, into a dark corner formed by one of the booths. Everingham, thinking that at last he had led Wessex into a graver train of thought, failed to notice the humorous twinkle of the eyes which had so palpably struggled to the surface.

"It is the fear of a woman has kept me away from Court," he whispered solemnly, "but that woman is not the Queen of England."

"Who is it then?"

"In your ear, friend ... 'tis the Lady Ursula Glynde."

Everingham could scarce suppress a movement of intense satisfaction. Lady Ursula! beautiful, exquisite Lady Ursula was the one stumbling-block on which the schemes of his faction might become hopelessly shattered.

Wessex was nominally plighted to the lady. True, 'twas an engagement undertaken by the lady's own father, without the consent of the parties chiefly concerned. But in Tudor England there was a curious adherence to such solemnly plighted troths, which might have proved a bar to the Duke's sense of absolute freedom.

If, however, he looked upon this unnatural and monstrous pledge with the lightness which it fully deserved, if he considered himself at liberty to break the imaginary bonds which held him to Lady Ursula, then the work of his partisans would become comparatively easy.

They had always hoped and fully intended to overcome His Grace's scruples in the matter, and fondly thought that they would succeed. But since the Duke himself looked indifferently upon this so-called troth, why, Everingham himself was the first to feel the keenest satisfaction at the thought.

"You dislike the lady then?" he asked with unfeigned delight.

"I have never seen her," retorted Wessex placidly. "At any rate, not since she was in her cradle. I certainly didn't like her then."

"She is very beautiful," remarked Everingham, with a somewhat shamefaced recollection of his previous adventure, "but——"

"She might be a veritable angel, yet she would frighten me."

A mock shudder passed through his tall, athletic frame, and taking his friend's arm in his, he whispered confidentially, "Think of it, my lord! A woman whom duty compels one to love—Brrr!—Her own father plighted our troth; I am left comparatively free, yet if I do not wed Lady Ursula, she is doomed to end her days in a convent.... A matter of honour—what? ... Yet I—I, who could love any woman," he added emphatically, "be she queen or peasant—that is—h'm!—if I were really put to it—find the very thought of my promised bride abhorrent. She is the one woman in all the world whom I could never love—never! ... I know it! So I ran away from Court, not because I feared one woman loved me too much, but because I knew I should love one woman too little."

He had spoken so light-heartedly, so gaily, that in spite of the grave issues at stake Everingham could not help but laugh.

"Nay! perhaps you exaggerate the danger," he said. "The Lady Ursula might prefer the convent to being a duchess. She has never seen Your Grace, she is rich and high-born, she may be pious——"

"Or perverse," responded Wessex. "I've never met a woman yet who didn't want—badly—the thing she mightn't get."

"Is England then a woman," queried Everingham with renewed earnestness, "since she wants Wessex?"

But the Duke was not prepared to follow his friend to-night into sentimental, ultra-patriotic bypaths. He was not altogether inclined to sacrifice his liberty for the sake of ousting the Spanish king from his proposed English throne.

Nevertheless he rejoined more gravely than was his wont.

"Does England really want me?" he said with gentle irony. "Nay!" he added, restraining with one hand Everingham's exuberant protests, "I know! I know! you all think so, and that I am an unhallowed idler, letting my country drift into the arms of the foreigner. Do not deny it, friend.... Perhaps I am.... Nay! we'll say, indeed I am.... There! there! calm your fears. Have I not told you that Her Majesty hath commanded my presence at Court? We'll set our poor wits to oust Spanish diplomacy, and I must trust my luckiest star to inspire in the Lady Ursula a wholesome desire for the convent; for I tell thee, friend, that if she holds me to my silken bonds, I will at once repair to the outermost corner of the earth and thence drop into vacancy, or take flight to the blue dome of heaven above."

"God protect Your Grace," rejoined Everingham with grave solemnity. "Ah! I fear no Spanish influence now," he added enthusiastically. "You'll save England, my lord, and the gratitude of the nation will be at your feet."

Wessex smiled, shrugged his shoulders, and without further allusion to more serious subjects the two men mingled once more among the crowd.

CHAPTER IX

THE VEILED WITCH

Outside the witch's tent all was silent and deserted. Darkness had gradually crept in, and with it—as far as the rest of the Fair was concerned—additional noise and exuberant gaiety.

Huge torches of gum and resin flickered at the entrance of every booth, throwing quaint red lights, and deep, mysterious shadows all round, distorting the faces of the gaping multitude, and of the criers, until they looked like fantastic figures, wizards all from some neighbouring Brocken.

Whether the world-famous necromancer, Mirrab, and her attendant genii were lacking in business or no, no one could say, for there was no torch outside their tent, and Abra had ceased to lure the passer-by. The open place in front of the platform was dark and still.

Suddenly from out the shadows something seemed to move forward, whilst a mysterious "Hist! hist!" came echoing from more than one direction.

Gradually the sound became more distinct, dark figures emerged from every side, and presently a compact group of moving, whispering people congregated some few yards away from the booth. Then a voice, still low and muffled, but firm and emphatic, detached itself from the ghostlike murmur around.

"My masters, I call upon you to witness! ... The Scriptures say, 'Let no witch live.' ... Shall we disobey the Scriptures and allow that witch to live? ... She is possessed, and the devil dwells in that booth."

Groans and threatening curses greeted this peroration. The speaker raised his voice somewhat.

"Will you allow Satan to remain amongst you?"

"No! no! no!" came in excited accents from the little crowd.

"And I say death to the witch!" added the leading voice solemnly.

"Death to the witch!" came in weird echoes from all around.

Then there was silence. The dark heads bent closer together.

"What wilt thou do, Matthew?" whispered one voice with awed timidity.

"Let her burn, I say," replied the learned village oracle; "'tis the only way of getting rid of Satan."

It had been a hot day. The heads of this pack of country folk had been overheated with sack and spiced ale; an unreasoning, maniacal terror, with superstition for its basis, had completed the work of completely addling their loutish brains. All day there had been talk of this veiled witch, these strange spirits and weird monsters which she was reputed to conjure up at will. Thoughts of poisoned wells, of sweating sickness, of hell-fire raged through these poor misguided fellows' minds.

What did they know of charlatanism or trickery? To them it was all real, living, awesome, terrible. The devil was a person with glowing eyes, two horns, and a forked tail, who caused innocent people to fall flat on their backs and foam at the mouth.

Every malady then unknown to science was ascribed to hellish agency. And here, within a few yards, was an unearthly creature who actually consorted with the creator of all evil, who wilfully brought him up from his burning abode below the earth, and let him loose upon this peaceful village and its God-fearing inhabitants.

"Nay! burn her! burn her!" they shouted, brandishing their sticks, emboldened through their very cowardice into deeds they would otherwise never have contemplated without a shudder.

And they shouted in order to keep up their exaltation and their excitement; the devil is known to favour whisperings.

"After me, my masters," continued Matthew, who was still the leader of this insane band of mischievous fools, "after me. Remember there's salvation for our sins if we burn the witch."

With another wild shout the little crowd made a rush for the platform of the booth, just as Abra and his henchman, attracted by the strangeness of the noise, came out of the tent to see what might be amiss.

Before they had time to utter a sound of protest the two men were seized by the crowd and dragged down the steps with violence. The people had no time to trouble about a lout such as he. They wanted the witch herself, now, at once, while their blood was up and boiling; and the guard might come round at any moment and frustrate them in their will.

"Out of the way, lout! out of the way! or thou'lt burn alongside of thy damned witch!"

Abra had fallen on his knees, understanding only too well the danger which was threatening him. He had known all along what terrible risks he was taking. 'Twas not well in these days to tamper with the supernatural. But he had trusted to the good temper of holiday-makers, whilst the certain patronage of rich burghers and Court gallants had proved an overwhelming temptation to his greed of gain. For the wench he cared but little. He had picked her out of the gutter one day, a starving little slut, and had used her as a tool—a willing one enough—for his own pecuniary ends.

Even now, with a cursing throng of maniacs round him, he only thought of his own safety. Mean, abject, and cowardly, he fell upon his knees.

"Merciful heavens, my masters," he pleaded.

But the crowd was not in a humour to listen. The men kicked him

31

on one side, and he fell up against his miserable companion, who was too terror-stricken to move.

Then there was another rush up to the platform. Without thought or pause, for these would have been fatal to the resolute purpose in view, and might give the devil time to look after his own.

From within the tent there came now a frantic shriek of terror. The next moment, the foremost among the crowd had pushed aside the gaudy draperies, and that one shriek was answered by a dozen awesome, horrified curses.

There was the witch at last. A poor trembling girl, scarce out of her teens, with beautiful, delicate features, and an abundance of golden hair falling round her shoulders; her mysterious veil—a bit of showy tinsel—lying in a heap on the floor. Nothing supernatural or devilish about her, surely. Quaint, perhaps, because of that singular beauty of face and skin which seemed so ill-assorted with the sordidness of her surroundings. One of Nature's curious freaks, this kitchen wench with a head which would have graced a duchess, her interesting personality merely the prey of a common charlatan, who used her for vulgar, senseless trickery.

For the moment her beauty was distorted through the dawning of an awful terror. To a sane man she would only have seemed a wretched, miserable, frightened woman. But not so to the ale-sodden, overheated minds of these excited creatures, blinded by an almost maniacal fear.

To them she looked supernaturally tall, supernaturally weird, with great glowing eyes and tongues of flame illumining her person.

"The witch!" they shouted, "the witch! the witch!"

"What do you want with me?" murmured the poor girl.

Egged on by their passions they smothered their terror. They seized her violently by the wrists and dragged her out of her lair and on to the platform, where the rest of the crowd were pressing.

A shout of exultation, of hellish triumph, greeted the appearance of the wretched woman. Not a spark of pity was aroused by her helplessness, her obvious, abject terror.

"The witch! the witch! death to the witch!"

They seemed to be fanning their own passions, adding fuel to the flames of their insensate wrath.

There was the source of all the evil which might have befallen the peaceful valley of the Thames! the creature with the evil eye, the dispenser of misery and death!

They had forgotten the guard now. Their lawlessness knew no bounds. But for the incessant din of the merry-makers at the Fair, the banging of the drums, and the shouts of the criers, their own yells of execration, their violent curses, and the shrieks of the captive girl could not have failed to attract attention.

But every one was busy laughing and enjoying the last hours of

32

this happy day. No one came to interfere in this devilish work which was about to be consummated.

And every word the poor woman uttered but brought further vituperation upon her.

She shouted, "Help!"

"Hark, my masters," sneered Matthew loftily, "she calls to Satan for help."

"What will you do with me?" she pleaded. "I've done you no wrong."

"Thou hast brought the devil in our midst."

"No! no!"

"I saw thee riding on a broomstick—going to thy Sabbath revels."

"'Tis false!"

"Tie her to the pole—quick!"

The so-called witch, the friend of Satan and of all the powers of darkness, fell upon her knees in an agony of the wildest despair. Realizing her position, the terrible doom which was awaiting her, her whole figure seemed to writhe with the agony of her horror. She dragged herself to Matthew's knees—he seemed to be leading the others—she wrenched her arms free from those who held her and threw them round him. She forced her voice to gentleness and pleading, tried to appeal to what was a stone wall of unconquerable prejudice.

"Sirs, kind sirs," she entreated, "you would not harm a poor girl who had done you no wrong? ... you won't harm me—you won't.... Oh, God!" she shrieked in her frenzy, "you wouldn't—you wouldn't—Holy Virgin, protect me——"

A rough hand was placed over her mouth and her last yells were smothered as she was ruthlessly dragged away.

Then with two or three leather belts she was securely tied to the flagstaff, whilst a thick woollen scarf was wound round her face and neck, leaving only the eyes free to roam wildly on the awful scene around.

Awful indeed!

Man turned to savage beast in the frenzy of his own fear.

Swift and silent, like so many rodents in the night, the men began collecting bits of wood, broke up their sticks into small pieces, tore branches down from the old elm tree.

Matthew the while, still the ringleader of this dastardly crew, was directing these gruesome operations.

"Hist!" he admonished incessantly, "not so much noise.... We don't want the guard to come this way, do we? ... Now, John the smith, quick, where's thy resin? ... James the wheelwright, thy tinder, friend.... Here! these faggots are not close enough.... Some more on the left there!"

And the men, as alert as their clumsy bodies would allow, as quick as the darkness would permit, groaning, sweating, falling up

33

against one another, worked with a will to accomplish the end which they had in view.

To burn the witch!

And she, the woman, her poor wits almost gone at sight of this fast approaching, inevitable doom, did not attempt to struggle. Had the gag been removed from her mouth she would not have uttered a sound.

Nature, more merciful than her own children, had paralysed the brain of the wretched girl and left her semi-imbecile, crazed, watching now with uncomprehending eyes the preparations for her own appalling death.

"Watch how the witch will burn!" said Matthew in a hoarse whisper. "Her soul will fly out of her mouth, and it'll be shaped like a black cat."

They had all descended the steps and were standing in a semicircle on the turf below, looking up at the miserable holocaust which they were about to offer up to their own cowardly superstition.

James the wheelwright was busy with his tinder, with John the smith bending over him, ready with a resin torch, which would start the conflagration.

And Mirrab, looking down on them with lack-lustre, idiotic eyes! Her body had fallen in a strange, shapeless heap across the leather bonds which held her, her feet were buried in the pile of faggots, whilst her fingers worked convulsively behind the flagstaff to which they were tied.

Ye gods, what a spectacle!

The Duke of Wessex, having taken leave of his friend, had been idly strolling towards the witch's booth, always closely followed by faithful Harry Plantagenet. At first sight of a group of men dimly outlined in the darkness he scarcely realized what was happening.

The fitful flicker of the torch, as the resin became ignited, threw the more distant figure of the woman into complete gloom.

Then there was a sudden shout of triumph. The torch was blazing at last.

"The holy fire! ... Burn the witch!"

John the smith, holding the torch aloft, inspired by the enthusiasm of his friends, had turned towards the steps.

For the space of one second the red glow illumined that helpless bundle of gaudy tinsel only dimly suggesting a woman's form beneath it, which hung limply from the flagstaff.

Then Wessex understood.

He had already drawn nigh, attracted by idle curiosity, but now with one bound he reached the steps. Striking out with his fists at two or three men who barred the way, he suddenly stood confronting these miscreants, the light of the torch glowing on the rich silk of his doublet, the jewelled agraffe of his hat, his proud, serious face almost distorted by overwhelming wrath.

"What damnable piece of mischief is this?" he said peremptorily.

He had scarcely raised his voice, for they were all silent, having retreated somewhat at sight of this stranger who barred the way.

The instinct of submission and deference to the lord was inborn in the country lout of these days. Their first movement was one of respectful awe. But this was only momentary. The excitement was too great, too real, to give way to this gallant, alone with only an elegant sword to stand between him and the mad desire for the witch's death.

"Out of the way, stranger!" shouted Matthew lustily from the rear of the group, "this is no place for fine gentlemen. Up with thy torch, John the smith! No one interferes here!"

"No! no! forward, John the smith!" exclaimed the others as with one voice.

But John the smith, torch in hand, could not very well advance. The fine gentleman was standing on the steps above him with a long pointed sword in his hand.

"The first one of you who sets foot on these steps is a dead man," he had said as soon as the shouts had subsided.

John the smith did not altogether care to be that notable first.

"Here! Harry, old friend," added the Duke, calling his dog to his side, "you see these miscreants there, when I say 'Go!' you have my permission to spring at the throat of the man who happens to be on these steps at the time."

Harry Plantagenet no doubt understood what was expected of him. His great jaws were slightly open, showing a powerful set of very unpleasant-looking teeth; otherwise for the moment he looked placid enough. He stood at the very top of the steps, his head on a level with his master's shoulder, and was wagging his tail in a pleasant, friendly spirit.

Matthew, however, had, not unjustly up to now, earned the respect of his friends. Whilst John the smith was still hesitating, he had already made a quick mental calculation that one Court gallant and his dog could be no real match against five-and-twenty lusty fellows with hard fists, who were determined to get their own way.

He elbowed his way to the front, pushed the smith aside, and began peremptorily—

"Stranger!——"

"Call me not stranger, dolt, I am the Duke of Wessex, and if thou dost not immediately betake thyself elsewhere, I'll have thee whipped till thou bleed. Now then, ye louts!" he added, addressing the now paralysed group of men, "off with your caps in my presence—quick's the word!"

There was dead silence, broken only by an occasional groan of real, tangible fright.

"The Duke of Wessex! Merciful heavens! he'll have us all hanged!" murmured Matthew as he fell on his knees.

35

One by one, still in complete silence, the caps were doffed. His Grace of Wessex! Future King of England mayhap! And they had dared to threaten him!

"Holy Virgin protect the lot of us!"

One man, more alert than his fellows, well in the rear of the group, began crawling away on hands and knees, hoping to escape unobserved. One or two saw his intention and immediately followed him. John the smith had already dropped his torch, which lay smouldering on the ground.

There was a distinct movement in the direction of general retreat.

"Well," laughed the Duke good-naturedly, "have you done enough mischief? ... Get ye gone, all of you!—or shall I have to call the guard and have you all whipped for a set of dastardly cowards, eh? ... Or better still, hanged, as your leader and friend here suggests—what?"

They had no need to be told twice. Still silently they picked up their caps, one or two of them scratched their addled pates. They were ashamed and really frightened, and had quite forgotten all about the witch.

There's nothing like real, personal danger to allay imaginary terrors. The devil was all very well, but he was a long way off, and for the moment invisible, whilst His Grace of Wessex was really there, and he was—well! he was His Grace of Wessex, and that's all about it.

One by one they edged away, and the darkness soon swallowed them up. The Duke never moved until the last of them had gone, leaving only Abra and his henchman cowering in terror beside the platform.

From behind a bank of clouds the pale, crescent moon suddenly emerged and threw a faint silvery light on the now deserted scene of the dastardly outrage.

"Well, Harry, my friend, I think that's the last of them ..." said Wessex lightly as he finally put up his sword and mounted the steps to the platform.

Mirrab's long strands of golden hair hung like a veil over her face and breast; she had straightened herself out somewhat, but her head was still bent. Her tottering reason was very slowly and gradually returning to her.

She did not even move whilst Wessex undid the leather belts which tied her to the flagstaff, and with his heel kicked the faggots to one side. She seemed as unconscious now of her safety as she had been a short while ago of her impending doom.

As her last bonds were severed she fell like a shapeless bundle on her knees.

He never looked at her. What was she but a poor tattered wreck of humanity, whom his timely interference had saved from an appalling death? But he was very sorry for her, because she was a woman, and had just gone through indescribable sufferings; in that gentle, impersonal pity, there was no room for the mere curiosity to know what she was like.

Before he finally turned to go, he placed a well-filled purse on the ground, not far from where she was cowering, and said very kindly—

"Take my advice, girl, and do not get thyself into any more mischief of this sort. Next time there might be no one nigh to get thee out of trouble. Come, Harry," he added, calling to his dog, "time is getting late."

At the foot of the steps he came across the shrinking forms of Abra and his companion. The Duke paused for a moment and said more sternly—

"As for thee, sirrah, get thee gone, bag and baggage, thy tents and thy trickeries, before the night is half an hour older. The guard shall be sent to protect thee; but if thou art still here an hour hence, those sobered ruffians will have returned, and nothing'll save thee and thy wench a second time."

He waited for no protestations from the abject wizard, and turned his steps towards the river.

As he was crossing the open space, however, he suddenly felt a tight grip on his cloak; he turned, yet could see nothing, for the capricious moon had once more hidden her light behind a passing cloud, and the darkness, by contrast, seemed all the more intense.

But he heard a sound which was very like a sob, and then a murmur which had a curious ring of passion in it—

"Thou hast saved my life ... 'tis thine ... I give it thee! ... Henceforth, whene'er I read the starlit firmament I'll pray to God that the most glorious star in heaven shall guide thy destiny!"

He gave a pleasant laugh, gently disengaged his cloak, and without another word went his way.

PART II

THE LADY URSULA

CHAPTER X

A BEVY OF FAIR MAIDENS

Never in all her life had Her Grace of Lincoln experienced anything so awful.

Her very coif, usually a pattern of propriety, looked awry and scarcely sober on her dear old head, whilst her round, chubby face, a beautiful forest of tangled wrinkles, expressed the most dire distress, coupled with hopeless, pathetic bewilderment.

"Well?" she repeated over and over again in breathless eagerness.

She seemed scarce to notice the pretty picture before her—two young girls standing with arms linked round one another's waists, eyes aglow with excitement, and cheeks made rosy with the palpitating intensity of the narrative.

Yet was not Her Grace justly proud of the flock of fair maids committed to her charge? What more charming than these two specimens of austere Queen Mary's dainty maids-of-honour, with their slim figures in the stiff corsets and unwieldy farthingales, their unruly curls held in becomingly by delicate lace coifs, and the sombre panelling of the room throwing up in harmonious contrast the vivid colouring of robes and kerchiefs, of lace and of complexion?

But to-day the Duchess of Lincoln had no eye for the charming sight. Leaning well forward in her high, straight-backed chair, her fat, be-ringed fingers were beating a veritable devil's tattoo against its brocaded arms.

"Alicia, girl, why don't you go on?" she added impatiently. "La! I vow the wench'll make me die of choler."

Alicia, in the eagerness of telling her thrilling story, had somewhat lost her breath; but now she made a vigorous effort to resume.

"Well," she said, "Your Grace must remember the night was very dark. Barbara and I were strolling by the low wall, when suddenly the clouds parted, the river was flooded with light, and just below us, not ten paces away, we saw——"

But here she broke off suddenly. A look of genuine distress crossed her piquant little face; she looked inquiringly at her

38

companion, then at the Duchess, whilst her merry eyes began to fill with tears.

"Oh! I scarce like to repeat it," she said hesitatingly at last, "for truly I love her so."

But Her Grace was in no mood to pander to girlish sentimentality just now. Her small round eyes, usually alive with good-nature and kindliness, were looking positively stern.

"Go on, child," she commanded, "cannot you see that I am verily sitting on pins? Was it—was it the Lady Ursula you saw?"

"Nay, madam," protested Alicia feebly, "'twas Barbara saw her—I do not believe that it was Ursula."

"She was wrapped in a dark cloak from head to foot," here interposed the other young maid. "When we called she looked up, but, seeing us, immediately fled along the bank."

"Then the clouds obscured the moon again, and we saw nothing more," resumed Alicia. "Barbara may have been mistaken."

Barbara nodded, quite longing to convince herself that she had indeed been mistaken. The two girls were getting more and more confused. Clearly they had no wish to get their absent friend into trouble, and, having been led into relating their experiences of the night before, they tardily realized that they were collecting storm-clouds over Lady Ursula's unsuspecting head.

With all her good-nature the Duchess was a stern disciplinarian, taking herself and her duties very seriously. When the Queen entrusted her with the formation of her own immediate feminine entourage, she also expressed a desire that her maids-of-honour and ladies-in-waiting should be models of decorum and veritable patterns of all the virtues.

The Court, which had been little else than a name in the old and gloomy palace of Richmond and the simple household at Esher, had seen some of its old glories revived since Mary's proclamation as sole and royal liege lady, Queen Sovereign of England.

Before and since the coronation, Hampton Court had once more become alive with merriment and laughter, with tennis and bowling games, jousts, suppers, and balls even, as in the best days of King Harry. Young people, who had been only temporarily sobered through the raging political conflicts of the past few months, quickly reasserted their desire for gaiety and splendour, and the Queen herself, somewhat softened with the joy of seeing England's loyalty towards her, tacitly acquiesced in this return to the ancient magnificence of her father's court.

Moreover, there were the foreign ambassadors to entertain, all eager to secure the Queen's hand for their respective royal masters, and in the meanwhile equally ready to be impressed with the luxuries of the English Court and the beauty and grace of its ladies.

The Duchess of Lincoln's task was certes no easy one, since it involved the keeping in order of a very attractive, pleasure-loving, highly unruly little flock.

So far, however, nothing serious had occurred to disturb her equanimity. The maids-of-honour placed under her charge had quickly succumbed to the charm of Her Grace's kindliness, and were easily ruled with the rod of good-nature.

Some scoldings and lectures, an admonition now and then, or a threat of more severe punishment, had readily quelled any incipient insubordination.

But since the arrival of Lady Ursula Glynde at the Palace matters had become more serious. The child was so terribly independent, so self-willed and unruly, and with it all so sweet and lovable, that the Duchess found all her scoldings of absolutely no avail.

Ursula defied her, then kissed and fondled her, rendering her absolutely helpless and defying her authority.

When it was discovered that the naughty child had, on the very day following Her Majesty's coronation, visited East Molesey Fair, masked and veiled, and attended only by weak-willed, silly Margaret Cobham, Her Grace felt nigh to having the palsy. But even that unseemly escapade was nothing in comparison with the terrible revelations which had recently come to Her Grace's ears. One or two rumours had already gained currency that one of Her Majesty's maids-of-honour had been seen alone and at night outside the purlieus of the Palace. So far, fortunately, the Queen knew nothing of this, nor had it been talked about among the gentlemen of the Court.

Heavens above! if such a thing were to happen! ...

"A scandal!" moaned the Duchess piteously, "a scandal in my department! Oh, I shall never survive it! If Her Majesty should hear of it, who is so austere, so pious! ... And with my lord Cardinal staying in the Palace just now.... What would he think of the morals of an English Court! ... Oh! the naughty, wicked child, thus to bring disgrace upon us all."

Some of the rumours anent Lady Ursula's mysterious nightly wanderings had already reached her; she had placed the other girls under severe cross-examination, and finally elicited from them the confirmation of her worst fears.

"Nay, madam," rejoined Alicia, tardily smitten with remorse, "I feel sure she means no harm. Ursula is gay, a madcap, full of fun, but she is too proud to stoop to an intrigue."

"Aye! but, child, she hath vanity," said the Duchess, shaking her grey curls, "and vanity is an evil counsellor. And, remember, 'tis not the first time she has been seen alone, at night, outside the purlieus of the garden. The Lord protect us! I should never survive a scandal."

"An Your Grace would believe me," added Barbara consolingly, "I think 'tis but a bit of foolish curiosity on the Lady Ursula's part."

But Her Grace would not be consoled.

"Curiosity?" she said. "Alas! 'tis an evil moment when curiosity leads a maiden out of doors at night ... alone ... Oh!"

And she made a gesture of such horror, there was such a look of stern condemnation in her kind old face, that the two girls began to feel really afraid as to what might befall that madcap, Ursula Glynde.

No one had ever seen the Duchess actually angry.

They were all ready to take up the cudgels for the absent girl now.

"Nay! 'tis harmless curiosity enough," said Alicia hotly. "Ursula is being very badly treated."

"Badly treated!" exclaimed Her Grace.

"Aye! she is affianced to the Duke of Wessex."

"Well, and what of it, child?"

"What of it?" retorted the girl indignantly, "she is never allowed to see him. The moment His Grace is expected to arrive in the Queen's presence, 'tis—'Lady Ursula, you may retire. I shall not need your services to-day.'"

And looking straight down her pretty nose, dainty Lady Alicia Wrenford pursed her lips and put on the starchy airs of a soured matron of forty.

The Duchess of Lincoln threw up her hands in horror.

"Fie on you, child!" she said sternly, "mimicking Her Majesty."

"'Tis quite true what Alicia says," here interposed Barbara, pouting; "everything is done to keep Ursula out of His Grace's way. And we, too, are made the scapegoats of this silly intrigue."

"Barbara, I forbid you to talk like that!"

"I mean nothing disrespectful, madam, yet 'tis patent to every one. Why are we relegated to this dreary old chamber this brilliant afternoon, when my lord the Cardinal and all the foreign ambassadors are at the Palace? Why are we not allowed to join the others at tennis, or watch the gentlemen at bowls? Why were Helen and Margaret kept from seeing the jousts? Why? Why? Why?"

She was stamping her little foot, eager, impatient, excited. The Duchess felt somewhat bewildered before this hurricane of girlish wrath.

"Because Her Majesty ordered it thus, child," she said in a more conciliatory spirit; "she hath not always need of all her maids-of-honour round her."

"Nay! that's not the reason," rejoined Barbara, "and Your Grace is too clever to believe it."

"You are a silly child and——"

"Then we are all silly, for 'tis patent to us all. 'Tis Ursula who is being kept wilfully away from the Court, or rather from seeing His Grace of Wessex, and in order not to make these machinations too obvious, some of us are also relegated in the background in her company."

41

"And 'tis small wonder that Ursula should wish to catch sight of the man whom her father vowed she should wed or else enter into a convent," concluded Alicia defiantly.

Her Grace was at her wits' ends. Too clever not to have noticed the intrigue to which the girls now made reference, she would sooner have died than owned that her Queen was acting wrongfully or even pettily.

However, for the moment she was spared the further discussion of this unpleasant topic, for a long, merry, girlish laugh was suddenly heard echoing through the great chambers beyond.

"Hush!" said the Duchess with reassumed severity, "'tis that misguided child herself. Now remember, ladies, not a word of all this. I must learn the truth on this scandal, and will set a watch to-night. But not a word to her."

The next moment the subject of all this animated conversation threw open the heavy oak door of the room. She came running in, with her fair hair flying in a deliriously mad tangle round her shoulders, her eyes dancing with glee, whilst above her head she was, with one small hand, flourishing a small piece of paper, the obvious cause of this apparently uncontrollable fit of girlish merriment.

CHAPTER XI

THE FAIREST OF THEM ALL

The Duchess was frowning for all she was worth. Alicia and Barbara tried to look serious, but were obviously only too ready to join in any frolic which happened to be passing in Ursula Glynde's lively little head.

"Oh!" said the latter, as soon as she had partially recovered her breath. "Oh! I vow 'tis the best of the bunch."

With the freedom of a spoilt child, who knows how welcome are its caresses, Ursula sidled up to the Duchess of Lincoln and sat down upon the arm of her chair.

"Your Grace, a share of your seat I entreat," she said gaily, heedless of stern looks. "Nay! I'll die of laughing unless you let me read you this."

"Child! child!" admonished the Duchess, still trying to look severe, "this loud laughter is most unseemly—and your cheeks all ablaze! What is it now?"

"What is it, sweet Grace?" responded the young girl. "A poem! Listen!"

She smoothed out the piece of paper, spread it out upon her knee and began reading solemnly:—

> *"If all the world were sought so farre*
> *Who could find such a wight?*
> *Her beauty twinkleth like a starre*
> *Within the frosty night.*
> *Her roseall colour comes and goes*
> *With such a comely grace,*
> *More ruddier too than doth the rose,*
> *Within her lively face."*

"And beneath this sonnet," she continued, "a drawing—see!—a heart pierced by a dagger. His heart—my beauty which twinkleth like a starre!"

Who could resist the joy and gladness, the freshness, the youth, the girlishness which emanated from Ursula's entire personality? The two other girls pressed closely round her, giggling like school-children at sight of the rough, sentimental device affixed to the love poem.

The Duchess vainly endeavoured to keep up a semblance of sternness, but she could not meet those laughing eyes, now dark, now blue, now an ever-changing grey, alive with irrepressible mischief, yet full of loving tenderness. She felt that her wrath would soon melt in the sunshine of that girlish smile.

"Lady Ursula, this is most unseemly," she said as coldly as she could. "How came you by this poem?"

Ursula threw her arms round the feebly-resisting old dame.

"Hush!" she whispered, "in your dear old ears! I found it, sweet Duchess ... beside my stockings ... when I came out of my bath!"

"Horror!"

"Now, Duchess! dear, sweet, darling, beautiful Duchess, tell me, who think you wrote this poem? And who—who think you placed it near my stockings?"

The Duchess was almost speechless, partly through genuine horror, but chiefly because a sweet, fresh face was pressed closely to her old cheek.

"'Twas not the Earl of Norfolk," continued Ursula meditatively. She seemed quite unconscious of the enormity of her offence, and sought the eyes of her young friends in confirmation of these various surmises. "He cannot write verses. Nor could it be my lord of Overcliffe, for he would not know where to find my stockings."

"The vanity of the child!" sighed Her Grace. "Think you these great gentlemen would write verses to a chit of a girl like you?"

But her kind eyes, resting with obvious pride on the dainty figure beside her, belied the severity of her words.

43

"Yes," replied Ursula decisively, "bad ones!—not such beautiful verses as these."

Then she went on with her conjectures.

"And there's my lord of Everingham, and the Marquis of Taunton, and——"

"His Grace of Wessex," suggested Alicia archly, despite the Duchess's warning frown.

"Alas, no!" sighed Ursula, "for he has never been allowed to see me."

"Ursula!" came in ever-recurring feeble protests from the old dowager.

But the young girl was wholly unabashed.

"But he will see me—before to-night," she said.

The others exchanged significant glances.

"To-night?"

"Yes! What have I said? Why do you all look like that?"

"Because your conduct, child, is positively wanton," said the Duchess.

But Ursula only hugged the kind old soul all the more closely.

"Now—now," she coaxed, "don't be angry, darling. There!—look!" she added with mock horror, "your coif is all awry."

With deft fingers she rearranged the delicate lace cap over Her Grace's white curls.

"So," she said, "now you look pretty again—and your nice, fat cheeks have the sweetest of dimples. Nay, I vow, all these young gallants only sigh with love for me because you frown on them so!"

"What a madcap!" sighed the Duchess, mollified.

"You won't be angry with me?" queried the girl earnestly.

"Nay! that depends what mad pranks you have been after."

"Sh—sh!—sh!—'tis a deadly secret. Barbara, Alicia, come a little closer."

She paused a moment, whilst all three of them crowded round Her Grace of Lincoln's chair.

Then Ursula said solemnly—

"The Queen is in love with my future husband!"

The Duchess of Lincoln nearly fell backwards in a faint.

"Ursula!" she gasped.

"Nay, that's not the secret," continued Ursula, quite unperturbed, "for that is town-talk, and every one at Court knows that she won't let him see me for fear he should fall in love with me. And my lord Cardinal is furious because he wants the Queen to marry Philip of Spain, and he is wishing His Grace of Wessex down there, where all naughty Cardinals go."

"Child! ... child! ..."

"But the days are slipping by, darling," added the young girl, with just a shade of seriousness in her eyes. "All these intriguers may fight as much as they like, but if I do not wed His Grace of Wessex, if he should be inveigled into marrying the Queen, I must to the convent. My dear father made me swear it on his deathbed, when I was beside myself with grief, and scarce knew what I did. 'There is but one true gentleman to whom I would trust my child,' he said to me; 'swear to me, Ursula, that if Wessex claims you not, that you will never marry any one else, but spend your days in happy singleness in a convent. Swear it, little one.' He was so ill, so dear, I swore and——"

"The convent is the proper place for such a feather-brain as yourself," concluded the Duchess with as gruff a voice as she could command.

"But I do not wish to be a nun," protested Ursula, as tears began to gather in her eyes, "and I do want to wed Wessex, who is handsome—and   gallant—and   witty—and—and," she added coquettishly, "when he sees me—I vow he'll not let me go to a convent either, so——"

She leant closer to the kind dowager and once more whispered confidentially in her ear.

"So, as the Queen is engaged in prayers for at least half an hour, I've sent His Grace word by one of the pages that the Duchess of Lincoln desired his presence in this chamber—here!"

But this was really past bearing.

"I! ..." exclaimed the Duchess in horror. "I? ... desire his presence? ... Merciful heavens! what will His Grace think?"

Once more Ursula, like the veritable child that she was, was dancing like mad round the room, now alone, clapping her tiny hands together, then seizing one of her companions by the waist, she whirled with her, round and round, until she fell back breathless against the Duchess's chair. And all the while her tongue went prattling on, now talking at top speed, anon singing out the words in the madness of her glee.

"And he is coming, dear Duchess," she said. "'He'll attend upon Her Grace at once!' these were his words to that pet of a page, and he'll see me—and—and——"

Now she paused, kneeling beside her old friend, putting coaxing arms round the bulky figure of the kind soul.

"But don't tell him my name all at once, Duchess darling," she whispered entreatingly; "let him fall in love with me without knowing that I am his affianced bride—for that might prejudice him against me. Just mumble something when he asks my name, and let me do the rest. Give me another kiss, darling. Alicia—Alicia," she cried in feverish anxiety, "is my kerchief straight at the back? and—and—oh, my hair!"

Still in that same madly-excited mood, she ran to a small oval mirror which hung on one of the walls, close to the great bay window.

The Duchess during that brief moment's respite tried to collect her scattered wits.

45

"But oh! what shall I say to His Grace?" she moaned distractedly. "Child! child! to your folly there is no end!"

A quickly smothered shriek from Ursula now brought the other girls to her side in the embrasure. She was pointing across the court to the gateway beneath the clock tower.

"He is coming!" she cried, with a slightly nervous tremor in her voice. "It is he, with my lord Everingham; they are laughing and talking together.... Oh, how handsome he looks!" she added enthusiastically. "My future husband, my lord, not the Queen's—mine own, mine own! Alicia, tell me, hast ever seen a more goodly sight than that of my future husband in that beautiful silken doublet and with that dear, dear dog of his walking so proudly behind him? Harry Plantagenet, thou'rt a lucky dog, and I'll kiss thee first, and—and——"

Then she ran back to the Duchess.

"Two minutes to mount the stairs, two more to cross the Great Hall, then the watching chamber, the presence chamber.... In six minutes he will be here—hush!—I hear a footstep! ... Holy Virgin, how my heart beats!"

There had come a discreet knock at the door. All four women were too excited to respond, but the next moment the door was opened and a young page, dressed in the same gorgeous livery which Henry VIII had originally prescribed, entered and bowed to the ladies.

Then he turned to the Duchess of Lincoln.

"Her Majesty the Queen desires the immediate presence of Her Grace and of her maids-of-honour in the Oratory."

There was dead silence in the room whilst the page once more bowed in the elaborate manner ordained by Court etiquette; then he walked backwards to the door, and stood there, holding it open ready for the ladies to pass.

"No, no, no!" whispered Ursula excitedly, as the Duchess immediately rose to obey.

"Ladies!" commanded Her Grace.

"One minute, darling," entreated Ursula, "just one short little minute!"

But where the Queen's commands were concerned Her Grace of Lincoln was adamant.

"Ladies!" she ordered once more.

Alicia and Barbara, though terribly disappointed at the failure of the exciting conspiracy, were ready enough to obey. Ursula wildly ran back to the window.

"I can see his silhouette and that of my lord Everingham slowly moving across the Great Hall," she said.

"Oh! why is he so slow?"

The Duchess turned to the page.

"Precede!" she commanded. "We'll follow."

She then pointed to the door. Alicia and Barbara, endeavouring to look grave, walked out with becoming dignity.

Her Grace went up to Ursula, who was still clinging to the window embrasure with passionate obstinacy.

"Lady Ursula Glynde," she said sternly, "if you do not obey Her Majesty's commands instantly, you'll be dismissed from the Court this very day."

And while His Grace of Wessex was slowly wending his way towards the chamber where he had been so eagerly expected, Lady Ursula, defiant and rebellious, was being peremptorily marshalled off in an opposite direction.

CHAPTER XII

INTRIGUES

When Wessex, accompanied by his friend, reached the room which so lately was echoing with merry girlish laughter, he was met by a page, deputed by the Duchess of Lincoln to present her excuses to His Grace for her non-appearance.

"Nay! marry, this is the bravest comedy ever witnessed," laughed the Duke, when the boy had gone.

"What, my lord?" asked Everingham with seeming unconcern.

"A comedy, friend, in which the Queen, Her Grace of Lincoln, you, and His Eminence the Cardinal, all play leading rôles."

"I don't understand."

"Well done, man! Nay! I know not yet which of you will win; but this I know, that whilst I do my best to whisper sweet nothings in Her Majesty's ear, you are pleased, the Cardinal is furious, and the Duchess of Lincoln discreetly keeps my affianced bride out of my way."

"For this at least Your Grace should be grateful," rejoined his friend with a smile.

"Grateful that other people should guide my destiny for me? Well, perhaps! 'Twould certes have been ungallant to flee from danger, when danger takes the form of a future wife. I cannot picture myself saying to a lady: 'Madam, honour demands that I should wed you, and thus hath put it out of my power ever to love you.' But since the Lady Ursula is so unapproachable, marry!—methinks I am almost free!"

"Perchance it is the lady herself who avoids Your Grace."

"Nay! undoubtedly she does. Poor girl! how she must hate the

47

very thought of me. Her dear father, I fear me, was wont to sing my praises in her childish ears; now that she hath arrived at years of discretion, my very name must have become an obsession to her. Obviously even a convent must be preferable. Then why this mad desire to keep us apart? Mutual understanding would do that soon enough."

The two men had once more turned to go back the way they came; slowly they strolled across the vast and lofty rooms and through the Great Hall, which, deserted at this time of day, was the scene of so much gaiety and magnificence during the evening hours.

"Your Grace, methinks, must be mistaken," said Everingham after a while; "there is, at any rate on the part of your friends, no desire to keep you and the Lady Ursula apart; you are best judge of your own honour, my lord, and no one would presume to dictate to you; but the most sensitive conscience in England could but hold the opinion that, whilst the lady may feel bound by her promise to her father, you are as free as air—free to wed whom you choose."

"By the mass! what an anomaly, friend! Free to wed! free to wear fetters! the most terrible chains ever devised by the turpitude of man."

"Marriage is a great institution——"

"Nay! 'tis an evil one, contrived out of malice by priests and old maids to enchain a woman who would rather be free to a man who speedily becomes bored."

"Nay! but when that woman is a queen?"

"Take off her crown and what is she, friend?" rejoined His Grace lightly. "A woman ... to be desired, of course, to be loved, by all means— but at whose feet we should only recline long enough to make all other men envious, and one woman jealous."

Everingham frowned. He hated this flippant, careless mood of his friend. He did not understand it. To him the idea of such a possibility as a union with the Queen of England was so great, so wonderful, so superhuman almost, that he felt that the man who deserved such incommensurate honour should spend half his days on his knees, thanking God for such a glorious destiny.

That Wessex hung back when Mary herself was holding out her hand to him seemed to this enthusiast almost a sacrilege.

"But surely you have ambition, my lord?" he said at last.

"Ambition?" replied Wessex with characteristic light-heartedness. "Yes, one!—to be a boy again."

"Nay! an you were that now, you could not understand all that England expects of you. The Queen is harassed by the Cardinal and the Spanish ambassador. Philip but desires her hand in order to lay the iron heel of Spain upon the neck of submissive England. Your Grace can save us all. Mary loves you, would wed you to-morrow."

"And send me to the block for my infidelities—supposed or real— the day after, and be free to wed Philip or the Dauphin after all."

"I'll not believe it."

"Friend! do you know what you ask of me? To marry—that is to say to give up all that makes life poetic, beautiful, amusing, the love which lasts a day, the delights which live one hour, woman in her most alluring aspect, the unattainable; and in exchange what do you offer me—the smaller half of a crown."

"The gratitude of a nation ..." protested Everingham.

"Ah! A woman, however fickle she may be, is more constant than a nation ... As for gratitude? ... nay, my lord ... let us not speak of the gratitude of nations."

"This is not your last word, friend," pleaded Lord Everingham earnestly.

They had reached the foot of the stairs, and were once more under the gateway of the clock tower, where Lady Ursula Glynde had caught sight of them from the great bay-window opposite.

It was a glorious afternoon. October, always lovely in England, was more beautiful and mellow this year than it had ever been. Wessex paused a moment, with his slender hand placed affectionately on his friend's shoulder. He looked round him—at the great windows of the hall, the vast enclosure of the Base Court beyond, the distant tower of the chapel visible above the fantastic roofs and gables of Henry VIII's chambers, the massive, imposing grandeur of the great pile which had seen so many tragedies, witnessed so many sorrows, so many downfalls, such treachery and such horrible deaths. A shudder seemed to go through his powerful frame, a look of resolution, of pride, and of absolute disdain crept into his lazy, deep-set eyes. Then he said quietly—

"That is my last word, friend. I'll never be made a puppet on which to hang the cloak of political factions and intrigues. My life belongs to my country, but neither my liberty nor my self-respect. If my friendship will help to influence the Queen into refusing to wed the King of Spain I'll continue to exert it to the best of my ability, but I'll not become Her Majesty's lapdog, nor the tool of my friends."

Then once more the hardness and determination vanished from his face; the nonchalance and careless idleness of the grand seigneur was alone visible now.

With easy familiarity he linked his arm through that of Everingham.

"Shall we rejoin Her Majesty on the terrace?" he said lightly. "She will have finished her orisons, and will be awaiting us. Come, Harry!"

CHAPTER XIII

HIS EMINENCE

A merry company was gathered on the terrace, which, fronting the ill-fated Cardinal Wolsey's rooms, descended in elegantly sloping grades down to the old Pond Garden, giving an exquisite view across the tall, trim hedges, the parterres gay with late summer flowers, and the green bosquets of lilac and yew, to the serpentine river and distant landscape beyond.

Mary Tudor had indeed finished her afternoon orisons. She had recited her rosary in the chapel, kneeling before the altar and surrounded by her maids-of-honour: no doubt she had prayed for the Virgin's help to aid her in the accomplishment of the one great wish which lay so near to her heart.

She was this afternoon expecting the arrival of a special envoy from His Holiness the Pope, and had to curtail her prayers in consequence. She had strolled back to the terrace, because His Eminence the Cardinal de Moreno was there, the ambassador of His Most Catholic Majesty the King of Spain, also the Duc de Noailles, who represented the King of France, and Scheyfne, who watched over the interests of the Emperor Charles V in this game of political conflicts, wherein the hand of the Queen of England was the guerdon.

Mary Tudor watched them all with a sleepy eye. She felt dreamy and contented this beautiful afternoon: was not the envoy from Rome bringing her a special blessing from His Holiness? and what could that blessing be but the love of the one man in all the world to whom she would gladly have given her hand to hold and her lips to kiss?

She sighed as she settled herself down on the straight-backed chair which she affected. Noailles and Scheyfne hurried eagerly towards her. His Eminence bowed low as she approached, but her eyes wandered restlessly round her in search of the one form dear to her, and she frowned impatiently when she missed the proud, handsome face, whose smile alone could bring hers forth in response.

She listened with but half an ear to Noailles' platitudes, or to His Eminence's smooth talk, until close by she heard the well-known step. She did not turn her head. Her heart, by its sudden, rapid beating, had told her that he was there.

Mary Tudor was not quite forty then, a woman full of the passionate intensity of feeling, characteristic of the Tudors, neither beautiful nor yet an adept at women's wiles; but when she heard Wessex' footsteps on the flagstones of the terrace, her whole face lighted up with that radiance which makes every woman fair—the radiance of a whole-hearted love.

50

"Nay, my lord Cardinal," she said with sudden impatience, "Your Eminence has vaunted the beauties of Spain long enough to-day. I feel sure," she added, half turning towards Wessex, "that His Grace, though a truant from our side, will hold a brief for Merrie England against you."

The Duke, as he approached, scanned with a lazy eye the brilliant company gathered round the Queen; an amused smile, made up partly of sarcasm, wholly of insouciance, glimmered in his eyes as he caught the frown, quickly suppressed, which appeared on the Cardinal's shrewd, clever face.

"Nay, His Eminence hath but to look on our Sovereign Lady," he said, as he gallantly kissed the tips of the royal hand, graciously extended to him, "to know that England hath naught to envy Spain."

Mary, with the rapid intuition of the woman who loves, seemed to detect a more serious tone in Wessex' voice than was his wont. She looked inquiringly at him. The thoughts, engendered in his mind by Everingham's earnestness and enthusiasm, had left their shadow over his lighter mood.

"You look troubled, my lord!" she said anxiously.

"What trouble I had Your Grace's presence has already dispelled," he replied gently.

It amused him to watch the discomfited faces of his political antagonists, whose presence now Mary seemed completely to ignore. Her whole personality was transformed in his presence: she looked ten years younger; her heavy, slow movements appeared suddenly to gain in elasticity.

She rose and beckoned to Wessex to accompany her. Neither Noailles nor Scheyfne cared to follow, fearing a rebuke.

His Eminence the Cardinal de Moreno alone, seeing her turn towards the gardens, ventured on a remark.

"At what hour will Your Majesty deign to receive the envoy of His Holiness?" he asked unctuously.

"As soon as he arrives," replied the Queen curtly.

His Eminence watched the two figures disappearing down the stone steps of the terrace. There was a troubled, anxious look in his keen eyes. The first inkling had just dawned upon him that perhaps he might fail in his mission after all.

A new experience for the Cardinal de Moreno.

When Philip of Spain desired to wed Mary of England he chose the one man in all Europe most able to carry his wishes through. A perfect grand seigneur, veritable prince of the Church, but a priest only in name, for he had never taken Holy Orders, His Eminence shone in every circle wherein he appeared, through the brilliancy of his intellect, the charm and suavity of his manner, and above all by that dominating personality of his, which willed so strongly what he desired to obtain.

Willed it at times—so his enemies said—without scruple. Well, perhaps! and if so, why not? would be His Eminence's own argument.

51

Heaven had given him certain weapons: these he used in order to get Heaven's own ends. And in the mind of the Cardinal de Moreno, Heaven was synonymous with the political interests of the Catholic Church. England was too fine a country to be handed over to the schismatic sect without a struggle, the people were too earnest, too deeply religious to be allowed to remain in the enemy's camp.

And His Eminence was not only fighting for an important political alliance for his royal master, but also for the reconquest of Catholic England. Wessex, a firm yet unostentatious adherent of the new faith, was to him an opponent in every sense.

When the Cardinal first landed in England he had been assured that the volatile and nonchalant Duke would never become a serious obstacle to Spanish plans.

The Duke? Perhaps not. But there was the Queen herself, half sick for love! and women's follies have ere now upset the most deeply laid, most important plans.

"Ah, my friend!" sighed His Eminence with ill-concealed irritation, as the Marquis de Suarez came idly lounging beside him, "alas! and alack-a-day! when diplomacy hath to reckon with women.... Look at that picture!" he added, pointing with be-ringed, slender, tapering finger to the figures of Wessex and Mary Tudor disappearing amid the bosquets of the park, "and think that the destinies of Europe depend upon how a woman of forty can succeed in chaining that butterfly."

Don Miguel too had followed with frowning eyes the little comedy just enacted upon the terrace. His intellect, though perhaps not so keen as that of his chief, was nevertheless sufficiently on the alert to recognize that Mary Tudor had distinctly intended to administer a snub to the entire diplomatic corps, by her marked preference for Wessex' sole company.

"Chance certainly, seems against your schemes and mine, my lord Cardinal," he said; "for that butterfly is heart-free and indolent, whilst the woman of forty is a queen."

"Indolent, yes," mused His Eminence, "but ambitious?"

"His friends will supply the ambition," rejoined Don Miguel; "and the Crown of England is a heavy prize."

The Cardinal did not speak for a moment. He seemed buried in thought.

"I was thinking of the beautiful Lady Ursula Glynde," he said meditatively after a while.

"Beautiful indeed. But His Grace is never allowed to see her."

"But when he does——".

"Oh! if I judge him rightly, when he does sée her—she is passing beautiful, remember—his roving fancy will no doubt be enchained for—shall we say—half an hour—perhaps half a day.... What then?"

"Half an hour!" mused the Cardinal. "Much may be done in half an hour, my lord Marquis."

52

"Bah!"

"In half an hour a woman, even if she be a queen, might become piqued and jealous, and the destinies of Europe will be shaped accordingly."

His keen grey eyes were searching the bosquets, trying to read what went on behind the dark yew hedges of the park.

"To think that the fate of Catholic Europe should depend upon the chance meeting of a young girl and a Court gallant," sighed Don Miguel impatiently.

"The fate of empires has hung on more slender threads than these ere now, my son," rejoined His Eminence quietly; "diplomacy is the art of seeming to ignore the great occasions whilst seizing the small opportunity."

He said nothing more, for at that same moment there came to his ears, gently echoing across the terrace, the sound of a half-gay, half-melancholy ditty. A pure, girlish voice was singing somewhere within the Palace, like a young caged bird behind the bars, at sight of the brilliant sunshine above.

Don Miguel gave a short sarcastic laugh.

"The Lady Ursula's voice," he said.

Then he pointed to the more distant portion of the garden, where Wessex and Mary were once more seen strolling slowly back towards the terrace.

A look of expectancy, of shrewd and sudden intuition crept into the Cardinal's handsome face. The eyes lighted up as if with a quick, bright, inward vision, whilst the thin lips seemed to close with a snap, as if bent on guarding the innermost workings of the mind.

He took his breviary from his pocket and began walking along the flagstones of the terrace in the direction whence the song had come. His head was bent; apparently he was deeply absorbed in the Latin text.

Don Miguel had not followed him. He knew that his chief wished to be alone. He watched the crimson robes slowly fading away into the distance. The Cardinal presently disappeared round the angle formed by Wolsey's rooms. Beyond these were the fine chambers built by Henry VIII. The sweet song still came from there, wafted lightly on the summer breeze.

CHAPTER XIV

THE DESTINIES OF EUROPE

Five minutes later His Eminence's brilliantly clad figure once more reappeared round the angle of the Palace. The breviary was no longer in his hands.

A few moments later he had joined Don Miguel, and together the two men watched the Queen and Wessex, as they drew nearer to the terrace steps.

A smile was on His Eminence's lips, suave, slightly sarcastic, and at the same time triumphant, yet at this very instant when he seemed so pleased with himself, or with events in general, Mary Tudor was looking with loving anxiety in His Grace of Wessex' eyes.

"I seem unable to cheer you to-day, my dear lord," she said. "What has become of your usual gay spirits?"

"Gone eavesdropping on my lord Cardinal," replied the Duke with a smile, as he spied the crimson robes on the top of the steps, "to find out how soon a King of Spain will rule over England and capture the heart of our Queen."

Mary paused and suddenly laid an eager hand on his wrist.

"Methought you cared nothing for the affairs of state," she said with some sadness, "and still less as to who shall rule over the heart of your Queen."

"Shall I dismiss the Spanish ambassador?" she added in an excited whisper, "and His Eminence?—and M. de Noailles? ... all of them? ... I have not yet given my answer. Will you dictate it, my lord?"

He looked up and saw the Cardinal's piercing eyes fixed steadily upon him. For one moment he hesitated. His Eminence looked so sure of himself, so proud of his ascendency over this impulsive woman, that just for the space of five seconds the thought crossed his mind that he would yield to the entreaties of his friends, and wrest the crown of England from the grasping hands of these foreigners, all eagerly waiting to snatch it for themselves.

As the Cardinal himself had said, but a short while ago, "the destinies of empires oft hang on more slender threads than these." No doubt none knew better than the shrewd Spaniard himself, how nigh he was at that moment to losing the great game which he played.

Who knows?—if at this instant the sudden commotion on the terrace had not stopped the words on Wessex' lips, how different might have been the destinies of England! But just as His Grace would have spoken, the major-domo's voice rang out:—

"The envoy of His Holiness the Pope awaits Her Majesty in the audience chamber."

"The envoy of His Holiness," said His Eminence with his usual suavity, as he stepped forward to meet the Queen, "and I am to have the honour of introducing him to your Majesty."

The major-domo, who had announced the news, was standing at some little distance with the pages who had accompanied him. The rest of the Court had dispersed when Mary strolled off with the Duke; only two or three ladies, in immediate attendance on the Queen, were laughing and chattering close by.

The Palace itself seemed astir with new movement and life, horses were stamping in the flagged courts, men were heard running and shouting, whilst the rhythmic sound of a brass trumpet at intervals announced the important arrival.

But through all this noise and bustle, the sweet, sad ditty sung by a fresh young voice still seemed to fill the air.

Mary was visibly chafing under this sudden restraint put upon her by rigid ceremonial. His Holiness' envoy could not be kept waiting, though she, poor woman, was burning with desire to prolong the happy tête-à-tête with the man she loved.

She felt His Eminence's eyes watching her every movement. She threw him a defiant look, then peremptorily ordered the major-domo and the pages to precede her.

His Grace of Wessex, on the other hand, seemed obviously relieved. He had turned his head in the direction whence came that girlish song, and appeared to be listening intently.

"Will you accompany us, my lord?" said the Queen in a tone of obvious command. "I must not keep the envoy of His Holiness waiting, and have need of your presence."

She placed her hand on his arm. Respect and chivalry compelled him to obey, yet he seemed loath to go.

"The Lady Ursula's song seems to fascinate His Grace of Wessex," whispered Don Miguel in His Eminence's ear.

"Hush! the small opportunity, my lord Marquis," whispered the Cardinal in reply.

"Have I the honour of following Your Majesty?" he added respectfully, bowing to the Queen.

"Nay, on our left, Your Eminence," rejoined Mary coldly.

Her right hand was still on Wessex' arm, and slowly, as if reluctantly, she began to move in the direction of the Palace. Don Miguel, at an almost imperceptible sign from his chief, had quickly disappeared down the terrace steps.

"Ah! my breviary!" suddenly exclaimed His Eminence in great perturbation. "I forgot it on the terrace!—the Nuncio will desire a prayer, and I am helpless without my Latin text! ... If Your Majesty will deign to forgive one moment ...."

He made a movement as if he would turn back.

From the further end of the terrace the young singer was continuing her song.

"Will Your Eminence allow me?" said the Duke of Wessex with alacrity.

"With pleasure, my dear lord," responded the Cardinal urbanely. "Ah! had I your years and you mine, 'twere my pleasure to serve you.... And Her Majesty will excuse ..." he added pointedly, for His Grace was quite ready to withdraw, whilst Mary was equally prepared to stop him with a look. "Will Your Majesty deign to place your hand on my arm? The envoy of His Holiness the Pope awaits your Most Catholic Majesty."

He was standing before her, outwardly respectful and full of deference. The pages and ladies had already disappeared within the Palace, whilst the Duke of Wessex, taking the Queen's silence for consent, had turned back towards the distant part of the terrace.

Mary, with all her weaknesses where her affections were concerned, was too proud to let this Spaniard see that she felt baffled and not a little humiliated. She guessed that this had been a ruse, a trap into which she had fallen. How it had all been done she knew not, but she could easily guess why.

She smothered the angry words which had risen to her lips, and without looking either to the right or left of her, she walked quickly towards the Palace.

CHAPTER XV

THE HAND OF FATE

Ursula had had a good cry.

She was a mere girl, only just out of her teens; she had been hideously disappointed and had given way to a paroxysm of tears, just like a child that has been cheated of its toys.

As far as her actual feelings for Wessex were concerned, she scarcely troubled to analyse them. As a tiny child she had worshipped the gallant boy, who had always been pointed out to her as the pattern of what an English nobleman should be, and moreover as the future husband who was to rule over her destiny.

No doubt that the Earl of Truro, lying on his deathbed, had but little real perception of what he was doing, when he forced his daughter to swear that she would marry Wessex or remain single to the end of her days.

But Ursula was thirteen years old then, and held an oath to her father to be the most sacred thing in the world. She had not seen Wessex for some years, but her girlish imagination had always endowed him with all those chivalrous attributes which her own father, whom she idolized, had already ascribed to him.

Love? Well, it scarce could be called that as yet. In spite of her score of years, Ursula had remained a child in thought, in feelings, in temperament. She had spent the last six or seven years within the precincts of old Truro Castle, watched over by her late father's faithful servants, who brought her up and worshipped her, taught her what they knew, and obeyed her implicitly.

Her one idea, however, had remained, that of a marriage with Wessex. By right and precedence she could claim a place in the Queen of England's immediate entourage. As soon as she was old enough she asserted this claim, and journeyed to Esher in charge of an old aunt, who had supervised her education since her father's death.

Since then her one desire had been to meet the man to whom she had pledged her troth. She had seen him, oh! scores of times, since the day on which he came back to the Court, but Mary Tudor, bent on winning his love, had resolutely kept him away from the beautiful girl who, she instinctively felt, would prove a formidable rival.

It had been easy enough up to now. His Grace, partly in order to please his friends, even if only half believing that his influence would prevent Mary Tudor from contracting an alien marriage, had been in constant attendance on the Queen.

Ursula, on the other hand, had been relegated into the background. She knew this well and chafed at the restraint. Something seemed to tell her that if she could but see the Duke he would easily realize that it would not be very hard to fulfil the old earl's promise. She knew that she was beautiful, her own mirror and the admiration of the Court gallants had already told her that, and at the same time she felt within herself a magnetism which must inevitably draw him towards her.

But time was speeding on. Ursula's quick intelligence had very soon grasped the threads of the present political situation, whilst Mary Tudor, on the other hand, made no secret of her love for Wessex. The young girl was well aware of the many intrigues which were being hatched round the personality of the man whom she looked upon as her affianced husband, and guessed how much these were aided by the enamoured Queen.

His Eminence the Cardinal, the Duc de Noailles, Scheyfne, Don Miguel de Suarez, all were seeking to obtain a definite promise from Mary. The English faction, on the other hand, hoped to force the Duke into a marriage which was obviously distasteful to him.

Ursula, in the midst of these contending parties, was, nevertheless, determined to gain her end. Too unsophisticated to attempt a serious intrigue, she relied on her woman's instinct to guide her to success. Her little plot to bring His Grace to her presence that afternoon had failed, probably owing to the Queen's keen acumen; and the young girl, for the first time since her arrival at Court, felt genuinely mortified and not a little despairing of ultimate triumph.

The Duke, evidently, had no desire to meet her, or he would have accomplished that end somehow. There was not much that His Grace wished that did not sooner or later come to pass.

Obviously, for the moment, he was glad enough to remain free of those bonds which truly were none of his making. Chivalry alone might tempt him to fulfil Lord Truro's dying wishes, for the late Earl and the Duke's own father had been the closest of friends. Ursula's pride, however, would not allow her to appeal to that chivalry; what she wanted was to gain his love.

Out of her childish admiration for the boy had grown a kind of poetic interest in the man, more than fostered by the great popularity enjoyed by Wessex, and the praises of his personality sung on every side. Ursula was still too young to be in love with aught else save with love itself, with her own imaginative fancy, her own conception of what her future husband should be.

He should be good to look at—like Wessex. High-born and gracious—like Wessex. A king among men, witty and accomplished— like Wessex.

"Holy Virgin! let me have him for mine own!" was her constant, childish prayer.

The girl was not yet a woman.

Thus musing and meditating, she strolled out into the garden, singing as she went. All the maids-of-honour had been bidden to wait on Her Majesty in the audience chamber, save Lady Ursula Glynde and Mistress Margaret Cobham, whose services would not be required. The Duchess of Lincoln, shrewdly guessing from this summons that His Grace of Wessex was in the Queen's company, had given the two young maids leave to wander whither they pleased.

Lazy Margaret had pleaded a headache and curled herself up in a window-embrasure with the express intention of doing nothing at all; but Ursula, with a burning desire for freedom and a longing for flowers, birds, and sunshine, had wandered out into the open.

A parterre of marguerites was laid out close to the terrace. Mooning, dreaming, singing, she had picked a bunch of these and was mechanically plucking their snow-white petals one by one.

Did she guess what a dainty picture she made, as she stood for one moment beside the pond, her shimmering gown of delicate white glistening against a background of dark green yews, her fair hair shining like gold beneath the soft rays of the October sun? Her sweet face was bent down, earnestly intent upon consulting the flowery oracle: a delicate shadow, that soft pearly grey tone beloved of Rubens, fell upon her girlish breast, her soft round arms, the dainty hands which held the marguerite.

"He loves me," she said, half audibly, "a little ... passionately ... not at all. He loves me ... a little ...."

So wrapped up was she in these important rites, that she did not hear a muffled footstep upon the gravel. The next moment she felt two firm hands upon her waist, whilst a laughing voice completed the daisy's prophecy,—

"Passionately!"

She gave a little gasp, but did not immediately turn to look who the intruder was. Her woman's instinct had told her that, and then she knew—or guessed—the sound of his voice. The moment had come at last. It had been none of her seeking; she did not pause to think how it had all happened, she only felt that he was near her and that her life's happiness depended on whether he thought her fair.

The pleasant little demon of girlish coquetry whispered to her that, in the midst of this poetic setting of an old-world garden, he would be hard to please indeed if he did not fall a victim to her smile.

She turned and faced him.

"Ah!" she said, with a little cry of feigned surprise, "His Grace of Wessex! ... I ... I vow you frightened me, my lord ... I thought this part of the garden quite deserted, and ... and the Duke of Wessex at the feet of the Queen."

She looked divinely pretty as she stood there before him, a delicate, nervous little blush suffusing her young cheeks, her eyes veiled by a fringe of lashes slightly darker than her golden hair. As dainty a picture as this fastidious man had ever gazed upon.

"At your feet, fair one," he replied, with undisguised admiration expressed in his every look, "and burning with jealousy at thought of him, for whose sake your sweet fingers plucked the petal of that marguerite."

She still held the flower, half stripped of its petals; he put out his hand in order to take it from her, or perhaps merely for the sake of touching for one second the soft velvet of her own.

Harry Plantagenet, close by, had stretched himself out lazily in the sun.

"Oh!" said Ursula, a little confused, still a little shy and nervous, "that ... that was for a favourite brother who is absent ... and I wished to know if he had not forgotten me."

"Impossible," he replied with deep conviction, "even for a brother."

"Your Grace is pleased to flatter."

"The truth spoken to one so fair must ever seem a flattery."

"Your Grace ...."

He loved to watch the colour come and go in her face, the dainty, girlish movements, simple and unaffected, that little curl which looked like living gold beside the small, shell-like ear. His passionate love for the beautiful was more than satiated at the exquisite picture before him, and then she had such a musical and tender voice; he had heard her singing just now.

"But you seem to know me, fair one," he said after a while.

"Who does not know His Grace of Wessex?" she responded, making a pretty curtsy.

"Then let me be even with you, sweet singer, and tell me your name."

Ursula darted a sudden shy look at him. Obviously he was conveying the truth; he did not know who she was.

A quick thought crossed her mind; she looked demurely down her nose and said placidly,—

"My name is Fanny."

"Fanny?"

"Yes ... you do not like it?"

"I didn't before," he said with a smile, "but now I adore it."

"I am getting to like it better too," she added thoughtfully.

"But, sweet Fanny, tell me how is it I never have seen you before."

"Your Grace does not know all the ladies of the Court."

"No! but I thought I knew all the pretty ones. Yet meseems that beauty was but an empty word now that I have seen its queen."

"Ah, my lord! I fear me your reputation doth not wrong you after all!" she added with a quaint little sigh.

"Why? What is my reputation?"

"They call you fickle, and say the Duke of Wessex loves many women a little ... but constantly, not at all."

He came a step closer to her, and tried to meet her eyes.

"Then will you let me prove them wrong?" he said with sudden seriousness, which perhaps then he could not himself have accounted for.

"I? ..." she said artlessly, "what must I do for that?"

"Anything you like," he replied.

"Nay, I have no power; for I fear me nothing short of putting Your Grace under lock and key would cure you of that fickleness."

"Then put me under lock and key," he suggested gaily.

"In an inaccessible tower?"

"Wherever you please."

She gave a merry, happy little laugh, for he was standing quite close to her now, his proud head slightly bent so that the quick, whispered words might easily reach her ears; and there was an unmistakable look of ardent admiration in his eyes. A demon of mischief suddenly seized her. She wondered whether he had guessed who she was and tried to nettle him into betraying himself.

60

"And to whom shall I give the key of that tower?" she said demurely. "To the Lady Ursula Glynde?"

"No," he replied. "Come inside and throw the key out of the window."

"But the Lady Ursula?" she persisted.

He made a quick gesture of mock impatience.

"What wanton cruelty to mention that name now," he said, "when mine ears are tuned to 'Fanny.'"

"'Tis wrong they should be so tuned—Lady Ursula, they say, is your promised wife."

"But I do not love her ... never could love her whilst——"

"They say she is not ill-favoured."

"Ill-favoured to me, like the bitter pills the medicine man gives us, whilst you——"

Once more she interrupted him quickly.

"You have never seen her," she protested, "you do not even know what she is like."

"Nay, I can guess. The Glyndes are all alike—sandy, angular, large-footed ...."

She laughed, a long, merry, rippling laugh which set his ears tingling with the desire to hear it once again. Ursula was indeed enjoying herself thoroughly.

"They all have brown eyes," he continued gaily, "and just now I feel as if I could not endure brown eyes."

She cast down her own, veiling them with her long lashes.

"What eyes could Your Grace best endure for the moment?" she said, with the same tantalizing demureness.

But something magnetic must have passed at that moment between these two young people, some subtle current from him to her, which forced the innocent young girl to raise her eyes almost against her will. He looked straight into their wonderful depths, and murmured softly,—

"The very bluest of the blue, and yet so grey, that I should feel they must somehow be green ...."

A little shudder had gone through her when first she met his ardent gaze; she tried to free herself from a sudden strange and delicious feeling of obsession, and said with somewhat forced merriment now:

"The Queen has greenish eyes, and Lady Ursula's are grey."

Then she held out the marguerite to him.

"Would you like to know which you love best?" she added. "Consult the marguerite, and take one petal at a time."

But he took the hand which held the flower.

"One petal at a time," he whispered. He took the slender fingers and kissed each in its turn: "This the softest ... that the whitest ... all rose-tipped ... and a feast for the gods ...."

"My lord! ..."

"Now you are frowning—you are not angry?"

"Very angry!"

"I'll make amends," he said humbly.

"How?"

"Give me the other hand, and I'll show you."

"Nay! I cannot do that, for we are told that the left hand must never know what the right hand doeth."

"It shall not," he rejoined earnestly, "for I'll tell it a different tale."

"What is it?"

"Give me the hand and you shall know."

Overhead in the green bosquets of yew a group of starlings began to twitter. The sun was just beginning to sink down in the west, throwing round the head of the fair young girl an aureole of gold. He stood watching her, happy in this the supreme moment of his life. A magic veil seemed to envelop him and her, shutting out all that portion of the world which was not poetic and beautiful; and she, the priestess of this exquisite new universe in which he had just entered, was smilingly holding out her dainty hand to him.

He seized it, and a sudden wave of passion caused him to bend over it and to kiss its soft rosy palm.

"Nay, my lord," she murmured, confused, "that Your Grace should think of such follies!"

"Yet, when you look at me," he said, "I think of worse follies still."

"Women say that there is no worse folly than to listen to His Grace of Wessex."

"Do you think they are right?"

"How can I tell?"

"By listening to me for half an hour."

"Here, in this garden?"

"No! ... there! ... by the river ...."

And he pointed beyond the enclosure of the garden, there where the soft evening breeze gently stirred the rushes in the stream.

"Oh! ... what would everybody say?" she exclaimed in mock alarm.

"Nothing! envy of my good fortune would make them dumb."

"But the Queen will be asking for you, and the Duchess of Lincoln wondering where I am."

"They shall not find us ... for we'll pull the boat beyond the reeds ... just you and I alone ... with the gloaming all round us ... and the twitter of the birds when they go to rest. Shall we go? ..."

Her heart had already consented. His voice was low and persuasive, a strange earnestness seemed to vibrate through it, as he begged her to come with him.

Slowly she began to walk by his side towards the stream. She seemed scarcely alive now, a being from another world wandering in the land of dreams. He said nothing more, for the world was too beautiful for speech. Youth, love, delight were coursing through his veins, and as he led the young girl towards the bank it seemed to him as if he were taking her away from this dull world of prose and humanity, far, far away through mysterious golden gates beyond the sunset, to a land where she would reign as queen.

The river beckoned to them, and the soft, misty horizon seemed to call. The intoxicating odour of summer's dying roses filled the air, whilst in the distance across the stream a nightingale began to sing.

CHAPTER XVI

THE ULTIMATUM

The envoy of His Holiness had departed.

Mary Tudor had dismissed her ladies, for she wished to speak with the Cardinal de Moreno alone.

Throughout the audience with the papal Nuncio, His Eminence had already seen the storm-clouds gathering thick and fast on the Queen's brow. His Grace of Wessex, gone to fetch a breviary left accidentally on the terrace-coping, had been gone half an hour, and moreover had not yet returned.

Her Majesty had sent a page to request His Grace's presence. The page returned with the intimation that His Grace could not be found.

Someone had spied him in the distance walking towards the river, in company with a lady dressed in white.

Then the storm-clouds had burst.

The Queen peremptorily ordered every one out of the room, then she turned with real Tudor-like fury upon His Eminence.

"My lord Cardinal," she said in a quivering voice, which she did not even try to steady, "an you had your master's wishes at heart, you have indeed gone the wrong way to work."

The Cardinal's keen grey eyes had watched Mary's growing wrath with much amusement. What was a woman's wrath to him? Nothing but an asset, an additional advantage in the political game which he was playing.

Never for a moment did he depart, however, from his attitude of deepest respect, nor from his tone of suave urbanity.

"I seem to have offended Your Majesty," he said gently; "unwittingly, I assure you ...."

But Mary was in no mood to bandy polite words with the man who had played her this clever trick. She was angered with herself for having fallen into so clumsy a trap. A thousand suggestions now occurred to her of what she might have done to prevent the meeting between Wessex and Ursula, which the Cardinal had obviously planned.

"Nay! masks off, I pray Your Eminence," she said, "that trick just now with your breviary ... Own to it, man! ... own to it ... are you not proud to have tricked Mary Tudor so easily?"

She was trembling with rage, yet looked nigh to bursting into tears. A shade almost of pity crossed His Eminence's cold and clever face. It seemed almost wantonly useless to have aided Fate in snatching a young and handsome lover from this ill-favoured, middle-aged woman.

But the Cardinal never allowed worldly sentiments of any kind to interfere, for more than one or two seconds, with the object he had in view. The look of pity quickly faded from his eyes, giving place to the same mask of respectful deference.

"My breviary?" he said blandly. "Nay! I am still at a loss to understand.... Ah, yes! I remember now.... I had left it on the balustrade. His Grace of Wessex, a pattern of chivalry, offered to fetch it for me, and——"

"A fine scheme indeed, my lord," interrupted the Queen impatiently, "to send the Duke of Wessex courting after my waiting-maid."

"The Duke of Wessex?" rejoined His Eminence with well-played astonishment. "Nay, methought I spied him just now in the distance, keeping the vows he once made to the Lady Ursula Glynde."

"I pray you do not repeat that silly fairy-tale. His Grace made no promise. 'Twas the Earl of Truro desired the marriage, and the Duke had half forgotten this, until Your Eminence chose to interfere."

"Nay! but Your Majesty does me grave injustice. What have the amours of His Grace of Wessex to do with me, who am the envoy of His Most Catholic Majesty the King of Spain?"

"'Twere wiser, certainly," retorted Mary coldly, "if the King of Spain's envoy did not concern himself with rousing the Queen of England's anger."

His Eminence smiled as amiably, as unconcernedly as before. Throughout the length of a very distinguished career he had often been obliged to weather storms of royal wrath. He was none the worse for it, and knew how to let the floods of princely anger pass over his shrewd head, without losing grip of the ground on which he stood. Nothing ever ruffled him. Supremely conscious of his own dignity, justly proud of his position and attainments, he had, at the bottom of his heart, a complete contempt for those exalted puppets of his own political schemes. Mary Tudor, a weak and soured woman, an all-too-ready prey of her own passions, swayed hither and thither by her loves and by her hates, was nothing to this proud prince of the Church but a pawn in a European game of chess. It was for his deft fingers to move this pawn in the direction in which he list.

"Nay," he said, with gentle suavity, "my only desire is to rouse in the heart of the Queen of England love for my royal master, the King of Spain. He is young and goodly to look at, a faithful and gallant gentleman, whom it will be difficult to lure from Your Grace's side, once you have deigned to allow him to kneel at your feet."

"You speak, my lord, as if you were sure of my answer."

"Sure is a momentous word, Your Majesty. But I hope——"

"Nay! 'tis not yet done, remember," retorted Mary, with ever-increasing vehemence, "and if this trick of yours should succeed, if Wessex weds the Lady Ursula, then I will send my answer to your master, and it shall be 'No!'"

There was a quick, sudden flash in the Cardinal's eye, a look of astonishment, perhaps, at this unexpected phase of feminine jealousy. Be that as it may, it was quickly veiled by an expression of pronounced sarcasm.

"As a trophy for the vanity of His Grace of Wessex?" he asked pointedly.

"No!—merely as a revenge against your interference. So look to it, my lord Cardinal; the tangle in the skein was made by your hand. See that you unravel it, or you and the Spanish ambassador leave my Court to-morrow."

With a curt nod of the head she dismissed him from her presence. He was far too shrewd to attempt another word just now. Perhaps for the first time in his life he felt somewhat baffled. He had allowed his own impatience to outrun his discretion—an unpardonable fault in a diplomatist. He blamed himself very severely for his attempt at brusquing Fate. Surely time and the Duke's own fastidious disposition would have parted him from Mary quite as readily as this sudden meeting with beautiful Lady Ursula.

The Cardinal had withdrawn from the Queen's presence after an obeisance marked with deep respect. He wished to be alone to think over this new aspect of the situation. Through the tall bay windows of the Great Hall which he traversed, the last rays of the setting sun came slanting in. His Eminence glided along the smooth oak floors, his crimson robes making but a gentle frou-frou of sound behind him, a ghostlike, whispering accompaniment to his perturbed thoughts. Somehow the softness of the evening air lured him towards the terrace and the gardens. There lacked an hour yet to supper-time, and Mary Tudor was scarce likely to be in immediate need of His Eminence's company.

He crossed the Clock Tower gates and soon found himself once more on the terrace. The gardens beyond looked tenderly poetic in the fast-gathering dusk. The Cardinal's shrewd eyes wandered restlessly over the parterres and bosquets, vainly endeavouring to spy the silhouettes of two young people, whom his diplomacy had brought together and whom his shrewd wit would have to part again.

He descended the terrace steps and slowly walked towards the pond, where, but an hour ago, a sweet and poetic idyll had been enacted. There was nothing to mark the passage of a fair young dream, born this lovely October afternoon, save a few dead marguerites and the scattered flakes of their snow-white petals.

The Cardinal's footsteps crushed them unheeded. He was thinking how best he could dispel that dream, which he himself had helped to call forth.

"Woman! woman!" he sighed impatiently as he looked back upon the graceful outline of the Palace behind him, "thy moods are many and thy logic scant."

"A tangled skein indeed," he mused, "which will take some unravelling. If Wessex weds the Lady Ursula, the Queen will say 'No' to Philip, out of revenge for my interference. She'll turn to Noailles mayhap and wed the Dauphin to spite me, or keep him and Scheyfne dangling on awhile whilst trying to reconquer the volatile Duke's allegiance. But if Wessex does not wed the Lady Ursula ... what then? Will his friends prevail? Yet there's more obstinacy than indolence in his composition, I fancy, and the dubious position of King Consort would scarce suit his proud Grace. Still, if I do not succeed in parting those two young people whom my diplomacy hath brought together, then Mary Tudor sends me and the Spanish Ambassador back to Philip to-morrow."

CHAPTER XVII

AN ARMED TRUCE

So intent was His Eminence in these complicated musings that he scarcely noticed how fast the shadows gathered round him. He had gradually wandered down towards the low wall which divided the Palace gardens from the river beyond.

He had always been very partial to this remote portion of the grounds, for it was little frequented, and he felt that here at least in his lonely walks he could lay aside that mask of perpetual blandness which he was obliged to wear all day, whatever his moods might be.

It was seldom that he met anybody when his footsteps led him thus far. Great was his astonishment therefore when he suddenly spied a figure leaning over the wall, evidently intent on prying into the darkness below.

The Cardinal drew nearer and recognized Lord Everingham, the closest friend, the most intimate companion His Grace of Wessex was known to have.

The young man had not heard His Eminence's footsteps on the sanded path; he started on hearing his name.

"Ah! my lord Everingham," said the Cardinal lightly. "I little thought to see any one here. I myself am fond of communing with Nature in these gathering shadows; but you are a young man, there are gayer attractions for you within the Palace."

It was too dark by now even for His Eminence's keen eyes to read the expression on Lord Everingham's face. The astute diplomatist, however, more than guessed what the young man's purpose was in thus scanning the river. His Grace of Wessex had not yet returned to the Palace, and it was generally known throughout the Court circle that Her Majesty was furious at his absence.

The Cardinal's ruse in the early part of the afternoon had been the subject of universal gossip; sundry rumours had also been current that the Duke had been seen in the company of the Queen's most beautiful maid-of-honour.

"Verily," thought His Eminence, "His Grace's partisans must be on tenterhooks. All along they must have dreaded this meeting, which chance and diplomacy has so unexpectedly brought about."

Was not Wessex' position with regard to the Lady Ursula a peculiar one? Tied to her and yet free, affianced, yet not necessarily bound, his own attitude towards her was sure to be influenced by the girl's own personality.

And every cavalier and diplomatist now at Hampton Court readily conceded that the daughter of the Earl of Truro was the most beautiful woman in England, and the most likely to captivate the roving fancy of His Grace.

No wonder that my lord of Everingham was anxious for the Duke's return, before the Queen's access of pique and jealousy had found vent in sudden revenge. But the young Englishman had no desire to display this anxiety before his triumphant opponent.

"Like your Eminence," he said carelessly, "I was lured into the garden by the softness of the air. The river looked so cool and placid, and 'tis not often one can hear the nightingale in October."

"Nay! your sudden fancy for the evening breeze is entirely my gain, my dear lord," rejoined the Cardinal in his most suave manner; "as a matter of fact I was, even at this moment, meditating how best I could secure an interview with you."

"With me?"

"Yes. Are you not His Grace of Wessex' most intimate friend?"

"I have indeed that honour," replied Everingham stiffly, "but I do not quite understand how——"

"How the matter concerns me?" interrupted His Eminence pleasantly. "An you will allow me, I can explain. Shall we walk along this path? I thank you," he added courteously, as the young man, after a moment's hesitation, turned to walk beside him.

"Have I been misinformed," continued the Cardinal, "or is it a fact that your lordship is about to quit Hampton Court?"

"Only for a very few weeks," rejoined Everingham. "Her Majesty has entrusted me with an amicable mission to the Queen Regent of Scotland. I start for town to-night on my way North."

"Ah! then I am only just in time," said His Eminence.

"In time for what?"

"In time to correct what we poor mortals are all liable to make, my lord—an error."

"Indeed!" said Everingham, with a touch of sarcasm. "Your Eminence must make so few."

"Nay! but the error this time is none of my making, my lord. 'Tis you, I think, who look upon me as an enemy."

"Oh! ... your Eminence ..." protested the young man.

"Well, an antagonist, if you will. Confess that you thought—and still think—that I have been scheming to bring the Duke of Wessex to the feet of Lady Ursula Glynde, his promised wife."

"A scheme in which Your Eminence succeeded over well, I fancy," retorted Everingham bitterly.

"But that is where you are in error, my dear lord; for, believe me, that, at the present moment, my sole desire is to put an insuperable barrier between His Grace and that beautiful young lady."

"Your sole desire, my lord?"

As the night was dark Everingham could see nothing of His Eminence's expression of face. If he had, he probably would only have seen the same mask of polite blandness which the Cardinal usually wore.

The young man, certes, was no match for these astute Spaniards, who had all the wiles and artifices of diplomacy at their finger-tips; his love for Wessex and the earnestness of his own political views gave him a certain amount of shrewdness, but even that shrewdness was at fault in the face of this extraordinary statement suddenly made by the Cardinal.

"You are surprised?" commented His Eminence.

"Boundlessly, I confess."

"Ah! Diplomacy is full of surprises. But you are pleased?"

Everingham, however, was not prepared to admit anything to this man, whose face he could not read, but whose tortuous ways he more than half mistrusted.

"I hardly know how to understand Your Eminence," he said guardedly. "I need hardly say that my fondest hope was to see Queen Mary wedded to Wessex, for that is common knowledge. But since His Grace's meeting with the beautiful Lady Ursula, I fully expect to hear him declare his intention of keeping his troth to her."

"You think her so very irresistible, then?—or His Grace so very susceptible?"

"I think that the Duke has always kept at the back of his mind an idea that he was in some measure bound to Lady Ursula."

"Let us add, my lord, that the charm and grace of the lady will inevitably tend to develop that idea. Eh?"

"And that Your Eminence will probably triumph in consequence."

"You, therefore, my lord, have by now set your heart on undoing what to-day's chance meeting may, perchance, have accomplished. By you I also mean your friends, the nobility and gentry of England, who would mourn to see His Grace wedded to Lady Ursula Glynde."

"Our loss will be your Eminence's gain, probably," rejoined Everingham with a sigh.

The Cardinal waited a moment before he continued the conversation. He had deliberately sought this interchange of ideas. Openness and frankness in matters political were not usually a part of His Eminence's programme, but this evening he seemed desirous to gain this young Englishman's confidence.

"But," he said after a while, with charming bonhomie, "but suppose that instead of gloating in the triumph which you, my lord, so readily prophesy—suppose that I were to ask you to let me help you— you and your friends—in parting the volatile Duke from his latest flame? ... Would you accept my help?"

"Your Eminence ... I ..." murmured Everingham, somewhat at a loss what to say.

"You would wish to consult with your friends, eh?" continued the Cardinal placidly. "Lord Derby, Lord Bath, the Earl of Oxford—nay, the whole string of patriotic Englishmen who desire to see one of their own kind on the English throne, and naturally look upon me as a monster of artifice and vice."

"Your Eminence ..." protested Everingham.

"Yet what are we but political antagonists, who can honour one another in private, whilst rending one another to pieces on the arena of public life? Do you not agree with me, my lord?"

"Certainly."

"Then why should you disdain my help, now that— momentarily—we have the same object in view?"

"I am hors de cause, Your Eminence, as I have only the next few hours at my disposal. After that I go to Scotland."

"Much may be done in a few hours, my lord, with an ounce of luck and a grain of tact."

"But I do not understand why Your Eminence should be at one with me and my friends over this."

The Cardinal smiled with gentle benevolence. Versed though he was in all the tricks and deceptions which were an integral part of his calling, no one knew better than he did the value of an occasional truth. With easy familiarity he linked his arm in that of his interlocutor.

"Nay! your lordship mocks me," he said with a light sigh. "From your conversation I have already gathered that you and your friends suspect me of having brought about this unwelcome meeting 'twixt His Grace of Wessex and Lady Ursula Glynde. Is it not so?"

"Marry ..." began Everingham with some hesitation.

"I pray you do not trouble to deny it. Let us admit that it is so. Do you not think then that Queen Mary will have a like suspicion as yourself?"

"Probably."

"And will, in consequence, turn the floods of her wrath on my innocent head. A woman angered is capable of anything, my lord. My position at this Court would become untenable. My mission probably would fail. Let us say that by endeavouring to part His Grace from the Lady Ursula, I would wish to give Her Majesty proof of the fact that I bore no part in their chance meeting."

"I understand," rejoined Everingham, still vaguely suspicious of any ulterior motive lurking behind the Cardinal's apparent frankness, "but ..."

"Once His Grace is effectually parted from his new flame, the game will stand once more as it did before the unfortunate episode of this afternoon ... unfortunate alike to your interests and to mine. Is that not so?"

"Certainly."

"I feel, therefore, that until then we ought to be ... well! if not friends exactly ... at least allies."

"Only to resume hostilities again, Your Eminence?"

"By all means."

"Once His Grace has ceased to think of Lady Ursula, I and my party will once more work heart and soul to bring about the alliance of Wessex with the Queen."

"And I to win the Queen's hand for Philip of Spain. Until then?..."

"Armed truce, Your Eminence."

"And you will accept my help? It may be worth having, you never can tell," quoth His Eminence with a sarcastic smile, which Everingham could not perceive in the darkness.

CHAPTER XVIII

THE VEILED WITCH

Lord Everingham felt not a little perplexed. The Cardinal seemed bent on pressing his point, and on obtaining a definite promise of friendship, whilst the young man would have preferred to leave the matter in statu quo, a condition of open and avowed enmity.

Moreover he would have wished to speak with some of his friends. Lord Sussex and the Earl of Oxford were staying at the Palace. Sir Henry Jerningham, Arundel, Cheyne, Paget, all hot partisans of Wessex, could easily be communicated with. In the meanwhile Everingham was racking his brain for the right word to say: the retort courteous, which would not hopelessly alienate His Eminence, if indeed he was seeking temporary friendship.

Chance and a zealous night watchman put an abrupt end to Lord Everingham's perplexity; even when he was about to speak, a gruff voice which seemed to come right out of the darkness interrupted him with the well-known call—

"Who goes there?"

Almost immediately afterwards the strong light of a lanthorn was projected on the figure of the Cardinal.

"How now, friend," quoth His Eminence presently, "art seeking for the truth with that lanthorn of thine?"

But already the knave, having recognized the brilliant crimson robes and realized the high quality of their august wearer, had lost himself in a veritable maze of humble apologies.

"I crave Your Eminence's merciful pardon," he stammered. "I did not think ... I am on duty ... I ..."

His thin, shrivelled form was scarce distinguishable in the gloom, only his old face, with large bottle-nose, and his pale, watery eyes appeared grotesque and quaint in the yellowish light of his lanthorn.

"Then fulfil thy duties, friend," rejoined the Cardinal, who made it a point always to speak kindly and urbanely, even to the meanest lout.

The man made a low obeisance and would have kissed His Eminence's hand, but the latter withdrew it gently.

"Are there marauders about, friend watchman?" he condescended to ask, as the man prepared to go. "Thou dost not appear to be very strong, nor yet stoutly armed."

"Your Eminence's pardon," replied the man, "'tis for a woman I am told to watch."

"A woman?"

"By Her Grace the Duchess of Lincoln's orders."

71

"Ah!" remarked His Eminence, with sudden interest.

"Mayhap some thief or vagrant, Your Eminence."

"Aye, mayhap! Then go thy way, good watchman; we'll not hinder thee."

Slowly the man shuffled off, dangling his lanthorn before him. The Cardinal watched the patch of brilliant light until it disappeared behind a projecting bosquet.

His Eminence had been exceedingly thoughtful.

"Know you aught of this, my lord?" he asked of Lord Everingham, who also seemed wrapped in meditation.

"I suspect something of it," replied the young man slowly. "There is a story afloat—gossip, I thought it—that one of the Queen's maids-of-honour has been playing some curious pranks at night ... and in disguise ...."

"Indeed? Know you who the lady is?"

"No! nor can I even guess. All the maids-of-honour are young and full of fun, and no doubt the girlish pranks were harmless enough, but Her Majesty is very austere and rigidly stern where questions of decorum are concerned."

"So the Duchess of Lincoln, like a watchful dragon, would catch the fair miscreant in flagrante delicto, eh?" continued His Eminence.

Mechanically he turned to walk along the path recently followed by the night watchman. His Eminence would have scorned the idea of any superstition influencing his precise, calculating mind, but, nevertheless, he had a strange belief in the guiding hand of Chance, and somehow at the present moment he had an unaccountable presentiment, that this gossip anent some young girl's frolic would in some way exercise an influence on his present schemes.

As if in immediate answer to these very thoughts a woman's frightened scream was suddenly heard close by, followed by muttered curses in the watchman's gruff voice.

"What was that?" exclaimed Everingham involuntarily.

"The lady in flagrante delicto, meseems," rejoined the Cardinal quietly.

And both men began to walk more rapidly in the direction whence had come the woman's scream. The next few moments brought them upon the scene, and soon in the gloom they distinguished the figure of the old watchman apparently struggling with a woman, whose head and shoulders were enveloped in some sort of veil or hood. The lanthorn, evidently violently thrown on the ground, had rolled down the path some little distance from this group.

The woman was making obvious and frantic efforts to get away, whilst the old watchman exerted all his strength to keep tight hold of her wrists.

"What is it to thee, man, what I am doing here?" the woman gasped in the midst of her struggles. "Let me go, I say!"

She was evidently not very strong, for the old watchman, shrivelled and shrunken though he was, had already mastered her. She had lost her balance, and was soon down on her knees. With a vigorous wrench the man contrived to force her arms behind her back; he held them there with one hand, and with the other was groping in his wallet for a length of rope.

"Not before thou hast given a good account of thyself before the Duchess of Lincoln, my wench!" he said, as he threw the rope round her shoulders and very dexterously contrived to pinion her arms behind her.

"Her Grace?" she murmured contemptuously. "I have naught to do with Her Grace.... Let me go, man; thou hast no right to tie me thus."

"Now then, my girl, get up, will ye? and come along quietly with me.... I'll not hurt ye ... if ye come along quietly."

The man helped her to struggle to her feet. Her veil or cloak had evidently fallen from her head, for the Cardinal and Lord Everingham, who were silently, and with no small measure of curiosity, watching the strange spectacle, caught the glint of a woman's face and of bright golden hair.

The watchman was trying to lead her away towards the Palace.

"Let me go, I tell thee," muttered the girl with persistent obstinacy. "I have important business here, and ..."

But the old man laughed derisively.

"Important business? ... and prithee with whom, wench?"

"With the Duke of Wessex ..." she retorted after a slight hesitation, "There! ... now wilt let me go?"

But the watchman laughed more immoderately than before.

"Oho! ... ho! ho! ho! that's a likely tale, my wench, there's many a young woman has business with His Grace, I'll warrant.... But thou'st best tell that tale to the Duchess of Lincoln first.... Business with the Duke of Wessex ... ha! ha! ha! ..."

"My friend," here interposed a gentle, very urbane voice, "meseems thy zeal somewhat outruns thy discretion. If this child has indeed business with the Duke of Wessex, His Grace might prefer that thou shouldst keep a quieter tongue in thy head."

The Cardinal, at sound of the Duke's name, had gradually drawn nearer to the group. Lord Everingham, impelled by the same natural curiosity, had followed him.

"You would wish to speak with His Grace, child?" continued His Eminence with that same gentle benevolence which inspired an infinity of confidence in the unwary. "Do you know him?"

The watchman, astonished, abashed, very highly perplexed at this unexpected interference, was rendered absolutely speechless. The girl had turned defiantly on her new interlocutor, whose outline she could but vaguely distinguish in the darkness.

73

"What's it to you?" she retorted with obvious suspicion and mistrust.

"Not much I own," replied the Cardinal with imperturbable kindliness; "I only thought that being alone and perhaps frightened you would be glad of some help."

"Your Eminence ..." stammered the watchman, who was trying to recover his speech.

"Silence!" commanded His Eminence. "I wish to speak with this young woman alone."

The worthy watchman had naught to do but to obey. There was no questioning an order given by so great a lord as the Cardinal de Moreno himself. The good man discreetly withdrew, His Eminence quietly waiting until he was out of earshot.

"Now, child, have no fear," said the Cardinal gently. "Tell me ... you wish to speak with the Duke of Wessex?"

She turned resolutely towards him.

"You'll take me to him?" she asked.

"Perhaps," he replied.

A great struggle must have been raging within her. Even through the gloom His Eminence could see her shoulders and breast working convulsively, whilst her breath came and went in quick, feverish gasps.

"I have been watching in the gardens at night," she murmured at last; "for he is a great lord, and I dared not approach him by day. He saved my life ... and I can read the stars.... I see that a great danger threatens him ....

"Oh! I must warn him," she added in a sudden outburst of passionate vehemence. "I must go to him ... I must."

Lord Everingham tried to interpose, but His Eminence restrained him with a quick touch upon his arm. The Cardinal's hands were beautiful, white and caressing as those of a woman, delicately scented and be-ringed. He passed them gently over the girl's head, whilst he whispered softly—

"So you shall, child ... so you shall.... Then, tell me ... His Grace saved your life, you say? and you are very grateful to him, of course ... more than that, perhaps ... you love him very dearly, eh? ..."

"What's that to you?" retorted the girl sullenly.

Lord Everingham once more made as if he would interrupt this curious interrogatory. His loyalty to his friend rebelled against this prying into matters which might prove unpleasant for Wessex.

That the girl was no Court lady out on some mad frolic was patent enough, whilst the passionate ring of her voice, when she mentioned the Duke's name, proved very clearly that she had seen him, and seeing him had perhaps learnt to love him.

Who knows? Some secret intrigue, not altogether avowable, might lie at the bottom of this strange adventure. Everingham's heart

74

misgave him at the thought that Wessex' most open enemy should perhaps learn a secret hitherto kept from all his friends.

The girl, on the other hand, seemed willing to trust the Cardinal. She repeated doggedly once or twice—

"You'll take me to him? ... at once? ..."

"If I can," replied His Eminence, still very protecting, very suave and kind, "but not just now.... His Grace is with the Queen ... you are too sensible and earnest, I feel sure, to wish to intrude upon him.... But will you not trust me a little while? ... and I promise you that you shall see him."

"Nay! I've nothing to lose by trusting you or any one," she replied. "If you do not take me to him, I'll find my way alone."

"Come, that's brave independence. But, child, if I am to help you with His Grace of Wessex, I must at least know who you are."

"They call me Mirrab."

At sound of the name Everingham started. One or two vague recollections, in connection with the soothsayer of East Molesey Fair, seemed to be chasing one another in his mind, but he could not give them definite shape.

A strange feeling, made up of uneasiness and shame, coupled with excitement and intense curiosity, caused him to go and pick up the watchman's lanthorn, which lay on the ground close by.

When he was near the girl again he held it up, and the light fell full on her face.

Then he remembered.

It was Mirrab, the necromancer, the kitchen wench, used by a vulgar trickster to hoodwink some gullible burgesses and their dames at the village fair, but whom Nature had, in one of her unaccountable freaks, endowed with the same golden hair, the same exquisite features, the same deep and wonderful eyes, as the most beautiful woman at Mary Tudor's court, the Lady Ursula Glynde.

The veil which usually enveloped Mirrab's head had fallen round her shoulders; her dress was of coarse woollen stuff, open at the neck and short in the sleeves; the arms and hands, rough and clumsy in shape, betrayed the girl's humble origin, and the likeness to Lady Ursula was confined to the face and hair. But it was there, nevertheless; quite unmistakable, even bewildering to the two men who were gazing, speechless, at this strange spectacle.

Then Everingham put down the lanthorn. He dared not look at the Cardinal, half fearing, perhaps, that the wild thoughts and schemes which had suddenly arisen in his mind at sight of this extraordinary freak of nature should have already found more definite shape in His Eminence's astute and far-seeing brain.

Strangely enough, at this moment, the practised diplomatist, the wily and unscrupulous Spaniard, met the more simple-souled

Englishman on common ground, and at once felt sure of his co-operation.

Both had the same end in view: a desire to break up any relationship which may have sprung up between the Duke of Wessex and the beautiful young girl, of whom this otherwise coarse wench was the perfect physical counterpart. But the Spaniard was the quicker in thought and in action. Whilst Everingham still vaguely wondered how the extraordinary resemblance might be utilized to gain that great end which he had in view, the Cardinal had already formed and matured a plan.

He took the veil from Mirrab's shoulders and once more drew it over her head. Then he undid the clumsy knot with which the watchman had pinioned her hands. Mirrab remained perfectly passive the while; she seemed under the magic spell of the soft, velvety hands, which had, as it were, taken possession of her person.

The two men had not exchanged one word since the light of the lanthorn had revealed the strange secret to them; they seemed to be acting in perfect accord. There was no longer any need for protestation of outward friendship, or for cementing the compact of temporary alliance.

Everingham once more picked up the lanthorn and went in search of the watchman, in order to dismiss him with a word of command and to ensure his silence with a threat and a few silver coins. The man, of course, knew nothing of the importance of the event which he had unwittingly brought about. He may have vaguely wondered in his mind why His Eminence the Spanish Cardinal should take such a keen interest in a female vagrant, found trespassing on royal ground. But the few pieces of silver given to him by the noble lord, soon silenced even this transitory astonishment.

Stolidly he resumed his nightly round, satisfied that he need no longer look for lurking thieves in the park.

When Everingham, having seen the last of the watchman, returned to the spot where he had left His Eminence and Mirrab, he found that both had disappeared.

PART III

A GAME OF CHESS

CHAPTER XIX

THE PAWNS

The evening banquet had been anything but gay.

The Queen, as was oft her wont, had hardly said a word. The Cardinal de Moreno looked thoughtful and His Grace of Wessex was singularly silent.

Directly after supper Her Majesty retired to her own apartments, accompanied by her ladies, leaving behind her that desultory atmosphere of dull and purposeless conversation, which hangs round a supper table in the absence of the fair sex.

The brilliant assembly broke up into small groups. The Earl of Pembroke and two or three other lords were leaving for Scotland towards midnight; their friends gathered round them to bid them God-speed. In the deep embrasure of the great bay His Grace of Wessex was in earnest conference with Lord Winchester and Sir William Drury, whilst at one end of the long centre table half a dozen young gallants were idling over a game of hazard.

But there was a feeling of obsession in the air—a sense as if something momentous was about to happen. Whispered rumours, more or less conflicting, were afloat, yet nothing definite was known. On the other hand, idle, far-stretched gossip was rife and was even growing in extravagance as the evening wore on.

No one had been present on the terrace to witness the little incident which occurred there earlier in the afternoon save the three distinguished actors in the brief comedy scene. Obviously from them nothing could be gleaned. The Queen and the Cardinal would not be like to enlighten the curious, whilst the Duke of Wessex, at all times reserved and unapproachable, could not be asked to give his version of the event.

The foreign envoys had very soon followed the example set by Her Majesty and withdrawn from the circle, which seemed more hostile to them than usual to-night. The Cardinal de Moreno and the Marquis de Suarez were the first to go. They occupied the magnificent suite of chambers wherein ill-fated Wolsey had lived, schemed, and fallen. The more sumptuous series of rooms beyond—those built with lavish extravagance by King Henry VIII for his own personal use—had been placed at the disposal of His Grace of Wessex and his numerous retinue.

Between the Duke's apartments and those allotted to the envoys of the King of Spain was the fine audience chamber, used by the Queen herself or by her more distinguished guests for the reception of important visitors. It was here that Lord Everingham, anxious, perturbed, vaguely ashamed of his own actions, had sought out the Cardinal de Moreno after the banquet and begged for an interview.

His Eminence, suave, urbane, a veritable mirror of benevolence, had received him with a smile of welcome on his lips and a wealth of kindly reproach in his eyes.

"Ah, my lord!" he said to the young man, as soon as the servants had withdrawn, "Nature, I fear me, hath not intended you for a diplomatist."

"How so?"

"This interview to-night, with me—was it necessary?"

"I could not rest," said Everingham impulsively, "until——"

"Until you had proclaimed it to the entire Court in general, and to His Grace of Wessex in particular, that you had a secret understanding with his political rival, the Spanish ambassador," rejoined His Eminence drily.

"An interview ..."

"Have you ever honoured me thus before, my lord?—you or any of your friends?"

"No ... perhaps not ... I only requested a brief tête-à-tête ...."

"And had I refused that dangerous tête-à-tête, what would you have done?"

"Demanded it," replied Everingham hotly. "I must know what has happened, and what you intend to do."

His Eminence threw a quick look at the young man, a look half of pity, half of contempt. For a moment it seemed as if an angry retort hovered upon his lips. But he merely shrugged his shoulders and said blandly—

"You are very expert at the game of chess, my lord, so they tell me."

"I have played it a great many times," rejoined Everingham, a little astonished at the sudden transition.

"Ah! and have become very proficient, I understand. Will you honour me by playing a game with me?"

"Now?"

"Why not?"

"The lateness of the hour ... I start for Scotland almost directly."

"Yet in spite of these difficulties you sought a casual interview with an avowed political enemy."

"No one need know ..." stammered the young man, slightly abashed.

"Every one inside this Palace knows by now that my lord of Everingham, the intimate friend at His Grace of Wessex, is closeted alone with the envoy of His Majesty the King of Spain," rejoined His Eminence with slow emphasis. "Believe me, my lord, a game of chess is the wisest course."

"Will you tell me first ..."

"I can tell your lordship nothing, except across the chess board."

"Well! ... since you wish it ..."

"My wishes have naught to do with this matter. I was following the most elementary dictates of prudence."

He touched the handbell and rang. A liveried servant appeared.

"Had I not told thee, sirrah," said His Eminence, "that my lord Everingham had kindly consented to give me my revanche at chess ere he departed? How is it that the board has not been prepared?"

"I crave Your Eminence's most humble pardon," protested the man in confusion. "I had not understood ..."

"Not understood?" laughed the Cardinal good-naturedly. "Marry! the knave doth impugn my knowledge of the English tongue."

"I would not presume, Your Eminence ..."

"Tush, man! hold thy tongue and repair thy negligence. Where's the board? His lordship hath but an hour to spare."

Everingham watched with ill-concealed impatience the elaborate preparations made for the game. He thought it quite unnecessary, and had he dared he would have refused to join in the senseless deception. But in this matter he had ceased to trust his own judgment, and, much against his will, was allowing the Cardinal to take the lead. He felt out of his own intellectual depths in this slough of intrigue wherein he had so impulsively ventured, and out of which he now felt incapable of extricating himself.

Simple-minded and loyal to the core, he had a horror of any treachery against his friend. No other consideration would ever have prompted him to join in an underhand scheme with the Spanish Cardinal, save his own earnest faith in the ultimate good which would accrue therefrom, both to the country at large and to Wessex himself. With his whole heart and soul he believed that, at this moment, the Duke's marriage with Lady Ursula Glynde would be nothing short of a national calamity.

Reluctantly, he sat down to the board at last. His Eminence, opposite to him, was shading his face with his delicate white hand, and at first seemed absorbed in the intricacies of the game. Two servitors were still busy about the room. One of them asked if His Eminence would desire more light.

But the Cardinal preferred the fitful flicker of a few wax tapers. He liked the fantastic shadows which left the greater part of the vast chamber in gloom. Lord Everingham was a noted and very proficient player; His Eminence was enjoying the game thoroughly.

"Check to your king, my lord Cardinal," said the young Englishman at last.

"Only a temporary check, you see, my lord," rejoined His Eminence, as with slender, tapering fingers he moved one of the ivory pieces on the board. "By the help of this one little pawn, the safety of the whole combination is assured, and 'tis your knight now which is in serious danger."

"Not serious, I think, Your Eminence, and once more check to your king."

Even as he spoke the two servitors finally left the room, closing the heavy doors noiselessly behind them.

"Oh!" said the Cardinal thoughtfully, "this will necessitate a bolder move on my part. You mark, my son," he added as soon as he had made a move, "how beautifully Nature herself plays into our hands: you and I desired to part His Grace of Wessex effectually and for ever from his beautiful affianced bride. Two hours ago this seemed impossible, and lo!—a girl comes across our path: low-born, brainless, probably a wanton, yet the very physical counterpart of virtuous Lady Ursula, and——"

"Check," said Everingham drily, as he moved his castle.

"Nay! nay! we'll once more move this little pawn," rejoined His Eminence, with his usual pleasant benevolence, "and see how simple the plan becomes."

"'Tis of that plan I longed to hear."

"So you shall, my son, so you shall," said the Cardinal very kindly. "What would you wish to know?"

"The girl Mirrab?—Where is she?"

"In Don Miguel de Suarez rooms, dressing herself in quaint finery, collected for the purpose by my faithful servant Pasquale, who has a valuable female friend in the Queen's own entourage. A silk kirtle, rich white robes, some fantastic ornaments for the hair, and the likeness 'twixt our Mirrab and the high-born Lady Ursula will be more strangely apparent than ever. Your turn to move, my lord. I pray you do not lose the thread of this interesting game."

"'Tis easy enough to lose oneself in the mazes of Your Eminence's diplomacy," quoth the young man anxiously. "Having dressed the girl up in all that finery, what do you propose to do?"

His Eminence was silent for awhile; he seemed absorbed in an elaborate strategical combination, directed against his opponent's king. Then he moved his queen right across the board and said quietly—

"What do I propose to do, my lord? Only, with the aid of that diplomacy which you English affect to despise, contrive that His Grace of Wessex should see a lady—whom he will naturally mistake for the

Lady Ursula Glynde—in a highly compromising situation, and the love idyll begun this afternoon will abruptly end to-night."

"But how?"

"Ah, my lord! surely we must trust Chance a little. The fickle jade has served us well already."

"I'll not allow a pure woman's reputation to be sullied by any dastardly trick ..." began Everingham hotly.

"Pray, my lord, what is your definition of a dastardly trick?" rejoined His Eminence suavely. "Is it the use made by a political opponent of every means, fair or foul, to accomplish his own aims, which he considers great and just? or is it the work of a friend—an intimate, confidential friend—joining issue for the like purpose? Nay, nay! understand me, my dear lord," he added, with an infinity of gentle kindliness expressed in the almost paternal tone of his voice, "'twas not I, remember, who ever thought to blame you. Your aims and ambitions are as selfless as mine own: for the moment our purpose is the same. Will you honour me by allowing me to show you the way of attaining that purpose, quickly and surely? I'll not ask you to lend me a hand. I would gladly have kept from you the knowledge of my own intricate diplomacy. Why should you fear for the Lady Ursula? Is her reputation in your eyes of greater moment than the success of your schemes?— yours and all your faction, remember."

"Ah! there you have me, my lord," rejoined Everingham with a sigh. "All England is at one with us in a burning desire to see Wessex wedded to our Queen. But this is where your diplomacy escapes me. Once Wessex is turned away from the Lady Ursula, he will, we hope, naturally turn to the Queen, who loves him passionately, and ... Check!" he added, moving one of his pieces.

"Ah! you press me hard. Your lordship is a skilful player," said the Cardinal, intently studying the board. "As for me, you see I seem to move my pawns somewhat aimlessly. For the moment, I wish to part His Grace of Wessex from Lady Ursula ... after that—we shall see."

Everingham was silent. A truly bitter conflict was raging in his simple heart. Loyalty to his friend, love for his country, and an overwhelming anxiety for its welfare, cried out loudly within him. The very thought of meeting Wessex face to face at this moment was terrible to him, and yet he would not undo what he had already done, and would not thwart the Spaniard's tortuous schemes by betraying them to the Duke.

The purpose which he had in view blinded him to everything save the hope of its ultimate achievement. At this moment he felt that, if Wessex shared Mary Tudor's throne with her, so much that was great and good would come to England thereby, that all petty considerations of temporary disloyalty, or the reputation of one innocent woman, would quickly vanish into insignificance.

The very feelings of remorse and of shame which he was

81

experiencing at this moment strengthened him in his faith, for he was suffering keenly and acutely to the very depths of his honest heart, and he imagined that he was earning a crown of martyrdom thereby; he believed that by trampling on his own prejudices and jeopardizing his friendship with the man he loved and honoured best in all the world, he was adding to the cause, which he held to be sacred, the additional lustre of self-sacrifice.

His Eminence no doubt knew all this. With his intimate knowledge of the foibles of mankind, he found it an easy task enough to probe the inner thoughts of the transparent soul before him. He divined the young man's doubts and fears, the battle waged within him betwixt an abstruse political aim and his own upright nature. The game was continued in silence, Everingham's state of mind being revealed in the one bitter sigh—

"Ah! I go away with a heavy heart, feeling that I have helped to commit a treachery."

The Cardinal looked benevolently compassionate. At heart he was more than glad to think that this blundering Englishman would be well out of the way. Could he have foreseen the marvellous turn by which Fate meant to aid him in his intrigue, he would never have made overtures to so clumsy an ally as Lord Everingham. But at the time he had been driven into a corner through the furious jealousy of the Queen, who had well-nigh staggered him.

His Eminence then did not know how to act. For the first time in his life he had been completely outwitted by the events which he himself had helped to bring about. They had shaped themselves in exact opposition to his keenest expectations. How to part Wessex from Lady Ursula, with whom his volatile Grace was probably by then more than half in love, became an almost insolvable problem.

The Queen's ultimatum was almost a fiat. His Eminence saw himself and his retinue ignominiously quitting the English Court and returning—baffled, vanquished, humbled—to the throne of an infuriated monarch, who never forgave and always knew how to punish.

In despair the Cardinal had turned to an ally. He knew that His Grace was quite inaccessible. Towards all the foreign ambassadors the Duke of Wessex was always ensconced behind a barrier of unbendable hauteur and of frigid reserve. It would have been impossible to attack the lady of his choice openly, and in offering his own help to Everingham His Eminence vaguely hoped to arrive at some half-hidden mystery, a secret perhaps in His Grace's life which would have helped him to strike in the dark.

Then Fate interposed: exactly ten minutes too late, and when the Cardinal had already saddled himself with an over-scrupulous, vacillating, ultra-honest ally. He could not now throw him over without endangering the success of his own schemes, and therefore brought all his powers of dissimulation into play to effectually hide the impatience which he felt.

The entrance of Don Miguel, Marquis de Suarez, created a diversion.

"Ah, my dear Marquis," said His Eminence, with a sigh of relief, "your arrival is most opportune. I pray you help me to persuade Lord Everingham that we are not scheming black treachery against His Grace of Wessex."

Don Miguel came forward, a smile of the keenest satisfaction upon his lips.

"Why treachery?" he said lightly.

But Everingham, having heard all that there was to know, was now in a hurry to depart. Having made up his mind to go through with his purpose to the end, he had but one wish—to turn his back upon the events which he had helped to bring about, and let them take their course.

With it all he felt a keen antipathy for these two plotters who had drawn him into their net. Whilst acting in concert with these Spaniards, he had an overwhelming desire to insult them or throw his contempt in their smooth, clever faces.

"Check and mate, my lord Cardinal," he said drily, as he took advantage of His Eminence's absence of mind to bring the game to a successful close. Then he rose to go. He was already booted and spurred for his journey northwards, and had unhitched his sword-belt when settling down to play. Whilst he was buckling it on again, Don Miguel approached him.

"I entreat you, milor, do not talk of treachery," said the young Spaniard earnestly. "Believe me that in this matter, your conscience is over-sensitive. After all, what does His Eminence propose? Only this, that for a little while—a few days only perhaps—His Grace of Wessex should be led to believe, through the testimony of his own eyes, that the Lady Ursula Glynde is not altogether worthy to become Duchess of Wessex. The wench Mirrab will play her part unconsciously, and therefore to perfection. No one but His Grace shall be witness of the scene which we propose to enact, and though his disenchantment will be complete, do you think that he will greatly suffer thereby? Surely you do not imagine that he has fallen seriously in love with Lady Ursula in one hour: his own amour-propre will suffer a very transitory pang et tout sera dit."

"The Duke of Wessex will never break his heart or quarrel with a friend for the sake of a woman," added the Cardinal in his smooth, gentle voice.

"Like the bee, His Grace lingers over a flower only whilst he finds the perfume sweet," continued Don Miguel. "If he thinks the Lady Ursula false, he will turn to some other pretty maid with an indulgent smile for woman's frailty."

All this sounded plausible enough, and Lord Everingham, at war with his own conscience, was only too willing to be persuaded that he was in no way wronging his friend. One scruple, however, still held him back and would not be denied.

"There is one person in all this, my lord Marquis," he said, "whom I notice you and His Eminence scarce trouble to think about."

"Who is that, milor?"

"The Lady Ursula Glynde!"

"Bah! What of her?"

"A girl's reputation, my lord, is in England held to be sacred."

"Why should her reputation suffer? Who will gossip of this affair? You? I'll not believe it! His Grace of Wessex?—perish the thought. Nay! to satisfy that over-sensitive conscience of yours, milor, may I remind you that you are not pledged to secrecy. If on your return from Scotland you find that the Lady Ursula's reputation has suffered in any way through the little scheme which we purpose, you will be at liberty to right the innocent and to confound the guilty. Is that not so, Your Eminence?"

"You have said it, my son," replied the Cardinal.

"Well, are you satisfied, milor?" queried Don Miguel, who at an impatient sign from the Cardinal was courteously leading Everingham towards the door.

"I feel somewhat easier in my mind, perhaps," responded the young man. "I dare admit that His Eminence and yourself are more right in your surmises than I am. But I have the honour of calling His Grace of Wessex my friend, and I have an earnest wish in my heart that I could stay another twenty-four hours here, to see that no grievous harm come to him from all this."

With a heavy sigh he finally took up his cloak and bade adieu to the two Spaniards.

Don Miguel escorted him as far as the cloisters, until a servitor took charge of his lordship. Then he turned back to the audience chamber, where he found His Eminence sitting placidly in a high-backed arm-chair.

"Marry! this was the most unprofitable half-hour I have ever spent in my life," quoth the Cardinal with a half-smothered yawn, and speaking in his own native tongue. "These English are indeed impossible with their scruples and their conscience, their friendships and their prejudices. Carramba! what would become of Europe if such follies had to be pandered to?"

"By the Mass! 'tis a mighty lucky chance which hath sent that blundering young fool to the frozen kingdom of Scotland to-night," rejoined Don Miguel with a laugh.

"Chance, my son, is an obedient slave and a cruel mistress. Let us yoke her to our war-chariot whilst she seems amenable to our schemes. I'll now retire to chapel and read my breviary there until Her Majesty hath need of me for her evening orisons. Her curiosity will not allow her to dispense with my services to-night, though she showed me the cold shoulder throughout the banquet. There's a good deal which devolves upon you, my son. Seek out His Grace of Wessex as soon as you can for the special interview which we have planned. I pray you be light-hearted and natural. It should not be a difficult task for Don Miguel de Suarez to play the part of a young and callous reprobate. I, the while, will watch my opportunity, and will have our dramatic little scene well in rehearsal by the time the Duke retires to his own apartments. He must cross this audience chamber to reach them.... There shall be no garish light ... only an open window and the moon if she will favour us.... One short glimpse at the wench shall be sufficient.... I will contrive that it be brief but decisive.... Your talk with His Grace will have paved the way.... I will contrive ... Chance will aid me, but I will contrive."

The voice was changed. It was no longer suave now, but harsh and determined, cruel too in its slow, cold monotones. His Eminence paused awhile, then said more quietly—

"What is the wench doing now?"

"Gazing in rapt admiration at her own face in the mirror," replied Don Miguel lightly, "and incessantly talking of the Duke of Wessex, whom she vows she will see before the dawn. She mutters a good deal about the stars, and some danger which she says threatens her dear lord. Ha! ha! ha!"

His laugh sounded hoarse and bitter, and there was a glimmer of hatred in his deep-set, dark Spanish eyes. There was obviously no love lost here 'twixt His Grace and these schemers, for His Eminence's bland unctuousness looked just now as dangerous as the younger man's hate.

"Does she talk intelligently?" asked the Cardinal.

"Intelligently? No!" quoth Don Miguel. "Awhile ago she talked intelligibly enough, but three bumpers of heavy Spanish wine have addled her feeble wits by now. I doubt me but the wench was always half crazed. I thought so when I saw her in that booth, covered with tinsel and uttering ridiculous incantations."

"She might prove dangerous too," remarked His Eminence softly.

"To the man who thwarted her—yes!"

"Then, if His Grace should find out the deception, and, mayhap, were none too lenient with her, she would ..."

He did not complete the sentence, and after a moment or two said blandly—

"In either case, meseems, chance is bound to favour us. Our good Pasquale shall see that the wench is provided with a short dagger, eh? ... of English make ... and with unerring and ... poisoned blade.... What?..."

There was silence between the two men after that. The thought

85

which now reigned in both their minds was too dark to be put into more precise words.

Don Miguel took up a cloak, which was lying on a chair, and wrapped it round him. His Eminence drew a breviary from his pocket and settled himself more comfortably in the high-backed chair. Don Miguel turned to go, but at the door he paused and came back close to where the Cardinal was sitting. Then he said quietly—

"Is Your Eminence prepared for that eventuality too?"

"We must always be prepared for any eventuality, my son," replied the Cardinal gently.

Then he became absorbed in his breviary, whilst Don Miguel slowly strolled out of the room.

CHAPTER XX

DEPARTURE

Everingham could not leave the Palace without bidding farewell to Wessex. For the first time in his life he wished to avoid his friend, yet feared to arouse suspicion, mistrust—what not? in the heart of the man whom he was so unwillingly helping to deceive. He half feared now the frank and searching eyes which had always rested on him with peculiar kindness and friendship; he almost dreaded having to grasp the slender, aristocratic hand, which had ever been extended to him in loyalty and truth.

Nevertheless in his heart there was no desire to draw back. During his lengthy colloquy with His Eminence he had weighed all the consequences of his own actions; though misguided perhaps as to the means, led away by a stronger will than his own, his purpose was pure and his aim high; and though he had tortured his brain with conjectures and fears, he could not see any danger to Wessex in the intrigue devised against him.

As for Lady Ursula, he swore to himself that no harm should ultimately come to her. She would be a tool, a necessary pawn in this game of cross-purposes, which had the freedom and greatness of England for its ultimate aim.

With a firm step Everingham reached the Great Hall, where one by one the company was slowly dispersing. The Earl of Pembroke had gone to his rooms to prepare for the journey; his friends were ready in the Fountain Court to bid him a final farewell. Some of the younger men were still whispering in groups in various parts of the hall, whilst others were continuing their game of hazard.

Everingham took a rapid look round. There, in the embrasure on the dais, Wessex was conversing with the Earl of Oxford, whilst faithful Harry Plantagenet lay calmly sleeping at his feet. The Duke's grave face lighted up at sight of his friend.

"I thought I should have missed you," he said, grasping the young man warmly by the hand. "My lord of Oxford was just telling me that he thought you would be starting anon."

"Should I have gone without your God-speed?"

"I trust not indeed. But your game of chess, meseems, must have been very engrossing."

Lord Everingham felt himself changing colour. Fortunately his back was to the light, and the Duke could not have seen the slight start of alarm which followed his simple remark. In a flash Everingham had realized how true had been His Eminence's conjecture. Wessex had already heard of the interview in the audience chamber. The game of chess had undoubtedly proved a useful explanation for so unusual an incident.

"Oh! His Eminence is passionately fond of the game," rejoined Everingham as lightly as he could, "and I could not help but accede to his request for a final battle of skill with him, since probably I may not see him on my return."

But he felt His Grace's earnest eyes fixed searchingly upon him. A wild longing seized him to throw off the mantle of diplomacy, which became him so ill, and to give a word of timely warning to his friend. The sight of the beautiful boarhound, so faithful, so watchful, at the feet of his master, became almost intolerable to his overwrought mind. Perhaps he would have spoken even now, at this eleventh hour, when from the court outside there came the sharp sound of bugle-call.

Harry Plantagenet, roused from his light sleep, had pricked his ears.

"I fear me 'tis to horse, friend," said Wessex, with a light tone of sadness, "Marry! it likes me not to see you depart. Harry Plantagenet and I will miss you sorely in this dull place, and I will miss your loyal hand amongst so many enemies."

"Enemies, my dear lord!" protested Everingham warmly. "Look around this Great Hall at this moment. Now that the foreign ambassadors have departed, do you see aught but friends? Nay more, adherents, partisans, faithful subjects, an you choose," he added significantly.

"Friends to-day," mused His Grace, "enemies perhaps to-morrow."

"Impossible."

"Even if ... But by the Lord Harry, this is no time to talk of my affairs," rejoined Wessex light-heartedly. "Farewell, friends, and God-speed.... Harry, make your bow to the most loyal man in England—you'll not see his like until he return from Scotland. In your ear, my dear lord, I pray you be not astonished if when that happy eventuality occurs, you find me no longer a free man. Come, Harry, shall we bid him adieu at the gates?"

He linked his arm in that of Everingham, the group of gentlemen parted to let him pass, then closed behind him, and followed him and his friend out of the hall. Every one was glad of a diversion from the oppressive atmosphere of the last few hours. Many murmured: "God bless Your Grace!" as he passed through the brilliant assembly exchanging a word, a merry jest with his friends, a courteous bow or gracious smile with the casual acquaintances.

His popularity at this moment was at its height. Nothing would have caused greater joy in England than the announcement of his plighted troth to the Queen. Yet if these gentlemen, who so eagerly pressed round him as he escorted his dearest friend through the hall, had been gifted with the knowledge of their fellow-creatures' innermost thoughts, they might have read in His Grace's heart the opening chapters of a romance which would have changed their enthusiasm into bitter disappointment. They would have seen that in that heart, wherein they hoped to see their Queen enthroned, there now reigned a dainty image, that of a young girl dressed in shimmering white, with ruddy golden hair falling loosely about her shoulders, and deep, dark eyes, now blue, now grey, now inscrutably black, the mirrors of a pure, innocent, joyous soul within.

As for Everingham, all his desire to warn Wessex had vanished with the latter's lightly spoken allusion to the incident of this afternoon. He was now only conscious of a desire to get away, and thus leave events to shape their course according to the dictates of my lord Cardinal.

Everything was ready for the departure. The gentlemen who composed the mission sent by Mary Tudor to the Queen Regent of Scotland were proceeding to Edinburgh by water. They would ride to Greenwich to-night, then embark in the early dawn.

The horses were pawing the ground impatiently; every one had assembled in the Fountain Court, which presented an animated and picturesque spectacle, with the crowd of servants and the numerous retinue which was to accompany the Earl of Pembroke to Scotland. A number of torch-bearers lent fantastic aspect to the scene, for a lively breeze had sprung up, blowing the fitful flames hither and thither, bringing into bold relief now the richly caparisoned steed of one of the noblemen, now the steel helmets of the military escort, anon throwing everything into deep, impenetrable shadow whilst touching with weird, red light some grotesque vane or leaden waterspout on the walls of the Palace.

The Earl of Pembroke took a long farewell from His Grace of

Wessex. Himself one of the most fervent adherents of the Duke, he was longing for a word, a promise however vague, that the much-desired alliance would indeed soon take place.

Wessex lingered some time beside Everingham. He seemed strangely loath to part from his fondest friend just now. The crowd around him were chattering merrily, the young men feeling the usual, natural exhilaration of manhood at sight of this goodly cavalcade, and the sound of clattering arms, the champing of bits, and quick, sharp calls to assemble.

Then, at a given moment, one of the bays of King Henry's presence chamber was thrown open, and the Queen herself appeared at the window. A shout of welcome was raised, such as could only come from faithful and loyal hearts.

Mary was surrounded by some of her ladies. The strong light of the room was behind her, so that she appeared as a silhouette, dignified, rather stiff in her corseted panier of rich brocade, her head slightly bent forward as if in anxious search of some one in the crowd.

"God bless our Queen," said the Duke of Wessex loudly, and the words were taken up again and again by two hundred lusty throats, gentlemen and servants all alike, and the cry echoed against the massive walls of old Hampton Court like a solemn prayer.

Not a few voices then added: "God bless His Grace of Wessex!" The Queen had recognized the Duke's voice. When she heard this second cry, every one noticed that she pressed her hand to her heart, as if overcome with emotion. Then she waved an adieu from the window and hastily retired within.

The signal for departure was given. A few belated gentlemen quickly sprang to the stirrup—Everingham being among the last. With a deafening noise of clattering steel the military escort led the way, the halberds gleaming like tongues of flame in the torchlight as the men-at-arms lowered them in order to pass through the gates.

Then followed the Earl of Pembroke with Lord Everingham by his side, and the other gentlemen of the mission in close proximity. The retinue of servants and another detachment of men-at-arms completed the cortège.

Some of the younger men followed the cavalcade on foot through the gate and thence across the Base Court, even as far as the bridge and beyond. The older ones, however, began to disperse. With a sigh, the Duke of Wessex called to his dog, who had followed the exciting proceedings with the keenest canine enthusiasm.

"Ah, Harry, old friend!" he said with a tinge of sadness. "Why did not Providence fashion my Grace into some humbler personality? You and I would have been the happier, methinks."

Harry Plantagenet yawned ostentatiously in acquiescence, then he blinked, and seemed to say, as if in echo of his master's thoughts—

"Marry! but there are compensations, you know!"

89

"Only since this afternoon!" commented His Grace under his breath, as he finally turned his steps in the direction of his own apartments.

CHAPTER XXI

THE BLACK KNIGHT

As the Duke of Wessex was crossing one of the large rooms of the wing which divides the old Fountain Court from the Cloister Green, he suddenly heard himself called by name.

"Luck favours me indeed," said a voice from out the gloom. "His Grace of Wessex an I mistake not."

At this hour of the evening these rooms were usually deserted, and left but dimly illumined by a few wax tapers placed in tall, many-armed candelabra, the flickering light of which failed to penetrate into the distant corners of the vast, panelled chambers. Wessex could only see the dim outline of a man coming towards him.

"At your service, fair sir, whoever you may be," he responded lightly, "but by the Mass! meseems you must claim kinship with the feline species to be able to distinguish my unworthy self in the dark."

"Nay! 'twas my wish which fathered my thoughts. I had hoped to meet Your Grace here, and was on the look out."

"The Marquis de Suarez," rejoined Wessex, as the young Spaniard now came within the circle of light projected by the candelabra. "You wished to speak with me, sir?"

"I would claim this privilege of Your Grace's courtesy."

"Indeed, I am ever at your service," replied the Duke, not a little astonished at the request.

Since his first meeting with Don Miguel at East Molesey Fair he had only exchanged a very few words with the Spaniard, and the latter seemed even to have purposely avoided him during the past few days. To this His Grace had paid no attention. The foreign envoys at present staying in the Palace were exceedingly antipathetic to him, and beyond the social amenities of Court life he had held no intercourse with any of them.

Rivals all of them, they nevertheless joined issue with one another in their hostile attitude towards the man, who was the formidable stumbling-block to all their diplomatic intrigues.

The Duke himself, in spite of his haughty aloofness from party

90

politics, knew full well how great was the enmity which his personality aroused in the minds of all the strangers at Mary's court.

He was certainly much more amused than disturbed by this generally hostile attitude towards himself, and many a time did the various ambassadors have to suffer, with seeming good-nature, the pointed and caustic shafts aimed at them by His Grace's ready wit.

No wonder, therefore, that Wessex looked with some suspicion on this sudden change of front on the part of one of his most avowed antagonists.

"How can I have the honour of serving an envoy of the King of Spain?" he continued lightly.

But Don Miguel appeared in no hurry to speak. His manner seemed to have completely altered. As a rule he was a perfect model of self-possession and easy confidence, with just a reflection of his distinguished chief's, the Cardinal's, own suavity of manner apparent in all his ways. Now he was obviously ill at ease, shy and nervous, and with a marked desire to be frank, yet too bashful to give vent to so boyish an outburst.

There was in his dark eyes, too, a look almost of appeal towards the Duke to meet his sudden access of friendliness half-way. All this Wessex had already noticed with the one quick glance which he cast at the young Spaniard. He motioned him to a chair and himself leant lightly against the edge of the table.

Don Miguel took this to be an encouragement to proceed.

"Firstly, your Grace's pardon if I should unwillingly transgress," he began.

"My pardon?" rejoined the Duke, much amused at the Marquis' obvious embarrassment. "'Tis yours already. But how transgress?"

"By the asking of a question which Your Grace might deem indiscreet."

"Nay, my lord," quoth the Duke gaily, "no question need be indiscreet, though answers often are."

"Your Grace is pleased to laugh ... but in this case ... I ... that is ... I hardly know how to put it ... yet I would assure Your Grace ..."

"By Our Lady, man!" cried Wessex with a slight show of impatience, "assure me no assurances, but tell me what you wish to say."

"Well then! since I have Your Grace's leave.... My object is this.... Court gossip has it that you are affianced to the Lady Ursula Glynde."

The Duke did not reply. Don Miguel looked up and saw a quaint smile hovering round His Grace's lips. The young Spaniard, though an earnest and even proficient reader of other men's thoughts, did not quite understand the meaning of that smile: it seemed wistful yet triumphant, full of gaiety and yet with a suspicion of that strange and delicious melancholy, which is never quite inseparable from a great happiness.

But as he seemingly was meeting with no rebuff, the Marquis continued more boldly—

"And ... but Your Grace must really pardon me.... I hardly know how to put it so as not to appear impertinent ... but 'tis also said that you do not wish to claim the lady's hand."

"Marry! ..." rejoined the Duke with a laugh. Then he paused, as if in the act of recalling his somewhat roving thoughts, and said more coldly—

"You must pardon me, my lord, if I do not quite perceive in what manner this may concern you."

"I pray Your Grace to have patience with me yet a while longer. I will explain my purpose directly. For the moment I will entreat you, an you will, to answer my question. It is a matter of serious moment to me, and you would render me eternally your debtor."

None knew better in these days than did the high-born Spaniards, all the many little tricks of voice and gesture which go to make up the abstruse and difficult art of diplomacy. Don Miguel at this juncture looked so frank, so boyish, and withal so earnest, that the Duke of Wessex—himself the soul of truth and candour—never even suspected that the young man was but playing a part and enacting a scene, which he had rehearsed under the skilful management of His Eminence the Spanish Cardinal.

Wessex, ever ready to see the merry side of life, ever ready for gaiety and brightness, felt completely disarmed, glad enough to lay aside the cold reserve which the foreign envoys themselves had called forth in him. He liked the Marquis under this new semblance of boyish guilelessness, and returned his tone of deferential frankness with one of easy familiarity.

"The question, my lord, is somewhat difficult to answer," he said with mock seriousness, the while a gay laugh was dancing in his eyes. "You see, there are certain difficulties in the way. The Lady Ursula is a Glynde ... and all the Glyndes have brown eyes.... Now at this moment I feel as if I could never love a brown eye again."

"The Lady Ursula is very beautiful," rejoined the Spaniard.

"Possibly—but you surprise me."

"Your Grace has never seen her?"

"Never, since she was out of her cradle."

"I have the advantage of Your Grace, then."

"You know her, my lord? ..."

"Intimately!" said Don Miguel, with what seemed an irresistible impulse.

Then he checked his enthusiasm with a visible effort, and stammered with a return of his previous nervousness—

"That is ... I ..."

"Yes?" queried the Duke.

"That is the purport of my importunity, my lord," said the young man, springing to his feet and speaking once more in tones of noble candour. "I would have asked Your Grace that, since you do not know the Lady Ursula, since you have no wish to claim her hand, if some one else ..."

"If the Lady Ursula honoured some one else than my unworthy self.... Is that your meaning, my lord?" queried Wessex, as Don Miguel had made a slight pause in his impetuous speech.

"If I ..."

"You, my lord?"

"I would wish to know if I should be offending Your Grace?"

"Offending me?" cried Wessex joyfully. "Nay, my lord, why were you so long in telling me this gladsome news? ... Offending me? ... you have succeeded in taking a load from my conscience, my dear Marquis. So you love the Lady Ursula Glynde? ... Ye heavens! what a number of circumlocutions to arrive at this simple little fact! You love her ... she is very beautiful ... and she loves you. Where did you first see her, my lord?"

"At East Molesey Fair.... Your Grace intervened ... you must remember!"

"Most inopportunely, meseems. I must indeed crave your pardon. And since then?"

"The acquaintanceship, perhaps somewhat unpleasantly begun, has ripened into ... friendship."

"And thence into love! Nay, you have my heartiest congratulations, my lord. The Glyndes are famous for their virtue, and since the Lady Ursula is beautiful, why! your Court will indeed be graced by such a pattern of English womanhood."

"Oh!" said the Spaniard, with a quick gesture of deprecation.

"Nay! you must have no fear, my lord. Since you have honoured me by consulting my feelings in the matter, it shall be my pride and my delight to further your cause, and that of the Lady Ursula ... if indeed she will deign to express her wishes to me.... I hereby give you a gentleman's word of honour that I consider the promise, which she made to her father in her childhood, in no way binding upon her now.... As for the future, I swear that I will obtain Her Majesty's consent to your immediate marriage."

"Nay! I pray you, not so fast!" laughed Don Miguel lightly. "Neither the Lady Ursula nor I have need of Her Majesty's consent ...."

"But methought——"

"'Twas not I who spoke of marriage, remember!"

"Then you have completely bewildered me, my lord," rejoined Wessex with a sudden frown. "I understood——"

"That I am the proudest of men, certainly," quoth Don Miguel with a sarcastic curl of his sensual lip, "but 'twas Your Grace who spoke of the lady's virtue. I merely wished to know if I should be offending Your Grace if ..."

93

He laughed and shrugged his shoulders. The laugh grated unpleasantly on Wessex' ear, and the gesture savoured of impertinence. The Marquis' manner had suddenly undergone a change, which caused the Duke's every nerve to tingle.

"If what?" he queried curtly. "The devil! sir, cannot you say what you do mean?"

"Why should I," replied the Spaniard, "since your Grace has already guessed? You will own that I have acted en galant homme, by thinking of your wishes. You will not surely desire to champion that much-vaunted virtue of the Glyndes."

"Then what you mean, sir, is that ..."

"I cannot speak more plainly, my lord, for that among gentlemen is quite impossible. But rumours fly about quickly at Court, and I feared that Your Grace might have caught one, ere I had the chance of assuring you that I recognize the priority of your claim. But now you tell me that you have no further interest in the lady, so I am reassured.... We foreigners, you know, take passing pleasures more lightly than you serious-minded English ... and if the lady be unattached ... and more than willing ... why should we play the part of Joseph? ... a ridiculous rôle at best, eh, my lord? ... and one, I think, which Your Grace would ever disdain to play.... As for me, I am quite reassured ... Au revoir to Your Grace ...."

And before Wessex had time to utter another word, Don Miguel, still laughing, went out of the room.

The Duke felt a little bewildered. The conversation had gone through such a sudden transition, that at the time, he had hardly realized whether it touched him deeply or not.

Owing to Ursula's girlish little ruse, he was totally unaware of her identity with the lady who had been the subject of this very distasteful discussion. To him Lady Ursula Glynde was both unknown and uninteresting. His meeting with beautiful, exquisite "Fanny" had driven all thoughts of other women from his mind.

But with all his volatile disposition, where women were concerned, the Duke of Wessex was nevertheless imbued with a strong and romantic feeling of chivalry towards the entire sex, and Don Miguel's disdainful allusions to the lady who might have been Duchess of Wessex had left his finger-tips itching with the desire to throw his glove in the impudent rascal's face.

Harry Plantagenet, who throughout the interview had openly expressed his disapproval of his master's interlocutor, gave an impatient little whine. He longed for the privacy of his own apartments, the warmth of the rugs laid out specially for him.

"Harry, old friend!" said Wessex thoughtfully, "what the devil, think you, that young reprobate meant?"

He took the dog's beautiful head between his hands and looked straight into the honest, faithful eyes of his dear and constant companion.

"Marry!" he continued more lightly, "you may well look doubtful, you wise philosopher, for you know the Glyndes as well as I do. You remember old Lady Annabel, whose very look would stop your tail from wagging, and Charles, stodgy, silent, serious Charles, who never drank, never laughed, had probably never seen a woman's ankle in his life. And then the Lady Ursula ... a Glynde ... do you mind me, old Harry? ... therefore as ugly, as a combination of virtue and Scotch descent can make any woman.... Yet, if I caught the rascal's meaning, neither Scotch descent nor ill looks have proved a shield for the lady's virtue! ... Well, 'tis no business of ours, is it, old Harry? Let us live and let live.... Perhaps Lady Ursula is not ugly ... perchance that unpleasant-looking Spaniard doth truly love her ... and who are we, Harry, you and I, that we should prove censorious? Let us to our apartments, friend, and meditate on woman's frailty and on our own ... especially on our own ... we are mere male creatures, and women are so adorable! even when they bristle with virtues like a hedgehog ... but like him too, are cushioned beneath those bristles with a hundred charming, fascinating sins.... Come along, friend, and let us meditate why sin ... sin of a certain type, remember, should be so enchantingly tempting."

Harry Plantagenet was a philosopher. He had seen his master in this kind of mood before. He wagged his tail as if to express his approval of the broad principles thus submitted for his consideration, but at the same time he showed a distinct desire that his master should talk less and come more speedily to bed.

CHAPTER XXII

THE WHITE QUEEN

Wessex after a while was ready enough to dismiss the unpleasant subject. Perhaps he had no right to be censorious or to resent the Spaniard's somewhat unusual attitude. In England, undoubtedly, a gentleman would never—except under very special circumstances—allude to any passing liaison he might have with a lady of his own rank. That was a strict code of honour which had existed from time immemorial, even in the days of King Harry's youth, when the virtue of high-born women had been but little thought of.

Abroad, perhaps, it was different. Spaniards, just then, were noted for the light way in which they regarded the favours of the fair sex, and Don Miguel's code of honour had evidently prompted him to consult Wessex' wishes in the matter of his own intrigue. Loyalty to their own sex is perhaps, on the whole, more general in men than is their chivalry towards women, and perhaps the Marquis' feelings would have revolted at the thought of seeing a lady of such light virtue in the position of Duchess of Wessex.

Be that as it may, His Grace had no wish to probe the matter further; with a shrug of the shoulders he dismissed it from his thoughts, whilst registering a vow to chastise the young blackguard if his impertinence showed signs of recurrence.

He was on the point of yielding to his faithful Harry's canine appeals by allowing him to lead the way towards his own distant lodgings, when his ear suddenly caught the sound of a silk dress rustling somewhere, not far from where he stood.

At the end of the room closest to him, a few steps led up to a gallery, which ran along the wall, finally abutting at a door, which gave access to the Duchess of Lincoln's and other ladies' lodgings. The rustle of a silk skirt seemed to come from there.

Perhaps Wessex would not have taken notice of it, except that his every thought was filled with a strange excitement since the rencontre of the afternoon. At times now he felt as if his very senses ached with the longing to see once more that entrancing, girlish figure, dressed all in white and crowned with the halo of her exquisite golden hair, to hear once more the sound of that fresh young voice, that merry, childlike laugh, through which there vibrated the thrill of a newly awakened passion.

Since he had met her he was conscious of a wonderful change in himself. He did not even analyse his feelings: he knew that he loved her now: that, in a sense, he had always loved her, for his poetic and romantic temperament had ever been in search of that perfect type of womanhood, which she seemed so completely to embody in herself.

He had only spoken to her for about half an hour, then had sat opposite to her in a boat among the reeds, in the cool of the afternoon, with the lazy river gently rocking the light skiff, and the water birds for sole witnesses of his happiness. They had hardly exchanged a word then, for he had enjoyed the delight—dear to every man who loves—of watching the blushes come and go upon her cheek in response to his ardent gaze. What did words matter? the music in their souls supplied all that they wished to say.

And he—who had been deemed so fickle, who had made of love a pastime, taking what joys women would give him with a grateful yet transient smile, His Grace of Wessex, in fact, who had loved so often yet so inconstantly—knew now that the stern little god, who will not for long brook defiance of his laws, had wounded him for life or death at last.

And even now, when he heard the rustle of a kirtle, he paused instinctively, vaguely, madly hoping that chance, and the great wild longing which was in him, had indeed drawn her footsteps hither.

The door above, at the end of the gallery, was tentatively opened. Wessex could see nothing, for those distant corners of the room were in complete darkness, but he heard a voice, low and sweet, humming the little ditty which she, his queen, had sung this afternoon.

> *"Disdaine me not that am your own,*
> *Refuse me not that am so true,*
> *Mistrust me not till all be knowen,*
> *Forsake me not now for no new."*

She walked slowly along the gallery, and paused not far from the top of the short flight of oak steps. She seemed to be hesitating a little, as if afraid to venture farther into the large, dimly lighted hall.

The flicker of the tall wax tapers now caught her dainty figure, casting golden lights and deep, ruddy shadows on her fair young face and on the whiteness of her gown. In her arms she held an enormous sheaf of pale pink monthly roses, the spoils of the garden, lavish in its autumnal glory.

Never had Wessex—fastidious, fickle, insouciant Wessex—seen anything more radiant, more exquisite, more poetic than this apparition which came towards him like the realization of all his maddest dreams.

For one moment more he lingered, his ardent, passionate soul was loath to give up these heaven-born seconds spent in looking at her. Her eyes shone darkly in the gleam of the candle light and had wondrous reflections in them, which looked ruddy and hot; her delicately chiselled features were suffused with a strange glow, which seemed to come from within; and her lips were slightly parted, moist and red like some ripe summer fruit. From her whole person there came an exhalation of youth and womanhood, of purity and soul-stirring passion.

"Come down, sweet singer," said Wessex to her at last.

She gave a startled little cry, leant over the balustrade, and the sheaf of flowers dropped from her arms, falling in a long cascade of leaves and blossoms, rose-coloured and sweet-scented, at his feet.

"Ah, Your Grace frightened me!" she whispered, with just a touch of feminine coquetry. "I ... I ... didn't know you were here."

"I swear you did not, sweet saint ... but now ... as I am here ... come down quickly ere I perish with longing for a nearer sight of your dear eyes."

"But my flowers," she said, with a sudden access of timidity, brought forth by the thrilling ardour of his voice. "I had picked them for Her Majesty's oratory."

"Nay! let them all wither save one ... which I will take from your hand. Come down ...."

One of the roses had remained fixed in the stiff fold of her panier. She took it between her fingers and sighed.

"Oh! I dare not," she said sadly. "Your Grace does not know,—cannot guess, what dire disgrace would befall me if I did."

"Perish the thought of disgrace," rejoined Wessex gaily. "Marry! the saints in Paradise must come down from heaven sometimes, else the world would be consumed by its own wickedness. Come down," he added more earnestly, seized with a mad, ungovernable desire to clasp her to his heart, "come down, or I swear that I'll bring you down in my arms."

"No ... no ... no!" she protested, alarmed at his vehemence. "I'll come down."

With a quaintly mischievous gesture she flung the rose at him; it hit him in the face, then fell; he had perforce to stoop in order to pick it up. When he once more straightened his tall figure she was standing quite close to him.

There she was, just as he had always thought of her, even as a boy when first he began to dream. She, the perfect woman whom one day he would meet, and on that day would love wholly, passionately, humbly, and proudly, his own and yet his queen; she the most perfect product of Nature, with just that tone of gold in her hair, just those eyes, so inscrutable, so full of colour, so infinite in their variety; not very tall, but graceful and slender, with her dainty head on a level with his shoulder, her fair young forehead on a level with his lips.

Now that she was so near, he was as if turned to stone. The wild longing was still in him to clasp her in his arms, to hold her closely, tenderly to his heart, yet he would not have touched her for a kingdom.

But as he looked at her he knew that she, herself, would come to him in all her purity, her innocence ... soon ... to-day perhaps ... but certainly one day ... and that she would come with every fibre in her entire being vibrating in responsive passion to him.

She looked up at him shyly, tentatively. His very soul went out to her as he returned her gaze. A great and glorious exultation thrilled every fibre of her being. She knew that she had conquered, that the love which in her girlish heart she had kept for him had borne fruit a thousandfold. Her heart seemed to stop beating at the immensity of her happiness.

But woman-like, she was more self-possessed than he was.

"I must not stay," she said gravely and with only an imperceptible quiver in her voice. "I am in disgrace, you know ... for that stroll on the river ... with you ... this afternoon."

"Why? what happened?" he asked with a smile.

She held up her little hand and counted on her fingers.

"Number one, a frown and a colder shoulder from Her Majesty! Two, a lecture from Her Grace of Lincoln! Twenty minutes! Three, four, and five, pin-pricks from the ladies and a lonely supper in my room to-night."

He loved her in this gayer mood which made her seem so young and childlike.

"Could you not have contrived to let me know?"

"Why? ... What would you have done?"

"Made it less lonely for you."

"You are doing that now. I thought I should be alone the rest of the evening. Her Grace of Lincoln and the others are at prayers with Her Majesty. I was confined to that room up there. How is it Your Grace happened to be in this hall just when I came out?"

"A moth is always to be found where the light happens to be," he replied gravely.

"But how did you know I should be here?"

"My eyes, since this afternoon, see you constantly where you are not—how could they fail to see you where you are?"

"Then, as Your Grace has seen me ..." she added with timid nervousness, seeing that he now stood between her and the steps, "will you allow me to go up again?"

"No."

"I entreat!" she pleaded.

"Impossible."

"Her Grace of Lincoln will be looking for me."

"Then stay here with me until she does."

"What to do?" she queried innocently.

"To make me happy."

"Happy?" she laughed merrily. "Ho! ho! ho! How can I, a humble waiting-maid, manage to make His Grace of Wessex happy?"

"By letting me look at you."

With quaint and artless coquetry she picked up the folds of her heavy brocaded paniers, right and left, with two delicate fingers, and executed a dainty pirouette in front of him.

"There!" she said merrily, "'tis done.... And now?"

"By letting me whisper to you ..." he murmured.

She drew back quickly, and said with mock severity—

"That which I must not hear."

"Why not?"

"Because Your Grace is not free," she rejoined archly. "Not free to whisper anything in any woman's ear, save in that of Lady Ursula Glynde."

"Then you guessed what I would have whispered to you?"

"Perhaps."

"What was it?"

She veiled the glory of her eyes with their fringe of dark lashes.

"That you loved me ..." she murmured, "for the moment ...."

How irresistible she was, with just that soupçon of coquetry to

99

whet the desire of this fastidious man of the world, and with it all so free from artifice, so young and fresh and pure:—a madonna, yet made to tempt mankind.

"Nay! if you would let me, sweet saint, I would whisper in your tiny ear that I worship you!" he said in all sincerity and truth, and with the ring of an ardent passion in every tone of his voice.

"Worship me? ..." she queried in mock astonishment, "and Your Grace does not even know who I am."

"Faith! but I do. You are the most beautiful woman on this earth."

"Oh! ... but my name! ..."

"Nay! as to that I care not ... You shall tell it me anon, if you like.... For the moment I love to think of you as I first beheld you in the garden this afternoon—a fairy or sprite ... I know not which ... an angel mayhap ... in your robes of white, surrounded with flowers and dark bosquets of hazelnut and of yew, with golden tints of ruddy autumn around you, less glorious than your hair. Let me worship blindly ... fettered ... your slave."

She sighed, a quaint little sigh, which had a tinge of melancholy in it.

"For how long?" she murmured.

"For my whole life," he replied earnestly. "Will you not try me?"

"How?"

"You love me, sweet saint?"

"I ..." she began shyly.

"Let me look into your eyes.... I will find my answer."

Her arms dropped by her side, she looked up and met his eyes, ardent, burning with passion, fixed longingly upon her. He came close to her, quite close, his presence thrilled her; she closed her eyes in order to shut out from her innermost soul everything from the outside world, save the exquisite feeling of her newly awakened love.

"Now, see how perverse I am," he whispered passionately. "I do not want you to tell me anything just now ... open your eyes, dear saint ... for I but want to stand like this ... and read in their blue depths ... enjoying every fraction of a second of this heavenly moment ...."

She tried to speak, but instinctively he stopped her.

"No ... no ... do not speak.... And yet ... 'tis from your sweet lips I'd have my final answer."

He took her in his arms. She lay against him, unresisting, her sweet face turned up to his, soul meeting soul at last in the ecstasy of a first kiss. He held her to his heart. It seemed as if he could never let her go from him again. Everything was forgotten, the world had ceased to be. For him there was but one woman on this earth, and she was his own.

100

CHAPTER XXIII

CHECK TO THE QUEEN

How long they stood thus, heart to heart, they themselves could never have said. The sound of many voices in the near distance roused them from their dream. Ursula started in alarm.

"Holy Virgin!" she exclaimed under her breath, "if it should be the Queen!"

But Wessex held her tightly, and she struggled in vain.

"Nay! then let the whole Court see that I hold my future wife in my arms," he said proudly.

But with an agitated little cry she contrived to escape him. He seemed much amused at her nervousness; what had she to fear? was she not his own, to protect even from the semblance of ill? But Ursula, now fully awakened to ordinary, everyday surroundings, was fearful lest her own innocent little deception should be too crudely, too suddenly unmasked.

She had so earnestly looked forward to the moment when she would say to him that she in sooth was none other than Lady Ursula Glynde, the woman whom every conventionality had decreed that he should marry, and whom—because of these conventionalities—he had secretly but certainly disliked.

Her woman's heart had already given her a clear insight into the character and the foibles of the man she loved. His passion for her now, sincere and great though it was, was partly dependent on that atmosphere of romance which his poetical temperament craved for, and which had surrounded the half-mysterious personality of exquisite, irresistible "Fanny."

Instinctively she dreaded the rough hand of commonplace, that ugly, coarse destroyer of poetic idylls. A few hastily uttered words might shatter in an hour the mystic shrine wherein Wessex had enthroned her. She had meant to tell him soon, to-morrow perhaps, perhaps only after a few days, but she wished to find her own time for this, when he knew her inner soul better, and the delicate cobwebs of this great love-at-first-sight had fallen away from his eyes.

She could not altogether have explained to herself why a sudden disclosure of her identity at this moment would have been peculiarly unpleasant to her. It was a weak, childish feeling no doubt. But such as it was, it was real, and strong, and genuine.

Barely a minute had elapsed whilst these quick thoughts and fears went wildly coursing through her mind. There was no time to tell him everything now. The voices came from the next room, within the next few seconds probably the great door would be open to admit a group of people: the Duchess of Lincoln and the ladies mayhap, or the Queen on her way to chapel. And His Grace of Wessex looked terribly determined.

"No! no! no!—not just this moment, sweet Grace," she entreated, "by your love! not just this moment.... The Queen would be so angry ... oh! not just now!"

She looked so genuinely disturbed, and so tenderly appealing, that he could not help but obey.

"But you cannot send me away like this," he urged. "Another word, sweet saint.... Faith! I could not live without another kiss ...."

"No, no, no, I entreat Your Grace ... not to-night," she protested feebly.

He thought, however, that he detected a sign of yielding in her voice, although she was already beginning to mount the steps ready for flight.

"Just one tiny word," he whispered hurriedly: "when the Queen has passed through, linger up there for one brief minute only. I'll wait in there!"

And he pointed to a small door close behind him, which led to an inner closet at right angles with the gallery. Before she had time to protest—nay! perhaps she had no wish to refuse—he had disappeared behind its heavy panels, quickly calling to his dog to follow him. But in that one moment's hesitation, those few brief and delicious words hastily exchanged, she had lost her opportunity for escape.

The next instant the door at the further end of the room was thrown open, and the Queen entered followed by some of her ladies. She was accompanied by the Duchess of Lincoln, and His Eminence the Cardinal de Moreno was on her left.

As chance or ill-luck would have it, the first sight which greeted Her Majesty's eyes was the figure of Lady Ursula, midway up the steps which led to the gallery, some mysterious imp of mischief having contrived that the light from the wax tapers should unaccountably and very vividly fall upon the white-clad form of the young girl. An exclamation of stern reproval from Her Grace of Lincoln brought Ursula to a standstill.

Flight now was no longer possible; she could but trust in her guardian angel, or in any of those protective genii who have in their keeping the special care of lovers in distress, and who happened to be hovering nigh.

It was not seemly to be half-way up a flight of stairs when Her Majesty was standing on the floor below. Ursula, with her cheeks aflame with vexation, slowly descended, whilst encountering as boldly as she could the artillery fire of half a dozen pairs of eyes fixed steadily upon her.

Mary Tudor looked coldly severe, Her Grace of Lincoln horror-struck, His Eminence ironical, and the ladies vastly amused.

"Ah, child!" said Her Majesty, in her iciest tone of voice, "all alone, and in this part of the Palace?"

She looked the dainty young figure disdainfully up and down, then her eye caught the sheaf of roses lying in a fragrant tangle close to the foot of the stairs. There was a quick flash of anger in her face, then a frown. Ursula wondered how much she guessed or what she suspected.

But the Queen, after that one quick wave of passionate wrath, made an obvious effort to control herself. She turned composedly to the Duchess of Lincoln.

"Your Grace is aware," she said drily, "that I deem it most indecorous for my maids-of-honour to wander about the Palace alone."

The wrinkled old face of the kindly Duchess expressed the most heartfelt sorrow.

"I crave Your Majesty's humble pardon ..." she stammered in an agony of misery at this public reproof. "I ..."

"Nay, Duchess, I know the difficulty of your task," rejoined Mary Tudor bitingly, "the other ladies are docile, and their behaviour is maidenly and chaste. 'Tis not always so with the Lady Ursula Glynde."

Mary's voice had been so trenchant and hard that it seemed to Ursula's sensitive ears as if its metallic tones must have penetrated to every corner of the Palace. She gave a quick, terrified look towards the door, longing with all her might for the gift to see through its massive panels—to know what went on within that inner closet, where Wessex was waiting and must have heard.

One pair of eyes, however, had caught that swift glance, and noted the sudden obvious fright which accompanied it. His Eminence had not taken his piercing eyes from off the young girl's face; he had seen every movement of the delicate nostril, every quiver of the eyelid.

What Mary Tudor only half suspected, what the good old Duchess could not even conjecture, that His Eminence had already more than guessed.

The delicate, rosy blush which suffused the young girl's cheeks, that indescribable something which emanated from her entire personality, the half-withered roses, all told their tale to this experienced diplomatist, accustomed to read his fellow-creatures' thoughts. Then that quick, apprehensive look towards the door had confirmed his every surmise.

"She has seen His Grace.... He is closeted in there!" were his immediate mental deductions. And whilst Ursula met Her Majesty's cold glances with as much boldness as she could command, and Her Grace of Lincoln lost herself in a maze of abject apologies, His Eminence, seemingly unconcerned, edged up to the low door, keeping the lock and handle thereof well in view.

"I crave Your Majesty's indulgence for the child," the Duchess of Lincoln was muttering. "She meant no harm, I'll take my oath on that, and she will, I know, return at once to her room, there to grieve over Your Majesty's disapproval of her. She——"

"Nay, Duchess," interrupted the Queen sternly, "repentance is far from Lady Ursula's thoughts, and her behaviour is not the thoughtlessness of a moment."

"Your Majesty ..." protested the Duchess, whilst Ursula threw her head back in token of proud denial.

"The rumour has already reached us," continued Mary, "of a maid-of-honour's strange wanderings at night and in disguise outside the purlieus of the Palace, and that the maiden who so far forgot her rank and her modesty was none other than the Lady Ursula Glynde."

Again that quick apprehensive glance directed towards the closet door at mention of her name, a glance unseen by any one present save by His Eminence's watchful eyes. To him it had revealed all that he wished to know, whilst the Queen, blinded by her own jealousy, saw nothing but a rival whom she desired to humiliate.

"Wessex is behind that door ..." mused His Eminence. "She starts every time her name is uttered ... ergo, he made love to her without knowing who she is."

It was natural and simple. The very logical sequence of a series of co-ordinated thoughts, together with a shrewd knowledge of human nature.

How this little incident would affect his own immediate plans His Eminence had not yet conjectured. That it would prove of vast importance, he was never for a moment in doubt. Therefore, at a moment when every one's eyes were fixed upon the Queen or Ursula, he quietly turned the key in the lock of that closet door, and slipped the key in his own pocket.

After that he rejoined the group of ladies, feeling that he could wait in peace until the close of the dramatic little episode.

"The rumour, if rumour there was," Ursula had retorted defiantly, "is a false one, Your Majesty."

"Indeed, child," said the Queen coldly, "did you not, then, some days ago leave the Palace with no other companion save weak-willed Margaret Cobham?"

"Verily, I ..."

"In order to visit, in disguise, or masked, or cloaked—we know not—some public entertainment, a country fair, methinks?"

"Of a truth, but ..."

"You do not deny that, meseems."

"I do not deny it, Your Majesty. I meant no harm."

"No harm! hark at the girl! Was there no harm then in your meeting certain gentlemen of our Court, under circumstances not altogether creditable to the fair fame of our English maidens?"

"Has the Marquis de Suarez dared ...."

"Nay! We did not name the Marquis, girl. Of a truth a gentleman will dare all, once a maid forgets her own dignity. But enough of this. I spoke a word of warning in your own interests. The Marquis—saving His Eminence's presence—has all the faults of his race. We warn you to cease this intercourse, which doth no credit to your modesty."

"Your Majesty ..." retorted Ursula, proud and rebellious at this slight put upon her, and forgetting for the moment even the invisible presence of the man she loved.

But Mary Tudor, though at times capable of noble and just impulses, was far too blinded by her own passion to give up the joy of this victory over the girl who had become her rival. At any rate, Fate had done one great thing for her: she was the Queen, ruling as every Tudor had ruled, by divine right, absolutely, unquestionably.

She would not let the girl speak, she would see her go, humiliated, with head bent, forcibly swallowing her tears of shame. Mary only regretted this: that Wessex could not be witness of this scene.

She threw back her head, drew herself up to her full height, and pointed peremptorily up towards the gallery.

"Silence, wench!" she commanded. "Go!"

And Ursula could not help but obey.

Slowly she mounted the stairs, her heart burning with defiance. To have angered Mary Tudor further by renewed rebellion would have been worse than madness; it would inevitably have brought more ignominy and worse perchance upon herself.

But the tears, which she tried in vain to suppress, were not caused by the Queen's harsh words, but by the terrible doubts which assailed her when she thought of Wessex.

Had he heard?

What would he think?

Would he understand the cause of her innocent deception, or would he believe—as indeed he must if he heard them—the evil insinuations so basely put forward by the Queen.

As she found her way along the gallery she heard Mary's voice once more.

"Duchess, I pray you see that in future more strict surveillance is kept over the young maids under your charge. Lady Ursula's conduct has put me verily to shame before the ambassadors of foreign Courts."

With a sob of impotent revolt Ursula disappeared within the upper room.

The Cardinal watched her until the door closed upon her and he was quite sure that she was well out of hearing. Then he approached the Queen and said in his most suave manner—

"Nay! Your Majesty, methinks, takes this trifling matter too much au sérieux. You deigned to mention the Marquis de Suarez just now. Believe me, he is far too proud of the favours bestowed upon him by Lady Ursula to look on England with any reproach."

The Duchess of Lincoln would have spoken, if she dared. Her loyal old soul rebelled against this insinuation, which she knew to be utterly false. But to tax His Eminence with the uttering of unfounded gossip and in the presence of the Queen of England—that task was quite beyond the worthy Duchess's powers.

But in her motherly heart she registered the resolution to take Ursula's part as hotly as she dared whenever Her Majesty would give her leave to speak, and in any case she would not allow the Cardinal's imputation to rest long upon the innocent young girl.

The Queen, on the other hand, had visibly brightened up when His Eminence himself mentioned the name of the young Spaniard in such close connection with that of Ursula. She seemed to drink in with delight the poisoned cup of thinly veiled slander which His Eminence held so temptingly before her.

She wanted to think of Ursula as base and wanton and had, until now, never quite dared to believe the many strange rumours which certainly had reached her ears.

With all her faults, Mary was a just woman and above all a proud one; she would never have allowed her rival to suffer long and seriously under a false calumny. The name of the Marquis de Suarez, when she uttered it, had been but a shaft hurled at random.

But since His Eminence so palpably hinted a confirmation of her hopes, she was more than ready to give his insinuations the fullest credence. So pleased was she that she gave him quite a pleasant smile, the first he had had from her since the afternoon.

"As Your Eminence justly remarks," she said graciously, "the matter is perhaps not of grave moment. But our interest in the young maidens who form our Court is a genuine one nevertheless. I pray you let it pass—Duchess, we'll speak of it all on the morrow. My lord Cardinal, we will wish you good night."

She was about to finally pass him and to leave the room when her curiosity got the better of her usual dignified reserve.

"Is it the last night Your Eminence will spend at our Court?" she asked pointedly.

"I think not, Your Majesty," replied the Cardinal blandly. "'Tis many days yet which I shall hope to spend in Your Majesty's company."

"Yet the skein is still entangled, my lord."

"'Twill be unravelled, Your Majesty."

"When?"

"Quien sabe?" he replied. "Perhaps to-night."

"To-night?"

She had allowed herself to be led away by the eagerness of her desire to know what was happening. Shrewd enough where her own wishes and plans were concerned, she could not help but notice the air of contentment, even of triumph, which the Cardinal had worn throughout the evening. He certainly did not look like a man about to

106

be sent back discomfited, to an irate master, there to explain that he had failed in the task allotted to him.

Mary's curiosity was very much on the alert, but His Eminence's monosyllabic answers were not intended to satisfy her, and perforce she had to desist from further questioning him. Obviously he did not mean to tell her anything just yet. She bade him good night with more graciousness than he could have anticipated, and his bow to her was full of the most profound respect.

A moment later she had passed out of the room, followed by Her Grace of Lincoln and her maids-of-honour.

CHAPTER XXIV

CHECK TO THE KING

The colloquy between Mary Tudor and Ursula Glynde had probably not lasted more than a few minutes.

To Wessex it seemed as if years had elapsed since he had closed the door of the small inner room behind him, shutting out from his sight the beautiful vision which had filled his soul with gladness.

Years! during which he had learnt chapter by chapter, the history of woman's frailty and deceit. Now, he suddenly felt old, all the buoyancy had gone out of his life, and he was left worn and weary, with a millstone of shattered illusions hung around his neck.

It had come about so strangely.

She was not exquisite "Fanny," mysterious, elusive, after all. She was Lady Ursula Glynde.

Well! what mattered that?

The name first pronounced by the Queen's trenchant voice had grated harshly on his ear. Why?

At first he could not remember.

Fanny or Ursula? Why not? The woman whom conventionality had in some sense ordained that he should marry. Why not?

Surely 'twas for him to thank conventionality for this kind decree.

But the Lady Ursula Glynde!

When did he last hear that name? Surely it was on that Spaniard's lips half an hour ago, accompanied by a thinly veiled, coarse jest and an impudent laugh.

But his "Fanny!"—that white-clad, poetic embodiment of his

most exalted dreams! Those guileless blue eyes—or were they black?—that childlike little head so fitly crowned with gold!

No! no! that was his "Fanny," not the other woman, whom the Queen was even now upbraiding for immodest conduct.

Now she was speaking ... stammering ... denying nothing.... Where was that Ursula Glynde? ... the other woman ... she who was false and wanton.... "Fanny" was pure and sweet and girlish.... Ursula alone was to blame. Where was she?

"Has the Marquis de Suarez dared ..."

It was her voice. Why did she name that man?

She knew him then? ... had met him at East Molesey Fair? ... she did not deny it ... she only asked if he had dared ... whilst the Spaniard had said, with a flippant shrug of the shoulders, that the acquaintanceship had ripened into ... friendship.

Wessex' whole soul rebelled at this suggestion. He had but one desire, to see her, to ask her—she would tell him the truth, and he would believe whatever she told him with those dear red lips of hers, which he had kissed.

He felt quite calm, still, firm in his faith, and sustained by his great love. He went to the door and found it locked.

A trifling matter surely, but why was it locked?

She had been upset, confused, ere the Queen had come. She would not allow him the great joy of proclaiming to all who were there to hear, that he had wooed and won her. Once more there came that torturing question: Why?

So averse was she to his appearing before the Queen, that she had locked the door for fear that the exuberant happiness which was in him, should cause him to precipitate a climax which she obviously dreaded.

Why? Why? Why?

But he would respect her wishes, and though his very sinews ached with the longing to break down that door, to see her then and there, not to endure for another second this maddening agony which made his temples throb and his brain reel, he made no attempt to touch the bolts again.

Just then there came the Queen's final words to her:

"The Marquis de Suarez has all the faults of his race. We warn you to cease this intercourse which doth no credit to your modesty."

And she—his love, his cherished dream—had said nothing in reply. Wessex strained his every sense to hear, but there came nothing save—

"Your Majesty ..."

And then the peremptory—

"Silence, wench!" from irate Mary Tudor.

And then nothing more.

She had gone evidently, bearing her humiliation, leaving him in

108

doubt and fear, to endure a torture of the soul which well-nigh unmanned him.

She must have known that he had heard, and yet she said nothing.

To the Duke of Wessex, the most favoured man in England, the grand seigneur with one foot on the throne, the idea of suffering a false accusation in silence was a thing absolutely beyond comprehension—weakness which must have its origin in guilt.

Human nature is so constituted that man is bound to measure his fellow-creatures by his own standard; else why doth charity think no evil? The goodness and purity which comes from the soul is always mirrored in the soul of others. Evil sees evil everywhere. Pride does not understand humility.

Thus in Wessex' heart!

Had his sovereign liege—that sovereign being a man—dared to put forth a base insinuation against him, he would have forgotten the kingship and struck the man, who impeached his honour, fearlessly in the face. Nothing but conscious guilt would have stayed his avenging hand, or silenced the indignant words on his lips.

Of course he could not see what was actually passing: he could but surmise, and a fevered, tortured brain is an uncertain counsellor.

He could not understand Ursula's attitude. The girlish weakness, the submission to the highest authority in the land born of centuries of tradition, the maidenly bashfulness at the monstrosity of the accusation, were so many little feminine traits which at this moment appeared to him as so many admissions of guilt.

He would have loved them at other times: loved them in her especially, because they were so characteristic of her simple nature, bred in the country, half woman and wholly child. Just now they were repellent to his pride, incomprehensible to his manhood, and for the first time his faith began to waver.

Pity him, my masters! for he suffered intensely.

Pity him, mistress, for he loved her with his whole soul.

Nay! do not sneer. Love-at-first-sight is a great and wonderful thing, and, more than that, it is real—genuinely, absolutely, completely real. But it is not immutable. It is the basis, the solid foundation of what will become the lasting passion. In itself it has one great weakness—the absence of knowledge.

Wessex loved with his soul, but not yet with his reason. How could he? Reason is always the last to fall into line with the other slaves of passion. At present he worshipped in her that which he had conceived her to be, and the very sublimity of this whole-hearted love was a bar to the existence of perfect trust and faith.

There had been a long silence whilst Ursula mounted the stairs and finally disappeared, but the rustle of her silk skirt did not penetrate through the solid panels of the closet door. Wessex did not know whether she had gone, or had been ordered to wait until Her Majesty had quitted the room. He wondered now how soon he would meet her, how she would look when she finally released him from this torture-chamber. He knew that he would not upbraid her, and feared but one awful eventuality, his own weakness if she were guilty.

Love such as his oft makes cowards of men.

To the Cardinal's poisoned shaft he paid but little heed. The weary soul had come to the end of its tether. It could not suffer more.

Beyond that lay madness or crime.

Silence became oppressive.

Then it seemed as if the key was being gently turned in the lock.

CHAPTER XXV

THE CARDINAL'S MOVE

His Eminence had been left all alone in the room after the passage of Her Majesty to her own apartments.

"And now, what is the next move in this game of chess?" he mused, as he took the key of the closet door from his pocket and thoughtfully contemplated this tiny engine of his far-reaching and elaborate schemes.

"For the moment my guess was a shrewd one. His Grace of Wessex is in there, and had I not locked that door he would have precipitated a climax, which had sent Queen Mary into a fever of jealous rage, and the Spanish ambassador and myself back to Spain to-morrow."

He listened intently for a second or so; no sound came from the inner room. Then he glanced up towards the gallery.

There was, of course, no sign of Lady Ursula. Even if she intended anon to rejoin His Grace, she would certainly wait a little while ere she once more ventured to sally forth.

The Cardinal very softly put the key back into the lock, and waited.

Very soon the door was vigorously shaken. His Eminence retired to the further end of the room and called loudly—

"Who goes there?"

"By Our Lady!" came in strong accents from the other side of the locked door, "whoever you may be, an you don't open this door, it shall fall in splinters atop of you."

110

Time to once more recross the room, and turn a small key, and a second later the Cardinal stood face to face with the Duke of Wessex.

"His Grace of Wessex!" he murmured, with an expression of boundless astonishment.

"Himself in person, my lord," rejoined Wessex, trying with all his might to appear unconcerned before this man, whom he knew to be his deadliest enemy. "Marry!" he added, with well-acted gaiety, "the next moment, an Your Eminence had not released me, I might have lost my temper."

"A precious trifle Your Grace would no doubt have quickly found again," said His Eminence with marked suavity. "Ah! I well recollect in my young days being locked in ... just like Your Grace ... by a lady who was no less fair."

Had he entertained the slightest doubt as to whether the little dramatic episode just enacted had borne its bitter fruit, he would have seen it summarily dispelled with the first glance which he had cast at Wessex.

The Duke's grave face was deadly pale, and the violent effort which he made to contain himself was apparent in the heavily swollen veins of his temples and the almost imperceptible tremor of his hands. But his voice was quite steady as he said lightly—

"Nay! why should Your Eminence speak of a lady in this case?"

"What have I said?" quoth the Cardinal, throwing up his be-ringed hands in mock alarm. "Nay! Your Grace need have no fear. Discretion is an integral portion of my calling. I was merely indulging in reminiscences. My purple robes do not, as you know, conceal a priest. Though a prince of the Church, I am an ecclesiastic only in name, and therefore may remember, without a blush, that I was twenty once and very hot-tempered. The lady in my case put me under lock and key whilst she went to another gallant."

"Again you speak of a lady, my lord," said the Duke, with the same light indifference. "May I ask——"

"Nay, nay! I pray you ask me nothing ... I saw nothing, believe me..."

He paused a moment. Wessex had turned to his dog, who, yawning and stretching, after the manner of his kind, and not the least upset by his recent incarceration, had just appeared in the doorway of the inner room.

"I saw nothing," continued the Cardinal, with a voice full of gentle, good-natured indulgence, "save a charming lady standing here alone, close to that door, when I entered with Her Majesty. What Queen Mary guessed or feared, alas! I cannot tell. The charming lady had just turned the key in the lock ... and this set me thinking of my own youth and follies.... But Your Grace must pardon an old man who has but one affection left in life. Don Miguel is as a son to me——"

111

"I pray you, my lord," here interrupted Wessex haughtily, "what has the Marquis de Suarez' name to do with me?"

"Only this, my son," rejoined the Cardinal with truly paternal benevolence, "Don Miguel is a stranger in England ... I had almost hoped that hospitality would prevent Your Grace from flying your hawk after his birds ...."

"Don Miguel would be hard hit," he added quickly, seeing that Wessex, at the end of his patience, was about to make an angry retort, "for we all know that where His Grace of Wessex desires to conquer, other vows and other lovers are very soon forgotten ... But the Marquis is young ... I would like to plead his cause ...."

His keen eyes had never for a moment strayed from the proud face of the Duke. He was shrewd enough to know that in speaking thus, he was reaching the outermost limits of His Grace's forbearance. His robes and his age rendered him to a certain extent immune from an actual quarrel with a man of Wessex' physique, nor did fear for his own personal safety ever enter into the far-seeing calculations of this astute diplomatist. Whatever his weaknesses might be, cowardice was not one of them, and he pursued his own aims boldly and relentlessly.

But he had had to endure a great deal through the personality and the presence of the Duke of Wessex: the humiliation put upon him this very afternoon by Mary Tudor still rankled deeply in his mind, and the vein of cruelty, almost inseparable from his nationality, rendered the present situation peculiarly pleasing to this dissector of human hearts.

Until this moment he had perhaps not quite realized that His Grace of Wessex had been hard hit. Having wilfully put away from his own life every tender sentiment, he did not understand the quick rise of a great and whole-souled passion. The Duke had been ever noted for his gallantry, his chivalry, and his numerous and light amourettes, and the Cardinal never imagined that in the daring game which he had planned, and which with the help of the wench Mirrab he was about to play, he would have to reckon with something more serious than a passing flirtation.

To his feline disposition, his callous estimate of human nature, his real hatred for this political rival, there was now a delicious satisfaction in dealing a really mortal wound to the man for whose sake he had oft been humiliated.

He felt a thrill of real and cruel delight in seeing this haughty Englishman half broken under the strain of this mental torture, which his slanderous words helped to aggravate. With half-closed eyes His Eminence was watching the quiver of the proud lip, ever ready with laughter and jest, the tremor of the slender hands, that peculiar stiffening of the whole figure which denotes a fierce struggle 'twixt raging passion and iron self-control. Was it not a joy to watch this

112

gaping wound, into which he himself was pouring a deadly poison with a steady and unerring hand?

The game had become doubly interesting now, and so much more important. The Duke, obviously deeply in love with Lady Ursula, would certainly never turn to another woman again. If the intrigue contrived by His Eminence and the Marquis de Suarez succeeded in accordance with their expectations, then not only would His Grace be parted from the lady in accordance with Queen Mary's ultimatum, but he would probably bury his disillusionment and sorrow on some remote estate of his, far from Court and political strife.

Chance had indeed been kind to the envoys of the King of Spain.

Chance, and the natural sequence of events, skilfully guided by the Cardinal's gentle hands.

But His Eminence was clever enough to know exactly how far he might dare venture. For the moment he certainly had said enough. The Duke seemed partly dazed and had altogether forgotten his presence.

Without a sound the Cardinal glided out of the room.

The closing of the door roused Wessex from the torpor into which he had fallen. The hall looked sombre and dreary, the wax tapers flickered feebly in their sockets, whilst strange shadows seemed to jeer at him from the dark corners around. He would not look up at the gallery, the steps whereon she stood, for it seemed to him as if some mocking witch wearing her face and her golden hair would look down at him from there, and laugh and sneer, until she finally faded from his sight in the arms of the Marquis de Suarez.

"Other vows and other lovers," he mused, whilst trying to shut away from his eyes the hellish visions which tortured him. "So my beautiful Fanny is not mine at all ... but the Spaniard's ... or another's ... what matter whose? Not true and proud, but a frisky wench, ready for intrigue, of whom these foreigners speak with a coarse laugh and a shrug of the shoulders."

"Harry Plantagenet, my friend," he added, as the dog, seeming to feel the presence of sorrow, gave his master's hand a gentle lick, "His Grace of Wessex has been made a fool of by a woman.... Ah, fortune! fickle fortune! one or two turns of your relentless wheel and a host of illusions ... the last I fear me ... have been scattered to the winds.... Shall we go, old Harry? Meseems you are the only honest person in this poison-infected Court. We'll not stay in it, friend, I promise you.... I am thirsting for the pure air of our Devon moors.... Come, now ... we must to bed ... and sleep.... Not dream, old Harry! ... whatever else we do ... for God's sake, let us not dream ...."

CHAPTER XXVI

THE PROVOCATION

When Ursula finally succeeded in escaping from her room, where she had been forcibly confined—almost a prisoner—in the charge of two waiting-women, she returned to the hall, vaguely hoping that Wessex would still be there. She found no one. The closet door was open; taking one of the wax tapers in her hand she peeped into the inner room and saw that it was empty.

On the fur rug, on the floor, was still the impress of Harry Plantagenet's body, as he had curled himself up patiently to wait and sleep.

A sudden draught extinguished the taper and left the small room in total darkness; to her overwrought nerves it seemed cold and lonely, like a newly opened grave. Wessex had gone because he had heard that she had deceived him. The slanders uttered against her had found credence in his heart. Thus she mused, guessing at the truth, perhaps not even realizing how much he had suffered.

She would not go back to her room just yet. She knew that she could not rest. Though the room was empty there seemed something of him still in it, even in its cold and deserted aspect.

She lingered here, sitting in the chair where he had sat and heard. She could not cry, she would not give way, for she wished to think. Therefore she lingered.

Thus fate worked its will in this strange history of that night.

Wessex did not know that she had returned. After the Cardinal had left him he waited awhile, but he never guessed that she would come back. Had he not heard that her kindest favours had been the Spaniard's, ere his noble Grace had come across her path? With that almost morbid humility which is such a peculiar and inalienable characteristic of a great love, he thought it quite natural that she should love Don Miguel, or any other man, rather than him, and now he was only too willing to suppose that she had gone to her favoured gallant, leaving him in the ridiculous and painful position in which she had wantonly placed him.

He had waited in a desultory fashion, not really hoping that she would come. Then, as silence began to fall more and more upon the Palace, and the clock in the great tower boomed the midnight hour, he had finally turned his steps towards his own apartments.

To reach them he had to go along the cloisters, and traverse the great audience chamber, which lay between his suite of rooms and that occupied by the Cardinal de Moreno and Don Miguel de Suarez.

As he entered the vast room he was unpleasantly surprised to see the young Spaniard standing beside the distant window.

The lights had been put out, but the two enormous bays were open, letting in a flood of brilliant moonlight. The night was peculiarly balmy and sweet, and through the window could be seen the exquisite panorama of the gardens and terraces of Hampton Court, with the river beyond bathed in silvery light.

Wessex had paused at the door, his eyes riveted on that distant picture, which recalled so vividly to his aching senses the poetic idyll of this afternoon.

It was strange that Don Miguel should be standing just where he was, between him and that vision so full of memories now.

Wessex turned his eyes on the Marquis, who had not moved when he entered, and seemed absorbed in thought.

"And there is the man who before me has looked in Ursula's eyes," mused the Duke. "To think that I have a fancy for killing that young reprobate, because he happens to be more attractive than myself ... or because ..."

He suddenly tried to check his thoughts. They were beginning to riot in his brain. Until this very moment, when he saw the Spaniard standing before him, he had not realized how much he hated him. All that is primitive, passionate, semi-savage in man rose in him at the sight of his rival. A wild desire seized him to grip that weakling by the throat, to make him quake and suffer, if only one thousandth part of the agony which had tortured him this past hour.

He deliberately crossed the room, then opened the door which led to his own apartments.

"Harry, old friend," he called to his dog, "go, wait for me within. I have no need for thy company just now."

The beautiful creature, with that peculiar unerring instinct of the faithful beast, seemed quite reluctant to obey. He stopped short, wagged his tail, indulged in all the tricks which he knew usually appealed to his master, begging in silent and pathetic language to be allowed to remain. But Wessex was quite inexorable, and Harry Plantagenet had perforce to go.

The door closed upon the Duke's most devoted friend. In the meanwhile Don Miguel had evidently perceived His Grace, and now when Wessex turned towards him he exclaimed half in surprise, half in tones of thinly veiled vexation—

"Ah! His Grace of Wessex? Still astir, my lord, at this hour?"

"At your service, Marquis," rejoined the Duke coldly. "Has His Eminence gone to his apartments? ... Can I do aught for you?"

"Nay, I thank Your Grace ... I thought you too had retired," stammered the young man, now in visible embarrassment. "I must confess I did not think to see you here."

"Whom did you expect to see, then?" queried Wessex curtly.

"Nay! methought Your Grace had said that questions could not be indiscreet."

"Well?"

"Marry! ... your question this time, my lord ..."

"Was indiscreet?"

"Oh!" said the Spaniard deprecatingly.

"Which means that you expect a lady."

"Has Your Grace any objection to that?" queried Don Miguel with thinly veiled sarcasm.

"None at all," replied Wessex, who felt his patience and self-control oozing away from him bit by bit. "I am not your guardian; yet, methinks, it ill becomes a guest of your rank to indulge in low amours beneath the roof of the Queen of England."

"Why should you call them low?" rejoined the Marquis, whose manner became more and more calm and bland, as Wessex seemed to wax more violent. "You, of all men, my lord, should know that we, at Court, seek for pleasure where we are most like to find it."

"Aye! and in finding the pleasure oft lose our honour."

"Your Grace is severe."

"If my words offend you, sir, I am at your service."

"Is this a quarrel?"

"As you please."

"Your Grace ..."

"Pardi, my lord Marquis," interrupted Wessex haughtily and in tones of withering contempt, "I did not know that there were any cowards among the grandees of Spain."

"By Our Lady, Your Grace is going too far," retorted the Spaniard.

And with a quick gesture he unsheathed his sword.

Wessex' eyes lighted up with the fire of satisfied desire. He knew now that this was what he had longed for ever since the young man's insolent laugh had first grated unpleasantly on his ear. For the moment all that was tender and poetic and noble in him was relegated to the very background of his soul. He was only a human creature who suffered and wished to be revenged, an animal who was wounded and was seeking to kill. He would have blushed to own that what he longed for now, above everything on earth, was the sight of that man's blood.

"Nay, my lord!" he said quietly, "are we children to give one another a pin-prick or so?"

And having drawn his sword, he unsheathed his long Italian dagger, and holding it in his left hand he quickly wrapped his cloak around that arm.

"You are mad," protested Don Miguel with a frown, for a sword and dagger fight meant death to one man at least, and a mortal combat with one so desperate as Wessex had not formed part of the programme so carefully arranged by the Cardinal de Moreno.

"By the Mass, man," was the Duke's calm answer, "art waiting to feel my glove on thy cheek?"

"As you will, then," retorted Don Miguel, reluctantly drawing his own dagger, "but I swear that this quarrel is none of my making."

"No! 'tis of mine! en garde!"

Don Miguel was pale to the lips. Not that he was a coward; he had fought more than one serious duel before now, and risked his life often enough for mere pastime or sport. But there was such a weird glitter in the eyes of this man, whom he and his chief had so wantonly wronged for the sake of their own political advancement, such a cold determination to kill, that, much against his will, the Spaniard felt an icy shiver running down his spine.

The room too! half in darkness, with only the strange, almost unreal brilliancy of the moon shedding a pallid light over one portion of the floor, that portion where one man was to die.

The Marquis de Suarez had been provoked; his was therefore the right of selecting his own position for the combat. In the case of such a peculiar illumination this was a great initial advantage.

The Spaniard, with his back towards the great open bay, had his antagonist before him in full light, whilst his own figure appeared only as a dark silhouette, elusive and intensely deceptive. Wessex, however, seemed totally unconscious of the disadvantage of his own position. He was still dressed in the rich white satin doublet in which he had appeared at the banquet a few hours ago. The broad ribbon of the Garter, the delicate lace at the throat, the jewels which he wore, all would help in the brilliant light to guide his enemy's dagger towards his breast.

But he seemed only impatient to begin; the issue, one way or the other, mattered to him not at all. The Spaniard's death or his own was all that he desired:—perhaps his own now—for choice. He felt less bitter, less humiliated since he held his sword in his hand, and only vaguely recollected that Spaniards made a boast these days of carrying poisoned daggers in their belts.

CHAPTER XXVII

THE FIGHT

Whilst Don Miguel was preparing for the fight, a slight sound suddenly caused him to turn towards that side of the room, from whence a tall oaken door led to his own and the Cardinal's apartments. His eyes, rendered peculiarly keen by the imminence of his own danger, quickly perceived a thin fillet of artificial light running upwards from the floor, which at once suggested to him that the door was slightly ajar.

It had certainly been closed when Wessex first entered the room. Behind it, as Don Miguel well knew, the Cardinal de Moreno had been watching; he was the great stage-manager of the drama which he had contrived should be enacted this night before His Grace. The young Marquis was only one of the chief actors; the principal actress being the wench Mirrab, who, surfeited with wine, impatient and violent, had been kept a close prisoner by His Eminence these last six hours past.

That little glimmer of light dispelled Don Miguel's strange obsession. The Cardinal, with the slight opening of that door, had plainly meant to indicate that he was on the alert, and that this unrehearsed scene of the drama would not be enacted without his interference. The Duke, who had his back to that portion of the room, had evidently seen and heard nothing, and the whole little episode had occurred in less than three seconds.

Now Don Miguel was ready, and the next moment the swords clashed against one another. Eye to eye these two enemies seemed to gauge one another's strength. For a moment their daggers, held in the left hand, only acted as weapons of defence, the cloaks wrapped round their arms were still efficient sheaths.

Very soon the Spaniard realized that his original fears had not been exaggerated. Wessex was a formidable opponent, absolutely calm, a skilful fencer, and with a wrist which seemed made of steel. His attack was quick and vigorous; step by step, slowly but unerringly, he forced the Marquis away from the stronghold of his position. Try how he might, parry how he could, the young Spaniard gradually found himself thrust more and more into full light, whilst his antagonist was equally steadily working his way round towards the more advantageous post.

No sound came from the Cardinal's apartments, and Don Miguel dared not even glance towards the door, for the swiftest look would have proved his undoing.

Wessex' face was like a mask, quite impassive, almost stony in its rigid expression of perfect determination. The Spaniard was still steadily losing ground, another few minutes and he would be in full light, whilst the Duke's figure would become the deceptive silhouette. Under those conditions, and against such a perfect swordsman, the Marquis knew that his doom was sealed. An icy sweat broke out from his forehead, he would have bartered half his fortune to know what was going on behind the door.

For one awful moment the thought crossed his mind that His Eminence perhaps had decreed his death at the hands of Wessex. Who knows? the ways of diplomacy are oft tortuous and ever cruel; none knew that better than Don Miguel de Suarez himself. How oft had he callously exercised the right given him by virtue of some important mission entrusted to him, in order to sweep ruthlessly aside the lesser pawns which stood in the way of his success?

Had he become the lesser pawn now in this gigantic game of chess, in which the hand of a Queen was the final prize for the victor? Was his death, at the hand of this man, of more importance to the success of the Cardinal's intrigues than his life would be? If so, Heaven alone could help him, for His Eminence would not hesitate to sacrifice him mercilessly.

The horror of these thoughts gave the young man the strength of despair. But he might just as well have tried to pierce a stone wall, as to break the garde of this impassive and deadly opponent. His own wrist was beginning to tire; the combat had lasted nigh on a quarter of an hour, and the next few minutes would inevitably see its fatal issue. The Duke's attacks became more swift and violent; once or twice already Don Miguel had all but felt His Grace's dagger at his throat.

Suddenly a piercing woman's shriek seemed to rend the air, the swift sound of running footsteps, the grating of a heavy door on its hinges, and then there came another cry, more definite this time—

"Wessex, have a care!"

Both the men had paused, of course. Even in this supreme moment when one life hung in the balance, how could they help turning towards the distant corner of the room whence had come that piercing shriek.

The door leading to the Marquis' apartments was wide open now; a flood of light came from the room beyond, and against this sudden glare, which seemed doubly brilliant to the dazed eyes of the combatants, there appeared a woman's figure, dressed in long flowing robes of clinging white, her golden hair hanging in a wild tangle over her shoulders. A quaint and weird figure! at first only a silhouette against a glowing background, but anon it came forward, disappeared completely for a while in the dense shadow of an angle of the room, but the next moment emerged again in the full light of the moon, ghostlike and fantastic; a girlish form, her white draperies half falling from her shoulders, revealing a white throat and one naked breast; on her hair a few green leaves, bacchante-like entwined and drooping, half hidden in the tangle of ruddy gold.

Wessex gazed on her, his sword dropped from his hand.

It was she! She, as a hellish vision had shown her to him half an hour ago, in the great room wherein he had first kissed her: a weird and witchlike creature, with eyes half veiled, and coarsened, sensuous lips. It was but a vision even now, for he could not see her very distinctly, his eyes were dazed with the play of the moonlight upon his sword, and she, after her second cry, had drawn back into the shadow.

Don Miguel on the other hand had not seemed very surprised at her apparition, only somewhat vexed, as he exclaimed—

"Lady Ursula, I pray you ..."

He placed his hand on her shoulder. It was the gesture of a master, and the tone in which he spoke to her was one of command.

"I pray you go within," he added curtly; "this is no place for women."

Wessex' whole soul writhed at the words, the touch, the attitude of the man towards her; an hour ago, when he stood beside her, he would have bartered a kingdom for the joy of taking her hand.

She seemed dazed, and her form swayed strangely to and fro; suddenly she appeared to be conscious of her garments, for with a certain shamed movement of tardy modesty she pulled a part of her draperies over her breast.

"I wish to speak with him," she whispered under her breath to Don Miguel.

But the Spaniard had no intention of prolonging this scene a second longer than was necessary. It had from the first been agreed between him and the Cardinal that the Duke should not obtain more than a glimpse at the wench. At any moment, after the first shock of surprise, Wessex might look more calmly, more steadily at the girl. She might begin to speak, and her voice—the hoarse voice of a gutter-bred girl—would betray the deception more quickly than anything else. The one brief vision had been all-sufficient: Don Miguel was satisfied. It had been admirably staged so far by the eminent manager who still remained out of sight, it was for the young man now to play his rôle skilfully to the end.

"Come!" he said peremptorily.

He seized the girl's wrist, whispered a few words in her ear which never reached her dull brain, and half led, half dragged her towards the door.

Wessex broke into a long, forced laugh, which expressed all the bitterness and anguish of his heart.

Oh! the humiliation of it all! Wessex suddenly felt that all his anger had vanished. The whole thing was so contemptible, the banality of the episode so low and degrading, that hatred fell away from him like a mantle, leaving in his soul a sense of unutterable disgust and even of abject ridicule. His pride alone was left to suffer. He who had always held himself disdainfully aloof from all the low intrigues inseparable from Court life, who had kept within his heart a reverent feeling of chivalry and veneration for all women, whether queen or peasant, constant or fickle, for him to have sunk to this! one of a trio of vulgar mountebanks, one of two aspirants for the favours of a wanton.

Of trickery, of deception, he had not one thought. How could he have? The events of the past hours had prepared him for this scene, and he had had only a brief vision in semi-darkness, whilst everything had been carefully prepared to blind him completely by this dastardly trick.

120

"By Our Lady," he said at last, with that same bitter, heartrending laugh, "the interruption was most opportune, and we must thank the Lady Ursula for her timely intervention. What! you and I, my lord, crossing swords for that?" and he pointed with a gesture of unutterable scorn towards the swaying figure of the woman. "A farce, my lord, a farce! Not a tragedy!"

He threw his dagger on to the floor and sheathed his sword, just as Don Miguel had succeeded in pushing the girl out of the room and closing the door on her.

The Spaniard began to stammer an apology.

"I pray you speak no more of it, my lord," said the Duke coldly, "'tis I owe you an apology for interfering in what doth not concern me. As His Eminence very pertinently remarked just now, hospitality should forbid me to fly my hawk after your lordship's birds. My congratulations, my lord Marquis!" he added with a sneer. "Your taste, I perceive, is unerring. Good night and pleasant dreams."

He bowed lightly and turned to go.

Don Miguel watched him until his tall figure had disappeared behind the door. Then he sighed a deep sigh of satisfaction.

"An admirably enacted comedy," he mused; "a thousand congratulations to His Eminence. Carramba! this is the best night's work we have accomplished since we trod this land of fogs."

CHAPTER XXVIII

THE SEQUEL OF THE COMEDY

Mirrab, during that very brief drama in which she herself had played the chief rôle, had vainly tried to collect her scattered wits. For the last few hours two noble gentlemen, one of whom wore gorgeous purple robes, had been plying her with wine and with promises that she should see the Duke of Wessex if she agreed to answer to the name of "Lady Ursula," seeing that His Grace never spoke to any one under the rank of a lady.

A clever and simple trick, which readily deceived this uneducated, half-crazy wench, whose life had been spent in gipsy booths, and whose intellect had long been quashed by the constant struggle for existence, which mostly consisted of senseless and fantastic exhibitions designed for the delectation of ignorant yokels.

She liked the idea of being called "my lady" even when it was

121

done in mockery, and was delighted at the thought of appearing in this new guise before the Duke of Wessex, for whom she had entertained a curious and passionate adoration ever since the dramatic episode of Molesey Fair. She liked still more the voluptuous garments which she was bidden to don, and was ready enough to concede to the young foreigner who thus embellished her, any favours which he chose to demand.

That had been her training, poor soul! her calling in life—a vulgar trickster by day, a wanton by night. Do not be too hard in your judgment, mistress! she knew nothing of home, very little of kindred; born in the gutter, her ambition did not soar beyond good food and a little money to spend.

The Duke of Wessex had saved her life; she was proud of that, and since that day she had had a burning ambition to see him again. She had hoped that a warning from the stars would prove a certain passport to his presence, but His Eminence the Cardinal and the other young gentleman had assured her that a noble name would alone lead her to him.

Thus she had been content to wait a few hours: the wine was good and the foreigner not too exacting. After awhile she had dropped to sleep like some tired animal, curled up on a rug on the floor. The clash of arms had roused her, and finding that every door yielded to her touch, she ran out, in eager curiosity to see whence came the sound. Her first cry, on seeing that strange moonlit combat, was one of sheer terror; then she recognized Wessex, and gave him a cry of warning.

But the wine which she had drunk had made her head heavy. She would have liked to go to the Duke, but the room seemed to be whirling unpleasantly around her. Ere she had time to utter another word the young foreigner had roughly seized her wrist and dragged her away. She was too weak to resist him, and was reluctantly compelled to follow his lead. The next moment he had closed the door on her, and she knew nothing more.

Excitement had somewhat dazed her, but a moment or two later she partially recovered and collected her scattered senses. She put her ear to the door and tried to listen, but she could hear nothing. Behind her was the corridor, out of which opened several doors, one of these being the one which gave into the room wherein she had been confined the whole evening. Not a sound came from there either. There was not a sign of my lord Cardinal.

Once more she tried the handle of the big door in front of her: it yielded, and she found herself back in the room where the fight had just taken place. The moonlight still streamed in through the open window. She could not see into the corners of the great hall, but straight in front of her was another massive door, exactly similar to the one in which she stood.

The room itself seemed empty. Wessex had gone, and she had

not spoken to him. That was the one great thought which detached itself from the turmoil which was going on in her brain. The door opposite fascinated her. Perhaps he had gone through there. Nay! surely so, for it almost seemed to her as if she could hear that strange, bitter laugh of his still echoing in the distance.

She ran across the room, fearful lest he should disappear altogether ere she could get to him. But even before she reached the door she felt her arm seized, her body dragged violently back. By the light of the moon, which fell full on him, she recognized the young foreign lord.

He had summarily placed himself before her, and he held her wrist in a tight grip.

"Let me go!" she murmured hoarsely.

"No!"

"I will go to him!"

"You cannot!"

He spoke from between his teeth, as if in a fury of rage or fear, she could not tell which, but as she, poor soul, had never inspired terror in any one she quaked before his rage.

Just then she heard, as if in the room beyond, a few footsteps, then a call: "Come, Harry!" and after that the opening and shutting of a distant door. It was the Duke of Wessex going again, somewhere where perhaps she could not find him again, and here was this man standing between her and the object of her adoration.

With a vigorous jerk she freed herself from Don Miguel's grasp.

"Have a care, man, have a care," she said in a low, trembling voice, in which a suppressed passion seemed suddenly to vibrate. "Let me pass, or ..."

"Silence, wench!" commanded Don Miguel. "Another word and I call the guard and have thee whipped as a disturber of the peace."

She started as if stung with the very lash with which he so callously threatened her. The fumes of wine and of excitement were being slowly expelled from her dull brain. A vague sense of bitter wrong crept into her heart; her own native shrewdness—the shrewdness of the country wench—made her dimly realize that she had been fooled: how and for what purpose she could not yet comprehend.

She pushed the tangled hair from her forehead, mechanically readjusting her cumbersome garments, then she stepped close up to the young Spaniard; she crossed her arms over her breast and looked him boldly in the eyes.

"Soho! my fine lord!" she said, speaking with a strange and pathetic effort at calmness, "that's it, is it? ... and do ye take me for a fool, that I do not see through your tricks? ... You and that purple-robed hypocrite there wanted to make use of me ... you cajoled me with soft words ... promises ... what? ... Bah! you tricked me, I say, do you hear?" she added with ever-increasing vehemence, "tricked me that you might trick him.... With all your talks of Ursula and Lady ... the devil alone knows what ye wanted.... Well! you've had your way ... he looked on me as he would on a plague-stricken cur ... mangy and dirty.... Was that what ye wanted? ... You've had your will ... are ye satisfied ... what more do ye want of me?"

Don Miguel, much astonished at this unexpected outburst of passion, gazed at her with a sneer, then he shrugged his shoulders and said coldly—

"Nothing, wench! His Grace of Wessex does not desire thy company, and I cannot allow thee to molest him. If thou'lt depart in peace, there'll be a well-filled purse for thee ... if not ... the whip, my girl ... the whip ... understand!"

"I will not go!" she repeated with dogged obstinacy. "I'll not ... I'll not ... I'll see him just once ... he was good to me.... I love his beautiful face and his kind, white hands; I want to kiss them.... I'll not go ... I'll not ... till I've kissed them.... So do not stand in my way, fine sir ... but let me get to him ...."

The obstinate desire, half a mania now, had grown upon her with this wanton thwarting of her wishes. A wholly unfettered passion seethed in her, half made up of hatred against this man who had fooled her and caused her to be spurned with unutterable contempt by Wessex.

"I'll give thee three minutes in which to get sober, my wench!" remarked Don Miguel placidly. "After that, take heed ...."

He laughed a long, cruel laugh, and looked at her with an evil leer, up and down.

"After that thou'lt go," he said slowly and significantly, "but not in peace. The Palace watch have a heavy hand ... three men to give thee ten lashes each ... till thy shoulders bleed, wench ... aye! I'll have thee whipped till thou die under it ... so go now or ..."

He looked so evil, so threatening, so full of baffled rage, that instinctively she drew back a few steps away from him, into the gloom.... As she did so her foot knocked against something on the floor, whilst the sharp point of some instrument of steel penetrated through the thin soles of her shoes.

She had enough presence of mind, enough determination, enough deadly hatred of him, not to give forth one sound; but when he, almost overcome with his own furious passion, had paused awhile and turned from her, she stooped very quickly and picked up that thing which had struck her foot. It was an unsheathed dagger.

Silently, surreptitiously, she hid it within the folds of her gown, whilst keeping a tight grip on its handle with her clenched right hand. Now she felt safe, and sure of herself and of ultimate success.

Don Miguel, seeing how quiet she had become, heaved a sigh of relief. For one moment he had had the fear that she meant to create a scandal, attract the guard with her screams, bring spectators upon the scene, and thus expose the whole despicable intrigue which had just been so successfully carried through.

But now she was standing quite rigid and mute, half hidden by the gloom, evidently terrorized by the cruel threats hurled against her.

"Well, which is it to be, wench," said the young man more calmly, "the purse of gold or the whipping-post?"

She did not reply at once, and a strange, almost awesome silence fell upon the scene. Not a sound from any portion of the Palace. Even from the gardens and terraces, beyond the night watchman's call had ceased to echo, only from far, very far away beyond the river and the distant meadows the melancholy hooting of an owl broke the intense stillness of the place.

Then the woman began to speak, slowly at first, very calmly, and in a voice deep and low, like the sound of muffled thunder, growing louder and louder, more violent, more passionate as she worked herself up into a very whirlwind of fury.

"Powers of Hell!" she said, "grant me patience! Man, listen. Ye don't understand me.... I am not one of your fine Court ladies, who simpers and trips along arrayed in silken kirtle.... I am called Mirrab, a witch, d'ye hear? ... a witch who knows naught about the law, and the guard, nor about queens and richly dressed lords. The Duke of Wessex saved my life ... and I want to go to him.... Do ye let me go.... What is it to ye if I see him? ... Do ye let me go ...."

Her voice broke into a sob of agonized entreaty and baffled desire.

"Shall I call the guard?" rejoined Don Miguel coldly.

She was now quite close to him, he, still between her and the door which she wished to reach, was half turned away from her, in obvious impatience, and looking at her over his shoulder with a sneer and a cruel frown.

"Do ye let me go!" she entreated once more.

For sole answer he made pretence at calling the guard.

"What ho there! the guard! What ho!"

But the last sound broke in a death rattle. Even as he spoke Mirrab had thrust the dagger with all her might between his shoulders. He fell forward on the floor, whilst with one last gasp of agony he called upon the man whom he had so deeply wronged.

"A moi! ... Wessex! ... I die! ... A moi! ..."

And the silvery moon, who had just gazed on so placidly whilst human passions ran riot in this vast audience chamber, who had shed her poetic light on hatred, revenge, and lust, suddenly veiled her brilliant face: the room was plunged in total darkness as the Marquis de Suarez breathed his last.

125

CHAPTER XXIX

CHECK-MATE

For some time already there had been a certain amount of commotion in the Palace. Mirrab's shouts when first she saw the combat, then her high-voiced altercation with Don Miguel, had roused the attention of some of the guard who were stationed in the cloister green court close by. Some of the gentlemen too were astir.

Wessex himself soon after he had reached his own apartments heard the sound of angry voices proceeding from the room which he had just quitted. He could hear nothing distinctly, but it seemed to him as if a woman and a man were quarrelling violently. He tried to shut his ears to the sound. He would hear nothing, know nothing more of the wanton who had fooled and mocked him.

But there are certain instincts in every chivalrous man, which will not be gainsaid; among these is the impulse to go at once to the assistance of a woman if she be in trouble or difficulty.

It was that impulse and nothing more which caused Wessex to retrace his footsteps. He had some difficulty in finding his way, now that there was no moonlight to guide him, but as soon as he re-entered the last room, which was next to the audience chamber, he heard the ominous "A moi!" of his dying opponent. Also all round him the obvious commotion of a number of footsteps all tending towards the same direction.

An icy horror suddenly gripped his heart. Not daring to imagine what had occurred, he hurried on. By instinct, for he could see nothing, he contrived to find and open the door, and still going forward he presently stumbled against something which lay heavy and inert at his feet.

In a moment he was on his knees, touching the prostrate body with a gentle hand; realizing that the unfortunate young man had fallen on his face, he tried with infinite care to lift and turn him as tenderly as he could.

Then suddenly he became conscious of another presence in the room. Nothing more than a ghostlike form of white, almost as rigid as the murdered man himself, whilst from the corridors close by the sound of approaching footsteps, still hesitating which way to go, became more and more distinct. A murmur of distant voices too gradually took on a definite sound.

"This way."

"No, that."

"In the court ..."

"No! the audience chamber!"

126

The ghostly white-clad figure appeared as if turned to stone.

"Through the window," whispered Wessex with sudden vehemence, "it is not high!—quick! fly, in the name of God! while there's yet time!"

That was his only instinct now. He could not think of her as the woman he had loved, he understood nothing, knew nothing; but in the intense gloom which surrounded him he had lost sight of the witchlike and horrible vision which had dealt a death-blow to his love, he seemed only to see the green bosquets of the park, the pond, the marguerites, and another white-clad figure, a girlish face crowned with the golden halo of purity and innocence.

The wild passion which he had felt for her changed to an agonizing horror, not only of her deed, but at the thought of seeing her surrounded, rough-handled by the guard, shamed and treated as a mad and drunken wanton.

He despised himself for his own weakness, but at this awful and supreme moment, when he realized that the idol which he had set up and worshipped was nothing but defiled mud, he felt for her only tenderness and pity.

Love had touched him once, and he knew now that nothing would ever tear her image completely from out his heart. Love, great, ardent, immutable, was dead; but death is oft more powerful than life, and his dead love pleaded for his chivalry, for his protection, with all the power of sweet memories, and aided by the agonizing grip of cold, stiff hands clinging to his heartstrings.

He pointed once more to the open window.

"Quick! in God's name!"

The girl moved towards him.

"Ah no, no, for pity's sake. Go!"

There was not a second to be lost. Mirrab, realizing her danger, was sobered and alert. The next moment she was clinging to the window-sill and measuring its height from the terrace below. It was but a few feet. As agile as a cat she flung herself over, and disappeared into the gloom just as the door leading into the audience chamber was thrown violently open, and a group of people—gentlemen, guard, servitors—bearing torches came rushing into the room.

"Water! ... a leech!—quick, some of you!" commanded Wessex, who held Don Miguel's head propped against his knee.

"What is it? ..." queried every one with unanimous breath.

Some pressed forward, snatching the flaming torches from the hands of the servitors. In a moment Wessex and the dead Marquis were surrounded, and the room flooded with weird, flickering light.

From the door of the apartments on the left a suave and urbane voice had sounded softly—

"What is it?"

"The Spanish Marquis," murmured the foremost man in the crowd.

"Wounded?" queried another.

"Nay! I fear me dead," said Wessex quietly.

Then the groups parted instinctively, for the same urbane voice had repeated its query in tones of the gravest anxiety.

"I was at prayers, and heard this noise.... What is it?"

The Cardinal de Moreno now stood beside the dead body of his friend.

"Your Grace! and? ..."

"Alas, Your Eminence!" replied Wessex, "Don Miguel de Suarez is dead."

"Alas, Your Eminence! Don Miguel de Suarez is dead."

The Cardinal made no comment, and the next moment was seen to stoop and pick up something from the ground.

"But how?" queried one of the gentlemen.

"A duel?" added another.

"No, not a duel, seemingly," said His Eminence softly. "Don Miguel's sword and dagger are both sheathed."

He turned to the captain of the guard, who was standing close beside him.

"Will this dagger explain the mystery, think you, my son?" he asked, handing a small weapon to the soldier. "I picked it up just now."

The guard—he was but a young man—took the dagger from His Eminence's hand, and looked at it attentively. Those who were nearest to him noticed that he suddenly started, and that the hand which held the narrow pointed blade trembled visibly.

"Your Grace's dagger!" he said at last, handing the weapon to Wessex. "It has Your Grace's arms upon the hilt."

Dead silence followed these simple words. The Duke seemed half dazed, and mechanically took the dagger from the captain's hand; the blade still bore on it the marks of Don Miguel's blood.

"Yes! it is my dagger," he murmured mechanically.

"But no doubt Your Grace can explain ..." suggested His Eminence indulgently.

Wessex was about to reply when one of the guard suddenly interposed.

"I seemed to see a woman flying through the gardens just now, captain," he said, addressing his officer.

"A woman?" asked His Eminence. "What woman?"

"Nay, my lord, I couldn't see distinctly," replied the soldier, "but she was dressed all in white, and ran very quickly along the terrace not far from this window."

"Then Your Grace will perhaps be able to tell us ..." suggested the Cardinal with utmost benevolence.

128

"I can tell Your Eminence nothing," replied Wessex coldly. "I was in this room all the time and saw no woman near."

"Your Grace was here?" said His Eminence in gentle tones of profound astonishment, "alone with Don Miguel de Suarez? ... The woman ..."

"There was no woman here," rejoined the Duke of Wessex firmly, "and I was alone with Don Miguel de Suarez."

There was dead silence now, the moon, pale, inquisitive, brilliant, peeped in through the window to see what was amiss. She saw a number of men recoiling, awestruck, from a small group composed of a dead man and of the first gentleman in the land self-confessed as a murderer. No one dared to speak, the moment was too solemn, too terrible, for any speech save a half-smothered sigh of horror.

The captain of the guard was the first to recollect his duty.

"Your Grace's sword ..." he began, somewhat shamefacedly.

"Ah yes! I had forgot," said Wessex quietly, as he rose to his feet. He drew his sword from its sheath, and with one quick, sudden wrench, broke the blade across his knee. Then he threw the pieces of steel on the ground.

"I am ready to follow you, friend captain," he said, with all the hauteur, all the light, easy graciousness so peculiar to himself.

The groups parted silently, almost respectfully, as His Grace of Wessex passed out of the room—a prisoner.

129

PART IV

HIS GRACE OF WESSEX

CHAPTER XXX

THOUGHTS

In the loneliness and silence of the Tower, the Duke of Wessex had had enough leisure to think.

One fatal autumn afternoon, and what a change in the destinies of his life! Yesterday he was the first gentleman in England, loved by many, feared by a few, reverenced by all as the perfect embodiment of national pride and national grandeur—almost a king.

And to-day?

But of himself, his own obvious fate, the shame and disgrace of his present position, he thought very little. Ever an easy-going philosopher, he had as yet kept the insouciance of the gamester who has staked and lost and is content to retire from the board. One thing more, remember! Life in those days was not the priceless treasure which later civilization would have us believe it. There was a greater simplicity of faith, a more childlike certitude in the great truths of futurity, which we in our epoch are so ready to cavil at.

If nations and individuals committed excesses of unparalleled cruelty in the name of their respective creeds, if men hated each other, tortured each other, destroyed one another, it was because they misunderstood the teachings of religion, and not because they ignored or disbelieved them.

The cruelties themselves are unjustifiable, the mind of twentieth-century civilization can but gaze at them in mute horror, history can but record and deplore. But the religion which prompted them—for it was religion—was not the feeble, anæmic plaything of an effete generation in search of new excitements; it was strong and virile, alike in the atrocity of its crimes and the sublimity of its virtues.

Thus with a man like Wessex. Life had been pleasant, of course, a bed of roses worthy even of one of our modern sybarites, but to him only the episode, which higher thoughts and Christian belief have ever suggested that it should be.

Perhaps it would be too much to say that faith alone caused him to look lightly upon this sudden, tragic ending of his brilliant career, but it undoubtedly helped him to preserve that easy and unembittered frame of mind of the philosopher, who, with life, loses that which hath but little value.

And now indeed, what worth would life have for him? This is where thoughts became bitter and cruel, not over death, not over disgrace, but over the treachery of a woman and the flight of an illusion. What did it all mean?

Sometimes now, when he sat looking straight before him at the cold grey walls of his prison, he seemed to see that strange dual personality mocking him with all the witchlike elusiveness which had mystified and tortured him from the first.

His "Fanny"! that beautiful vision of innocent girlhood; arch, coquettish, tender yet passionate, the clear depths of those blue eyes, the purity of that radiant smile!

And then she! Ursula Glynde! with bare shoulder and breast, cheeks flushed, but not with shame, eyes moist, yet not with tears, submitting with feeble, hoarse protests to the masterful touch of an insolent Spaniard, only to take revenge later with the elemental barbarity of the street wench, too drunk to understand her crime.

Every fibre within him cried out that this was not the woman who had plucked a marguerite petal by petal, and quivered with delight at sound of the nightingale's voice among the willows; not the woman on whose soft girlish cheeks he had loved to call forth, with an ardent gaze or a bold word, a tender blush of rosy red, not the woman whom in one brief second he had learnt to love, whom in one mad, heavenly moment he had kissed.

Every sense in him clamoured for the belief that it had all been an ugly dream, an autumn madness from which he would presently wake at her feet.

Every sense! yet his eyes had seen her! his ears had heard her respond to her name, when uttered roughly by the man who seemed to be her master.

The truth itself never once dawned upon him. The whole trick had been managed with such devilish cunning, every piece in the intricate mechanism of that intrigue had been so carefully adjusted, that it would have required superhuman insight, or the cold, calculating mind of an unemotional mathematician, to have hit upon its natural explanation.

Wessex possessed neither. He was just a man touched for the first time in his life with the strongest passion of which human creatures are capable. He loved a woman with all the ardour, all the unreasoning instincts, all the sublime weakness and folly of which a loyal and strong heart is capable. That woman had proved a liar and a wanton in his sight.

He was forced to believe that; had he not seen her? Which of us hath ever really grasped the fact that one human being may be fashioned line for line, feature for feature, exactly like another? Yet such a thing is. Nature hath every freak. Why not that one?

He thought of everything, of every solution, of every possibility. Heaven help him! of every excuse, but never of that. That Nature, in one of those wayward moods in which no one would dare deny that she at times indulges, had fashioned a kitchen wench as a lifelike replica of one of the most beautiful women in England—that one simple, indisputable, easily verified fact, never once entered his tortured mind.

She was mad! yes!—irresponsible for her own actions, yes!—wilfully wanton! no! a thousand times no! Hers was a dual nature, wherein angels and devils alternately held sway!

He, poor fool, had fallen under the spell of the angels, and the devils had then turned him away from his shrine, shattered his illusions, shown him his idol's feet of clay, then dared him ever to worship again, ever to forget the mud which cloyed the bottom of the limpid stream.

With Harry Plantagenet for sole companion, during the brief days which preceded his trial, Wessex had indeed leisure for his thoughts. The faithful animal knew quite well that his master suffered and could not now be comforted, but he would sit for hours with his wise head resting on Wessex' knee, his gentle eyes fixed in mute sympathy upon the grave face of the Duke.

He knew better than any one that his master was in serious trouble, for when they were alone together, when no one was there who could see, no one but this true and silent companion, then philosophy, pride, and bitterness would fly to the winds and a few hot tears would ease the oppression which made Wessex' heart ache almost to breaking.

And Harry Plantagenet, when he saw those tears, would curl himself up and go to sleep. With his keen, canine instinct, he felt no doubt only that an atmosphere of peace and rest had descended on the gloomy Tower prison.

The faithful creature could not understand that it was the visit of the angel of sorrow, who, in passing, had lulled a weary man's agonizing soul with the gentle, soothing touch of his wing.

CHAPTER XXXI

MARYE, THE QUEENE

Thus day followed day, whilst in the great world without, England was preparing to see her premier lord arraigned before his peers on a charge of murder. And in one of the smaller chambers of her own private apartments at Hampton Court, Mary Tudor sat alone, praying and thinking, thinking and praying again.

Not a queen now, not a proud and wilful Tudor, passionate, cruel, or capricious, but only a middle-aged, broken-hearted woman, with eyes swollen with weeping, and brain heavy with eternally reiterated desires.

To save him! to save him!

But how?

That he had committed so foul a crime as to stab an enemy in the back, this in the very face of his own confession Mary still obstinately refused to believe. The rumours anent the presence of a woman in that part of the Palace and at that fatal hour had of course reached her ears. Jealousy and hatred, which had raged within her, had readily fastened on Ursula Glynde as the cause, if not the actual perpetrator of the dastardly crime.

That a woman was somehow or other connected with the terrible events of that night, every one was of course ready to admit, but in what manner no one was able to conjecture.

A murder had been committed. Of that there could be no doubt. Don Miguel de Suarez had been stabbed in the back! Not in fair fight, but brutally, callously stabbed! and he a guest at the English Court!

Of this barbarous, abominable act the Duke of Wessex stood self-convicted.

Impossible, of course! Preposterous! pronounced his friends. He! the first gentleman in England, brave to a fault, fastidious, artistic, and a perfect swordsman to boot! The very accusation was ridiculous.

Yet he stood self-convicted.

Why? in the name of Heaven! Why?

"To shield a woman," said His Grace's friends.

"What woman?" retorted his enemies.

The name of Lady Ursula Glynde had been faintly whispered, yet it seemed almost as preposterous to suppose that a beautiful young girl—refined, gentle, poetic, scarce out of her teens—would have the physical strength to commit so foul a deed, as to think of His Grace in connection with it.

Yet, in spite of that, the idea had gained ground, that the Lady Ursula Glynde could, an she would, throw some light on the mystery which surrounded the events of that terrible night, and no one brooded over that idea more determinedly than did Mary Tudor.

The young girl had of course denied all knowledge of what had or had not occurred. There was not a single definite fact that might even remotely connect her with the supposed enmity between Wessex and Don Miguel.

The Cardinal was not likely to speak, for the present turn of events suited his own plans to perfection.

My lord of Everingham was away in Scotland, and news travelled slowly these days. As for the Queen, she had nothing on which to found her suspicions, save her own hatred of the girl and the firm conviction that on that same night, an hour or two before the murder, Ursula and Wessex had met. She had then seen and upbraided the girl in the presence of my lord Cardinal and the ladies; His Grace was not there then, but what happened immediately afterwards?

Had she but dared, Mary Tudor would have submitted her rival to mental and bodily torture, until she had extracted a confession from her. All she could do was to confine her to her own room in the Palace; she would not lose sight of her, although the young girl had begged for permission to quit the Court and retire to a convent, for the silence and peace of which she felt an unutterable longing.

The Duke's trial by his peers was fixed for the morrow.

It was but a fortnight since that fateful evening. His Grace had been in the Tower since then, and by virtue of his high influence and of his exceptional position had demanded and readily obtained a speedy trial.

Twenty-four hours in which a queen might perchance still save the man she loved from a shameful and ignominious death. And she had thought and schemed and suffered during fourteen days, as perhaps no other woman had ever thought and suffered before. She was queen, yet felt herself powerless to accomplish the one desire of her life, which she would have bartered her kingdom to obtain: the life of the man she loved.

But to-day she had pluckily dried her tears. The whole morning she had spent at her toilette, carefully selecting—with an agitation which would have been ridiculous, considering her age and appearance, had it not been so intensely pathetic—the raiment which she thought would become her most. She had a burning desire to appear attractive.

Earnestly she studied the lines of her face, covered incipient wrinkles and faded cheeks with cosmetics, spent nigh on an hour in the arrangement of her coif. Then she repaired to a small room, which was hung with tapestry of a dull red, and into which the fading afternoon light would only peep very gently and discreetly.

Since then she had paced that narrow room incessantly and

134

impatiently. Every few moments she rang a handbell, and to the stolid page or servitor in attendance she repeated the same anxious query—

"Is the guard in sight yet?"

"Not yet, Your Majesty," reiterated the page for the tenth time that day.

It was nigh on three o'clock in the afternoon when the Duchess of Lincoln at last came with the welcome news.

"The captain of the guard desires to report to Your Majesty that the Tower Guard, with His Grace the Duke of Wessex, are at the gates of the Palace."

Mary, with her usual characteristic gesture, pressed her hand to her heart, unable to speak with the sudden emotion which had sent the blood throbbing in her veins. The kind old Duchess, her wrinkled face expressive of the deepest sorrow and the most respectful sympathy, waited patiently until the Queen had recovered herself.

"'Tis well," said Mary, after a while. "I pray you, Duchess, to see that His Grace is introduced in here at once."

When she was alone she fell upon her knees, a great sob shook her delicate frame. She took her rosary from her girdle and with passionate fervour kissed the jewelled beads.

"Holy Mary, Mother of God!" she murmured amidst her tears, "make him listen to me! ... pray for me ... intercede for me, Queen of Heaven, mystic rose, tower of ivory, holy virgin, our mother ... pray for me now ... I would save him, and I would make him King.... Queen of Heaven, aid me ... Mother of God, make him to love me ... make him ... to love me! ..."

After that she rose, and carefully wiped her tears. She cast a glance at a small mirror which stood on the table, smoothed her hair and coif and forced her lips to smile.

The next moment there was a knock at the door, a clash of arms, the sound of voices, and two minutes later His Grace of Wessex was in the presence of the Queen.

She held out her hand to him and he stooped to kiss it. This gave her time to recover outward composure. Her fond heart ached at sight of him, for he seemed so altered. All the gaiety, the joy of life, that buoyancy of youth and ever-ready laughter which had always been his own peculiar charm, had completely gone from him: he looked older too, she thought, whilst his step even had lost its elasticity.

Mary motioned him to a seat close beside her. She herself had wisely chosen so to place her chair that the light from the window, whilst falling full on him, left her own figure in shadow.

"I trust, my lord," she began with a trembling voice, "that my guard at the Tower are showing you all the deference and doing you all the honour which I have commanded, and that your every comfort in that abode of evil hath been well looked to?"

"Your Majesty is ever gracious," replied Wessex, "far more than I

135

deserve. The kindness shown me by every one at the Tower hath been a source of the deepest happiness to me."

"Nay! if I could ..." began Mary impulsively.

Then she checked herself, determined not to let emotion get the better of her, ere she had told him all that she wished to say.

"My lord of Wessex," she resumed more firmly, "will you try to think that you are before a sincere and devoted friend; not before your Queen, but beside a woman who hath naught so much at heart as ... your happiness? ... Will you try?"

"The effort will not be great," he replied with a smile. "Your Majesty's kindness hath oft shamed me ere this."

"Then, if you value my friendship, my lord," rejoined Mary vehemently, "give me some assurance that to-morrow, before your judges and your peers, you will refute this odious charge which is brought against you."

"I crave Your Majesty's most humble pardon," said Wessex. "I have made confession of the crime imputed to me and can refute nothing."

"Nay, my lord, this is madness. You, the most gallant gentleman in England, you, to have done a deed so foul as would shame the lowest churl! Bah!" she added, with a bitter laugh, "'twere a grim farce, if it were not so terrible a tragedy!"

"Nay! not a tragedy, Your Majesty. Better men than I have made a failure of their lives. So I pray you, think no more of me."

"Think no more of you, dear lord," said Mary, with an infinity of reproach in her voice. "Ah me, I think of naught else since that awful night when they came and told me that you ..."

There was a catch in her throat and perforce she had to pause. Oh! the irony of fate! The bitter satire of that wanton god, called Love!

Wessex looked at this proud Tudor Queen with a deep reverence, in which there was almost a thought of pity. This lonely, middle-aged woman, passionate, self-willed, who loved him with all the tenderness of pent-up motherhood! yet, try how he might! he could only respond to her true affection with cold respect and deep but unimpassioned gratitude! Yet was not her worth ten thousandfold more great than that of the wanton, whose image still filled his heart?

The one woman he honoured, the other he must perforce despise, and yet—such is the heart of man—he was more ready than ever to give up life, honour, a great name, and still greater destiny, so that the worthless object of his whole-hearted affection should be spared public disgrace.

He would not have named Ursula Glynde in this chaste, virgin Queen's presence, the very remembrance of that awful night was a pollution, but proud and haughty as he was, he dwelt on that memory, for it was the last which he had of her.

Mad, foolish, criminal, sublime Love! The sin of the loved one was dearer to him than all the virtues of which other women were capable, and whilst Mary Tudor would have given him a crown, he found it sweeter far to accept ignominy for Ursula's sake.

Perhaps something of all these thoughts which went on in his mind was reflected in his face, for Mary, who had been watching him keenly, said after a while with a tone of bitter resentment—

"My lord, I know that your silence over this mysterious affair is maintained out of a chivalrous desire to shield another ... a woman.... Ah, consider ...."

"I have considered," replied Wessex firmly, "and I entreat Your Majesty ..."

"Nay! 'tis I who entreat," she interrupted him vehemently. "Let us look facts in the face, my lord. Think you we are all fools to believe in your cock-and-bull story? A woman was seen that night flying from the Palace across the terrace ... who was she? ... whence did she come? ... None of the watch could see her face, and the louts were too stupid to run after her ... but there are those within this Court at this moment who will swear that that woman was Ursula Glynde."

Strangely enough this was the first time, since that fatal night, that this name was actually spoken in Wessex' hearing: it seemed to sting him like the cut of a lash across his face. For that one brief instant he lost his icy self-control, and Mary saw him wince.

"Ursula has been questioned," she continued, "but she remains obdurately silent. Believe me, my lord, you waste your chivalry in defence of a wanton."

But already Wessex had recovered himself.

"Your Majesty is mistaken," he rejoined calmly. "I know naught of Lady Ursula Glynde, and I defend no one by confessing my crime."

"You'll not persist in that insensate confession."

"'Twill not be necessary, Your Majesty, my judges have it in full, writ by mine own hand."

"You'll recant it."

"Why should I? 'Twas done willingly, in full possession of my faculties, under no compulsion."

"You'll recant it!" she persisted obstinately.

"Why should I?"

"Because I ask it of you," she said with great gentleness, "because I ..."

She rose from her chair, and came closer to him. Then as he, respectfully, would have risen too, she placed a detaining hand upon his shoulder.

"Listen, my lord," she said, "for I've thought of it all.... This is not a moment when foolish prejudices and mock modesty should stand in the way of so great an issue.... I would throw my soul, my future life, my chances of paradise on that one stake—your innocence ...."

"Your Majesty ..."

137

"Nay, I pray you, do not waste these few valuable minutes in vain protestations, which I'll not believe.... There's not a sane man in this country who thinks you guilty.... Yet on this confession your judges and peers will condemn you to death ... must condemn you, so that the law of England is satisfied—and you, my lord, will suffer death with a lie upon your lips."

"The truth," rejoined Wessex firmly; "'twas I killed the Marquis de Suarez."

"A lie, my lord, a lie," protested Mary passionately; "the first you've ever told, the last you'll be allowed to breathe.... But let it pass.... I'll not torture your pride by forcing you to repeat that monstrous tale again. Would I could wrench her secret from the cowardly lips of that hussy.... Oh! if I were a man ... a king like my father! ... I'd have her broken on the wheel, tortured on the rack, whipped, lacerated, burnt, but I'd have the truth from her!"

Wessex took her hand in his. She was trembling from head to foot. The inward, real Mary Tudor had risen to the surface for this one brief moment. All the cruelty in her, which in after life made this wretched woman's name the byword of history, seemed just then to smother her very womanhood, her every tender thought. At the touch of Wessex' hand she paused suddenly, shamed and in tears, that he should have seen her like this.

"Before she came you said many sweet words to me," she murmured, as if trying to find an excuse for her terrible outburst. "Ah! I know ... I know ..." she added, with a bitter tone of melancholy, "you never loved me ... how could you? ... Men like you do not love an ill-favoured creature like me, old, bad-tempered ... with something of the brute under the queenly robes.... But ... you had affection for me once, my dear lord ... and an unimpassioned love can bring happiness sometimes.... I would soon make you forget these last terrible days ... and ..."

Her voice had sunk down very low, almost to a whisper now, the hand, which he still held in his own, trembled violently and became burning hot.

"And no one would dare to whisper ill of the King Consort of England."

He turned to her; she was standing beside him, her hand imprisoned in his, her face bent so that he could not meet her eyes. But there was such an infinity of pathos in the attitude of this domineering, haughty woman wilfully humbling her pride before her love, that with a tender feeling of reverence he bent the knee before her and tenderly kissed her hand.

"Ah, my sweet Queen," he said with gentle sadness, "I am and always will be your most devoted subject—but do you not see how impossible it is that I should accept this great honour, which you would deign to confer upon me?"

138

"You refuse? Is it that you have not one spark of love for me?"

"I have far too much veneration for my Queen to allow her to sully her fair name. If being avowedly guilty I were acquitted by Your Majesty's desire, 'twould be said the Queen had saved her lover ... and then married a felon."

"I would stake mine honour, that no one shall dare ..."

"Honour is already lost, my Queen, once it is at stake."

"But I will save you," cried Mary with ever-increasing vehemence, "in spite of yourself, in spite of your confessions, in spite of all these lies and deceptions.... I'll save you in the very teeth of your judges and your peers, and proclaim to the whole world that I saved you—guilty or not guilty, proud gentleman or felon—because my name is Mary Tudor, and that there is no law in England outside my will."

Pride and passion almost beautified her. Her love for this man was the one soft, tender trait in her strange and complex character, but Tudor-like she would have her way, she would rule his destiny, command his fate, tear and destroy everything around her so long as her caprice held sway. But he had suddenly risen to his feet, and stood confronting her now, tall and erect, with a pride as great, as obstinate as her own, a haughty dignity which neither Queen nor destiny, neither sorrow, disgrace or fear had the power to bend.

"Ere that dishonour fall upon us both, Your Majesty," he said firmly, "the last Duke of Wessex will lie in a suicide's grave."

Her eyes were fixed upon his, and he, carried away by the poignancy of this supreme battle fought by his pride against her passion, allowed her to read his innermost thoughts. He had nothing to hide from her now, not even his love, miserable and desperate as it was: but he wanted her to know that not even at this fateful moment, when he stood 'twixt a scaffold and a crown, did he waver in the firm resolve which had guided him throughout his life.

He would not become the tool and minion of a Tudor queen—loving enough now, but endowed with all the vices and all the arrogance of her race; he would not barter his life in order to become the butt of contending political factions, the toy of ambitious parties, flattered by some, hated by most, despised by all. A courtier, a lapdog, an invertebrate creature without power or dignity.

Bah! the hangman's rope was less degrading!

And Mary, as she read all this in the expressive eyes which met hers fully and unwaveringly, realized that her cause was lost. She had staked everything on this one final appeal, but she, a Tudor, had struck against an obstinacy greater than her own. She could not flatter, she could not bribe, and he was—by the very hopelessness of his present position—beyond the reach of threats or punishment.

He saw that her heart was admitting that she was vanquished. The hardness within him melted into pity.

"Believe me, my Queen," he said gently, "the memory of your

kind words will accompany me to my life's end, it will cheer me to-morrow and sustain me to the last. And now for pity's sake," he added earnestly, "may I entreat Your Majesty to order the guard ... and to let me go."

"That is not your last word, my lord," urged Mary with the insistence of a desperate cause. "Think ...."

"I have thought—much," he replied quietly. "Life holds nothing very tempting at best, does it? The honour of the Queen of England and mine own self-esteem were too heavy a price to pay for so worthless a trifle."

Mary would have spoken again, but just then there was a discreet knock at the door twice repeated. She had perforce to say—

"Enter!" and the next moment a page-in-waiting stood bowing before her.

"What is it?" she demanded.

"The Lord High Steward has arrived at the Palace, Your Majesty," announced the page, "and the Lieutenant of the Tower demands the prisoner."

"'Tis well! you may go."

"The Lieutenant of the Tower awaits Your Majesty's pleasure and His Grace of Wessex in the next room."

"'Tis well. The Lieutenant may wait."

The page bowed again and retired.

Then only did Mary Tudor's self-control entirely desert her. Forgetting all her dignity and pride, her self-will and masterfulness, she clung to the man she loved with passionate ardour, sobbing and entreating.

"No! no!—they shall not take you!—they dare not! Say but one word to me, my dear lord ... what is it to you?—'twere all my life to me.... What should we care for the opinion of the world?—Am I not above it? ... so will you be when you are King of England ...."

Wessex had need of all his firmness, and of all his courage, to free himself as gently as he could from her clinging arms. He waited until her half-hysterical paroxysm of grief had subsided, smoothing with tender hand her moist hair and burning forehead. She was a woman beside herself with grief, almost sublime in this hour of madness.

"I will not let you go!" she repeated persistently.

Through the door there came the sound of a slight clash of arms. The Lieutenant of the Tower and his guard were impatiently waiting for their prisoner. Wessex saw Mary's whole figure stiffen at this muffled sound. Like an enraged animal she turned towards the door. For one second he wondered what she would do, how much humiliation her uncontrolled passion would heap upon him, through some mad, impulsive action. He jumped to his feet, and, regardless of all save the imminence of this critical moment, he seized both her wrists in an iron

140

grip, striving through the infliction of this physical pain to bring back her wandering senses.

She looked him straight in the face with a tender and appealing gaze...

"Did you not know that I loved you even to humiliation?" she said.

"May God and all His angels bless you for that love," he replied earnestly, "but before Him and them I swear to you that if you do not allow the justice of your realm to have its will with me, I'll not survive your own disgrace and mine."

She closed her eyes, trying to shut out that picture of unbendable determination expressed in his whole attitude, and which she at last felt that nothing would conquer. The rigidity of her figure relaxed, the fury died out from her heart, she only felt inexpressibly sorrowful, helpless and broken-hearted.

"God be with you, my dear lord," she whispered.

He kissed her hands: all the fever had gone out of them, they were icy cold: there was neither arrogance nor obstinacy in her face now, her eyes were still closed, and one by one, heavy tears fell down her wan cheeks.

The pathos of her helplessness and of her crushed pride made a strong appeal to the sentiments of tender loyalty which he had always felt for her, who was his Queen and Liege Lady. He saw that she was determined not to break down, that she was gathering all her courage for the supreme farewell.

"I beseech Your Majesty to allow me to order the guard," he urged.

She tottered and would have fallen, had he not put out his arm to support her.

"Do not forget that you are a Tudor and a Queen, and remember," he added quaintly, as her head fell against his shoulder, "remember ... I am only a man!"

He led her back to her seat, then he touched the handbell, and when the page appeared he said firmly—

"I am at the Lieutenant's service."

He knelt once more before the Queen and finally bade her farewell. She could neither speak nor move, and scarcely had the strength to take a last look at the loved one, as with a firm step he passed out of her sight.

There was a clash of steel against steel, a few words of command, the sound of retreating footsteps, then silence.

Queen Mary Tudor was alone with her grief.

CHAPTER XXXII

A BARGAIN

But Mary would not have been the woman she was if she admitted a failure, whilst there was still a chance of victory.

The first half-hour after Wessex' departure she gave way to weakness and to a flood of tears, she turned to her prie-Dieu and prayed fervently for resignation to the heavenly will, for strength to bear her cross.

"Holy Mother of our crucified Lord, pray for me now and at the hour of his death," was the burden of her passionate orisons.

"Take my life since he must die," she added, striking her breast and falling prostrate before the holy images.

And then reaction set in. She felt more calm after her prayers, and began to think more clearly. The inevitableness of a catastrophe seemed to become less tangible, a persistent and hopeful "if" crept in amongst her desperate litanies. She dried her tears, rang for her waiting-woman, had her face bathed with soothing, scented waters, her temples rubbed with perfumed vinegar.

All the while now she repeated to herself—

"I will save him ... I will save him ... but how? ... how?"

She had less than twenty-four hours in which to do it, and she had spent fourteen days previously in the same endeavour, without arriving at any definite plan, save the one which had so signally failed just now.

"If being found guilty I were acquitted at Your Majesty's desire, 'twould be said the Queen had saved her lover—and then married a felon!" was his sole reply to her impassioned query whether he loved her and would be saved by her command.

She would have been content to lose her honour for his sake, he would not even jeopardize his own self-esteem for hers. If he had one spark of love for her he would have been content to challenge the opinion of the world, whilst accepting his life at her hands, but he cared naught about death, and all the world for another woman who was false, a coward, a wanton, and who boldly allowed him to sacrifice his honour for her, whilst she herself had none to lose.

"Then I will save him in spite of himself," repeated Mary for the hundredth time.

Suddenly a thought struck her. She rang her hand-bell, and to the servitor who appeared at the door she commanded briefly—

"His Eminence the Cardinal de Moreno;—I desire his presence here at once."

The servitor retired, and she waited in seeming calm, sitting at

142

her desk, her trembling hand alone betraying the excitement of her mind.

Five minutes later, the Cardinal stood before her, placid, urbane, picturesque in his brilliant, flowing robes, with one white, richly be-ringed hand raised in benediction, as he stood waiting for the Queen to speak.

"I pray Your Eminence to be seated," began Mary, speaking with feverish haste. "I have something of grave import to say to you, which brooks of no delay, else I had not interrupted you at your orisons."

"My time is ever at Your Majesty's service," replied the Cardinal humbly. "In what way may I have the honour to serve the Queen of England to-day?"

He was looking keenly at her face: not a single sign of her intense mental agitation escaped his shrewd observation. A satisfied smile lurked round the corners of his thin lips, and a flash of triumph lit up the depths of his piercing eyes.

That searching glance at Mary Tudor had told the envoy of the King of Spain that victory was at last within his grasp.

"My lord Cardinal," rejoined Mary firmly, "you are aware of the fact that His Grace of Wessex is on the eve of being tried by his peers, for a heinous crime of which he is innocent."

"I am aware," replied the Cardinal gently, "that His Grace stands self-convicted of the murder of my friend and colleague Don Miguel, Marquis de Suarez, a guest at Your Majesty's Court."

"Truce on this folly, my lord," retorted Mary impatiently, "you know just as well as I do, that His Grace is incapable of any such act of cowardice, and that some mystery, which no one can fathom, lies at the bottom of this monstrous self-accusation."

"Whatever may be my own feelings in this matter, Your Majesty," said His Eminence, still speaking very guardedly, "I was forced to accomplish my duty, when I made and signed my deposition, which I fear me has gone far towards confirming the guilt of His Grace."

"I have heard of your deposition, my lord. It rests on your finding His Grace's dagger ...."

"Beside the body of the murdered man, and still stained with Don Miguel's blood."

"What of that? Some one else must have used the dagger."

"Possibly."

"You did not suggest this in your deposition."

"It was not asked of me by His Grace's judges."

"There is time to make a further statement."

"It could but be in consonance with what I have already said."

"And your servant?"

"Pasquale?"

"He lied when he averred that he heard angry words 'twixt His Grace and Don Miguel."

143

"He has sworn it upon oath. Pasquale is a good Catholic, and would not commit the deadly sin of perjury."

"You are fencing with me, my lord," said Mary Tudor with sudden vehemence.

"I but await Your Majesty's command!" rejoined His Eminence blandly.

"My command?" she said firmly. "This, my lord, that you save His Grace of Wessex from the consequences of this crime, in which he had no hand."

"To save His Grace of Wessex?" he ejaculated with the greatest astonishment, "I? and at this eleventh hour? Nay! meseems that were impossible."

"Then Your Eminence can set your wits to attempt the impossible," rejoined Mary curtly.

"But why should Your Majesty suggest this strange task to me?" he urged with the same well-feigned surprise.

"Because Your Eminence hath more brains than most."

"Your Majesty is too gracious."

"And because you have the success of your own schemes more at heart than most," added the Queen significantly.

"Then, if I do not succeed in effecting the impossible, Your Majesty, am I to be sent back to Spain ignominiously to-morrow?" queried the Cardinal with more than a soupçon of sarcasm.

"No!" rejoined Mary quietly, "but if you succeed I will give you in reward anything which you may ask."

"Anything, my daughter? Even your hand in marriage to King Philip of Spain?"

"If Your Eminence succeeds in effecting the impossible," replied Mary firmly, "I will marry King Philip of Spain."

There was silence for a moment or two. His Eminence was meditating. Not that he had been taken unawares. For the past fortnight he had been expecting some such interview as the Queen had now demanded at the eleventh hour. He was far-seeing and shrewd enough to have anticipated that, sooner or later, Mary Tudor would propose a bargain, whereby he would be expected to pit his wits against Fate, and thereby earn the victory which she knew he coveted. The task was a difficult one; not impossible—for the Cardinal never admitted that anything was impossible. But he was peculiarly placed, and he knew the value of royal promises and of royal compacts. This one he thought he could enforce, but only if his methods were above suspicion. To have confessed the whole dastardly intrigue of that eventful night would certainly have saved the Duke from condemnation, but the tale itself would so disgust these stiff-necked Britishers, that Mary would see herself easily released from her promise through unanimous public opinion.

That simple and sure method of obtaining the Duke's acquittal was

144

therefore barred to him, and he had perforce to reflect seriously, ere he closed with the bargain which Mary Tudor held so temptingly before him. His mind was clearer, less scrupulous than that of his colleagues, and he had most at stake now, for nothing but ultimate success could justify the heinousness of his methods. If his schemes failed, then these methods became monstrous and criminal beyond hope of pardon.

For the moment the Cardinal had no remorse. The sacrifice of every piece in the great human game of chess was of no importance if the final mating of his enemies were gained. Don Miguel was dead, Lord Everingham far away; the wench Mirrab, terrified at her own act probably, had disappeared and no doubt would not be heard of again until His Eminence's victory was assured. This he had hoped to attain with the death of the Duke of Wessex and Mary's consequent grief and feebleness of will, always supposing that Lord Everingham did not return in time to ruin the whole scaffolding of his tortuous diplomacy.

That was the great danger and one which was ever present before the Cardinal's mind: the return of Lord Everingham. Every day added to the danger, and it was Wessex' own impatience to see the end of his own shattered existence, which had up to now saved His Eminence from exposure.

The Duke had urged that his trial should come on speedily. This was readily granted, for he was the Duke of Wessex still. The trial itself would not last more than the one day, seeing that the accused had made full confession and only a few secondary depositions were to be read for form's sake. His Grace had refused counsel, there could be no argument. The judges on the face of the circumstantial self-accusation were bound, in the name of justice, to convict and condemn, in spite of public opinion, in spite of the machinations of the Duke's friends, in spite even of the Queen's commands.

Once His Grace was out of the way, His Eminence had felt that he would be able to breathe more freely, but until then he was living at the edge of a volcano, and often wondered how it had not broken out ere now.

The news of the crime and of Wessex' arrest had been sent to Scotland, he knew that; but the way thither was long, the late October gales would make the journey by sea difficult, whilst the overland roads, sodden with the rain, were unusually bad; but in any event, Everingham was bound to arrive in England within the next ten days, for, of a surety, he would travel with mad speed on hearing the terrible news.

But now Mary Tudor suddenly offered him a definite promise, a bargain which he could clinch before exposure had shamed him publicly. The task proposed was indeed difficult, but it was not impossible to such a far-reaching mind as that of my lord Cardinal.

A few moments' deep reflection, whilst the Queen watched him eagerly, and he had already formed a plan.

145

"Does Your Eminence accept the bargain?" asked Mary impatiently at last, seeing that he seemed disinclined to break the silence.

"I accept it, Your Majesty," he replied quietly.

"You have my royal promise if you succeed."

"If His Grace to-morrow is acquitted by his judges, through my intervention," said His Eminence, "I will claim Your Majesty's promise in the evening."

"Your Eminence can have a document ready and I will sign it."

"It shall be done as Your Majesty directs."

"Then I'll bid Your Eminence farewell, until to-morrow."

"I am ever at Your Majesty's service. But before retiring I would crave one favour."

"I pray you speak."

"To speak to the Lady Ursula Glynde."

A long bitter laugh of the keenest disappointment came from Mary Tudor's oppressed heart.

"Nay!" she said in a tone of deep discouragement, "an you pin your faith on that hussy, Your Eminence had best give up the attempt at once."

"Did I not say that I would attempt the impossible?" said the Cardinal, unperturbed.

"The impossible indeed, an you wish to appeal to that wench," retorted Mary drily.

"Have I Your Majesty's permission to speak to the lady?" persisted the Cardinal blandly.

Mary shrugged her shoulders impatiently. She was terribly disappointed. All her hopes had been built on the clever machinations of this man, on some tortuous means which his brain would surely evolve if she held out a sufficiently tempting bait to him. She had half endowed him with supernatural powers ... and now ... an empty scheme to make an appeal to that heartless coward, who might save Wessex, yet refused to do it!

But the Cardinal was smiling: he looked a rare picture of benevolence and dignity, with those white hands of his which seemed ever ready for a caress. He looked triumphant too, his eyes were eagerly fixed upon her as if her consent to the useless interview was of great and supreme moment. To her the appeal to Ursula did not even seem to be a last straw, but something far more ephemeral, intangible, a breath from some mocking demon. Yet the Cardinal looked so satisfied. She shrugged her shoulders again, as if dismissing all hope, all responsibility, all interest, but she said nevertheless—

"When does Your Eminence desire to see her?"

"To-morrow in the Lord Chancellor's Court," he replied, "half an hour before the arrival of the Lord High Steward. Can that be done?"

"It shall be, since Your Eminence wishes it."

"And to-night I will announce the joyful news by special messenger to the King of Spain," he added significantly.

"Is Your Eminence so sure of success then?"

"As sure as I am of the fact that the Queen of England is the most gracious lady in Europe," he replied, with all the courtly grace which he knew so well how to assume. "I pray you then to trust in God," he concluded earnestly, "and in the devotion of Your Majesty's humble servant."

He took his leave ceremoniously, with pompous dignity, as was his wont. She did not care to prolong the interview, and nodded listlessly when he prepared to go. She felt more than ever hopeless and angered with herself for having clinched a bargain with that man.

But His Eminence the Cardinal de Moreno left the presence of the Queen of England with a smile of satisfaction and a sigh of anticipated triumph.

It was not an appeal which he meant to address to the Lady Ursula Glynde.

CHAPTER XXXIII

IN THE LORD CHANCELLOR'S COURT

The great Hall at Westminster was already thronged with people at an early hour of the morning, and the servants of the Knight Marshal and the Lord Warden of the Fleet had much ado to keep the crowd back with their tipstaves.

All London was taking a holiday to-day: an enforced holiday as far as the workers and merchants were concerned, for there surely would be no business doing in the City when such great goings-on were occurring at Westminster.

The trial of His Grace the Duke of Wessex on a charge of murder! A trial which, seeing that the accused had confessed to the crime, could but end in a sentence of death.

It is not every day that it is given to humbler folk to see so proud a gentleman arraigned as any common vagabond might be, and to note how a great nobleman may look when threatened with the hangman's rope.

Is there aught in the world half so cruel as a crowd?

And His Grace had been very popular: always looked upon, even by the meanest in the land, as the most perfect embodiment of English

147

pride and English grandeur, he had always had withal that certain graciousness of manner which the populace will love, and which disarms envy.

But with the exception of his own friends, people of his own rank and station, who knew him and his character intimately, the people at large never for a moment questioned his guilt.

He had confessed! surely that was enough! The loutish brains of the lower proletariat did not care to go beyond that obvious self-evident fact. The meaner the nature of a man, the more ready is he to acknowledge evil, he seeks it out, recognizes it under every garb. Who, among the majority of people, cared to seek for sublime self-sacrifice in an ordinary confession of crime?

The wiseacres and learned men, the more wealthy burgesses, and people of more consideration, were content with a few philosophical reflections anent the instability of human nature and the evil influences of Court life and of great wealth.

No one cared about the man! it was the pageant they all liked. What thought had the mob of the agonizing rack to which a proud soul would necessarily be subjected during the course of a wearisome and elaborate trial? They only wanted to see a show, the robes of the judges, the assembly of peers, and that one central figure, the first gentleman in England, once almost a king—now a felon!

A fine sight, my masters! His Grace of Wessex in a criminal dock!

Places in the Hall were at a premium. The 'prentices were well to the fore as usual; like so many eel-like creatures, they had slipped into the front rank as soon as the great doors had been opened. Some few waifs and vagrants—acute and greedy of gain—were making good trade with small wooden benches, which they sold at threepence the piece to those who desired a better view.

The women were all wearing becoming gowns, sombre of hue as befitted the occasion. His Grace of Wessex was noted for his avowed admiration for the beautiful sex. They had all brought large white kerchiefs, for they anticipated some exquisite emotions. His Grace was so handsome! there was sure to be an occasion for tears.

But only as a pleasurable sentiment! Like one feels at the play, where the actor expresses feelings, yet is himself cold and unimpassioned. What His Grace himself would feel was never considered. The crowd had come to see, some had paid threepence for a clearer sight of the accused, and all meant to enjoy themselves this day.

Proud Wessex! thou hast sunk to this, a spectacle for a common holiday! Thy face will be scanned lest one twitch escape! thy shoulders if they stoop, thy neck if it bend! A thousand eyes will be fixed upon thee in curiosity, in derision—perchance in pity!

Ye gods, what a fall!

The Lord High Steward of England was expected to arrive at ten o'clock. In the centre of the great court a large scaffold had been erected, not far from the Lord Chancellor's Court. In the middle of this there was placed a chair higher than the rest and covered with a cloth, which bore the royal arms embroidered at the four corners.

This was for my Lord High Steward.

Each side of him were the seats for the peers who were to be the triers. Great names were whispered, as the servants of the Knight Marshal arranged these in their respective places. There was the chair for the Earl of Kent, and my lord of Sussex, the Earl of Hertford, and Lord Saint John of Basing, and a score of others, for there were twenty-four triers in all.

On a lower form were the seats for the judges, and in a hollow place cut in the scaffold itself, and immediately at the feet of my Lord High Steward, the Clerk of the Crown would sit with his secondary.

And facing the judges and the peers was the bar, where presently the exalted prisoner would stand.

No one was here yet of the greater personages, the servants were still busy putting everything to right, but some gentlemen of the Queen's household had already arrived, and several noble lords who would be mere spectators. His Grace's friends could easily be distinguished by the sombreness of their garb and the air of grief upon their faces. Mr. Thomas Norton, the Queen's printer, was sorting his papers and cutting his pens, and two gentlemen ushers were receiving final instructions from Garter King-at-Arms.

There was indeed plenty for the idlers to see. Great ropes had been drawn across the further portions of the Hall, leaving a wide passage from the main entrance right down the centre and up to the Lord High Steward's seat. Behind these ropes the crowd was forcibly kept back. And the gossip and the noise went on apace. Laughter too and merry jests, for this was a holiday, my masters, presently to be brought to a close—after the death sentence had been passed and every one dispersed—with lively jousts and copious sacks of ale.

But of all this excitement and bustle not a sound penetrated within the precincts of the Lord Chancellor's Court, where His Eminence the Cardinal de Moreno sat patiently waiting.

Desirous above all things of escaping observation, he had driven over from Hampton Court in the early dawn, and wrapped in a flowing black cloak, which effectually hid his purple robes, he had slipped into the Hall and thence into the Inner Court, even before the crowd had begun to collect. Since then he had sat here quietly buried in thoughts, calmly looking forward to the interview, which was destined finally to unravel the tangled skein of his own diplomacy. Once more the destinies of Europe were hanging on a thread: a girl's love for a man.

Well! so be it! His Eminence loved these palpitating situations, these hairbreadth escapes from perilous positions which were the wine and salt of his existence. He was ready to stake his whole future career

149

upon a woman's love! He, who had scoffed all his life at sentimental passions, who had used every emotion of the human heart, aye! and its every suffering, merely as so many assets in the account of his far-reaching policy, he now saw his whole future depending on the strength of a girl's feelings.

That she would certainly come, he never for a moment held in doubt. In these days the commands of a sovereign were akin to the dictates of God; to disobey was a matter of treason. Aye! she would come, sure enough! not only because of her allegiance to the Queen, but because of her intense, vital interest in the great trial of the day.

So His Eminence waited patiently in the Lord Chancellor's Court, which gave straight into the great Hall itself, until the appointed time.

Exactly at half-past nine the door of the room was opened, and Ursula Glynde walked in. The Cardinal rose from his seat and would have approached her, but she retreated a step or two as he came near and said coldly—

"'Tis Your Eminence who desired my presence?"

"And 'tis well that you came, my daughter," he replied kindly.

"I was commanded by Her Majesty to attend; I had not come of my own free will."

She spoke quietly but very stiffly, as one who is merely performing a social duty, without either pleasure or dislike. The Cardinal studied her face keenly, but obviously she had been told nothing by the Queen as to the precise object of this interview.

She looked pale and wan: there was a look of acute suffering round the childlike mouth, which would have seemed pathetic to any one save to this callous dissector of human hearts. Her eyes appeared unnaturally large, with great dilated pupils and dry eyelids. She was dressed in deep black, with a thick veil over her golden hair, which gave her a nunlike appearance, and altogether made her look older, and strangely different from the gay and girlish figure so full of life and animation which had been one of the brightest ornaments of old Hampton Court Palace. The Cardinal motioned her to a seat, which she took, then she waited with perfect composure until His Eminence chose to speak.

"My child," he said at last, bringing his voice down to tones of the greatest gentleness, "I would wish you to remember that it is an old man who speaks to you: one who has seen much of the world, learnt much, understood much. Will you try and trust him?"

"What does Your Eminence desire of me?" she rejoined coldly.

"Nay! 'tis not a question of desire, my daughter, I would merely wish to give you some advice."

"I am listening to Your Eminence."

The Cardinal had taken the precaution of placing himself with his back to the light which entered, grey and mournful, through the tall leaded window above. He was sitting near a table covered with writing materials, and in a large high-backed tapestried chair, which further enhanced the ponderous dignity of his appearance, whilst helping to envelop his face in complete shadow. Ursula sat opposite to him on a low stool, that same grey light falling full upon her pale face, which was turned serenely, quite impassively upon her interlocutor.

His Eminence rested his elbow on the arm of his chair and his head in his delicate white hands. The purple robes fell round him in majestic folds, the gold crucifix at his breast sparkled with jewels: he was a past master in the art of mise-en-scène, and knew the full value of impressive pauses and of effective attitudes during a momentous conversation, more especially when he had to deal with a woman. His present silence helped to set the young girl's aching nerves on edge, and he noticed with a sense of inward satisfaction that her composure was not as profound as she would have him think: there was a distinct tremor in the delicate nostrils, a jerkiness in the movements of her hand, as she smoothed out the folds of her sombre gown.

"My dear child," he began once more, and this time in tones of more pronounced severity, "a brave man, a good and chivalrous gentleman, is about to suffer not only death, but horrible disgrace.... On the other side of these thin walls the preparations are ready for his trial by a group of men, whose duty it will be anon to allow the justice of this realm to take its relentless course. The accused will stand self-convicted, yet innocent, before them."

Once more the Cardinal paused: only for a second this time. He noticed that the young girl had visibly shuddered, but she made no attempt to speak.

"Innocent, I repeat it," he resumed after a while. "His Grace has many friends; not one of them will believe that he could be capable of so foul a crime. But he has confessed to it. He will be condemned, and he—the proudest man in England—will die a felon's death ...."

"I knew all that, Your Eminence," she said quietly. "Why should you repeat it now?"

"Only because ..." said the Cardinal with seeming hesitation, "you must forgive an old man, my child ... methought you loved His Grace of Wessex and ..."

"Why does Your Eminence pause?" she rejoined. "You thought that I loved His Grace of Wessex ... and ... ?"

"And yet, my child, through a strange, nay, a culpable obstinacy, you, who could save him not only from death, but also from dishonour, you remain silent!"

"Your Eminence errs, as every one else has erred," she replied with the same cold placidity; "I am silent because I have naught to say."

The Cardinal smiled with kind indulgence, like a father who understands and forgives the sins of his child.

"Let us explain, my daughter," he said. "That fatal night, when

151

the Marquis de Suarez was killed, a woman was seen to fly from that part of the Palace where the tragedy had just taken place ...."

"Well?"

"Do you not see that if that woman came forward fearlessly and owned the truth, that it was from jealousy or even to defend her honour that His Grace killed Don Miguel, do you not see that no judge then will find him guilty of a wilful and premeditated crime?"

"Then why does not that woman come forward?" she retorted with the first sign of vehemence, noticeable in the quiver of her voice and the sudden flash in her pale cheeks, "why does she not speak? she for whose sake His Grace of Wessex not only took a man's life but is willing to sacrifice his honour?"

"She seems to have disappeared," said His Eminence softly, "perhaps she is dead.... Some say it was you," he added, leaning slightly forward and dropping his voice to a whisper.

"They lie," she replied. "I was not there. 'Tis not for me His Grace of Wessex will suffer both death and disgrace in silence."

This time His Eminence did not smile. There had been a sudden flash in his eyes at this quick, sharp retort—a sudden flash as suddenly veiled again. Then his heavy lids drooped; once more he looked paternal, benevolent, only just with a soupçon of sternness in his impassive face, the aloofness of an austere man towards the weaknesses of more mundane creatures.

Never for a moment did he reveal to the unwary young girl all that he had guessed through her last unguarded speech.

Her love for Wessex! that he knew already! Its depth alone was a revelation to him. But her jealousy! How her lips had trembled and her hand twitched when speaking of another, an unknown woman who had called forth in Wessex that spirit of noble self-sacrifice, that immolation of his own honour and dignity, which had finally landed him in a criminal dock.

A woman's passion and a woman's jealousy! Two precious assets in His Eminence's present balance. He pondered over what he had learned, and victory loomed more certain than before. He loved this present situation, the acute tension of this palpitating moment, when he seemed to hold this beautiful woman's soul, bare and fettered, writhing with agony and self-torture.

To dissect a human heart! to watch its every quiver, to note the effect of every searing iron applied with a skilful hand! then to achieve success in the end through subtle arts and devices seemingly so full of benevolence, yet instinct with the most refined, most far-reaching cruelty! This was the form of enjoyment which more than any other appealed to the jaded mind of this blasé diplomatist. The feline nature within him loved this game with the trembling mouse.

But outwardly he sighed, a deep sigh of disappointment.

"Ah! if they lie!" he said, a gentle tone of melancholy pervading

152

his entire attitude, "if indeed it was not you, my daughter, who were with Don Miguel that night ... then naught can save His Grace.... He has suffered in silence.... He will die to-morrow in silence ... and innocent."

He had risen from his chair, and began wandering about the narrow room—aimlessly—as if lost in thought. Ursula was staring straight before her. The first revelation of her present danger had suddenly come to her. As in a flash she had suddenly realized that this man had sent for her in order to use her for his own ends. She felt that she was literally in the position of the mouse about to be sacrificed to the greedy ambition of this feline creature, who had neither rectitude nor compunction where his ambition was at stake.

Yet after that one betrayal of her emotions she had made a vigorous effort to regain her self-control. Every instinct of self-preservation was on the alert now, and yet she knew already that she was bound to succumb. To what she could not guess, but she felt herself the weaker vessel of the two. He was calm and cruel, passionless and tortuous, whilst she felt with all her heart and soul and with all her senses.

And though he could not now see her face the Cardinal studied her every movement. He could see her figure stiffen with the iron determination to retain her self-possession, and inwardly he smiled, for he knew that the next moment all that rigidity would vanish, the marble statue would become living clay, the palsied nerves would quiver with horror, and she herself would fall, a weeping, wailing creature, supplicating at his feet.

And this by such a simple method!

Just the opening of a door! gently, noiselessly, until the sound from the Great Hall entered into this inner room, and voices clearly detached themselves from the confusing hubbub.

Then His Eminence whispered, "Hush, my daughter! listen! my Lord High Steward is speaking."

At first perhaps she did not hear, certainly she did not understand, for her attitude did not relax its uncompromising stiffness.

Lord Chandois was delivering his first speech.

"My lords and gentlemen," he said, "ye are here assembled this day that ye may try Robert d'Esclade, Duke of Wessex, for a grievous and heinous crime, which he hath wilfully committed."

It was just the opening and shutting of a door—the claw of the cat upon the neck of the mouse. At first sound of Wessex' name Ursula had risen to her feet, straight and rigid like a machine. She did not look towards the door, but fixed her eyes on him—her tormentor—fascinated as a bird, to whom a snake has beckoned and bade it to come nigh.

The colour rose to her cheeks, the reality was gradually dawning upon her. That man who spoke in the Great Hall beyond was a judge—there were other judges there too. When she arrived at Westminster she had seen a great concourse of people, heard the names of great legal dignitaries whispered round her, and of peers who had been summoned for a great occasion.

That occasion was the trial of the Duke of Wessex on a charge of murder.

"No, no, no," she whispered hoarsely, somewhat wildly, as she took a step forward; "no, no, no ... not yet ... it is not true ... not yet——"

The thin crust of ice which had enveloped her heart was melting in the broad garish light of the actual, awful fact—the commencement of Wessex' trial.

She tottered and might have fallen but for the table close beside her, against which she leant.

Her calm and composure were flying from her bit by bit. She had at last begun to understand—to realize. Up to now it had all been so shadowy, so remote, almost like a dream. She had not seen Wessex since that last happy moment when he had pressed her against his heart ... since then she had only heard rumours ... wild statements ... she knew of his self-accusation—the terrible crime which had been committed—but her heart had been numbed through the very appalling nature of the catastrophe following so closely upon her budding happiness ... it had all been intangible all this while ... whilst now ...

"The Duke hath made confession," said the Cardinal, and his voice seemed to come as if in direct answer to her thoughts. "In an hour at most judgment will be pronounced against him, and then sentence of death."

She passed her hand across her moist forehead, trying to collect her scattered senses. She looked once or twice at him in helpless, appealing misery, but his face now was stern and implacable, he seemed to her to be the presentment of a relentless justice about to fall on an innocent man. Her throat felt parched, her lips were dry, yet she tried to speak.

"It cannot be ..." she repeated mechanically, "it cannot be ... no, no, my lord, you are powerful ... you are great and clever ... you will find a means to save him ... you will ... you will ... you sent for me.... Oh! was it in order to torture me like this that you sent for me?"

"My child ...."

"That woman?" she continued wildly, not heeding him, "that woman ... where is she? ... find her, my lord ... find her, and let me speak to her.... Oh! I'll find the right words to melt her heart ... she must speak ... she must tell the truth ... she cannot let him die ... no, no ... not like that ...."

Gone was all her pride, all her icy reserve, even jealousy had vanished before the awful inevitableness of his dishonour and his death. She would have dragged herself at the feet of those judges who were about to condemn him, of this man who was taking a cruel delight in torturing her; nay! she would have knelt and kissed the hands of that

154

unknown rival, for whose sake she had endured the terrible mental tortures of the past few days, if only she could wrench from her the truth which would set him free from all this disgrace.

"That woman!" she repeated with agonizing passion, "that woman ... where is she? ..."

"She stands now before me," said the Cardinal sternly, "repentant, I hope, ready to speak the truth."

"No! no! it is false!" she protested vehemently, "false I tell you! It was not I ..."

Her voice broke in a pitiable, wistful sob, which would have melted a heart less stony than that which beat in the Cardinal's ambitious breast.

"Oh! have I not endured enough?" she murmured half to herself, half in appealing misery to him. "Jealousy—hate for that woman whom he loves as he never hath loved me ... whom he loves better than his honour ... for whose sake he will stand there anon, branded with infamy ...."

Her knees gave way under her, she fell half prostrate on the floor at the very feet of her tormentor.

"Find her, my lord," she sobbed passionately, "find her ... you can ... you can ...."

But for sole answer he once more pushed the door ajar.

Another voice came from the body of the hall now, that of Mr. Barham, the Queen's Serjeant—

"And having proved Robert d'Esclade, Duke of Wessex, guilty of this most heinous murder, I, on behalf of the Crown, will presently ask you, my lord, to pass sentence of death upon him."

"No, no, no—not death!" she moaned, "not death.... They are mad, my lord—are they not mad? ... He guilty of murder! Oh! will no one come forward to prove him innocent?"

"No one can do that but you, my daughter," replied His Eminence sternly, as he once more closed the door.

"But you do not understand. In God's name, what would you have me do? I loved him, it is true, but ... it was another woman ... not I! another woman, whose honour is dearer to him than his own ... for whose sake he killed ... for whose sake he is silent ... for whose sake he will die ... but that woman was not I ... not I!"

"Alas!" he replied placidly, "then indeed nothing can save His Grace from the block ...."

He sighed and returned to his former place beside the table, like a man who has done all that duty demanded of him, and now is weary and ready to let destiny take its course.

Ursula watched him dully, stupidly; she could not read just then what went on behind that mask of suave benevolence. Could she have read the Cardinal's innermost thoughts she would have seen that complete satisfaction filled his ambitious heart. He knew that he had

155

succeeded, it was but a question of time ... a few minutes, perhaps; but he had a good quarter of an hour to spare, in which the tortured soul before him would fight its last fight with despair. There was the long arraignment to be read out by the Clerk of the Crown, then the names of the triers to be called out in their order—all that, before the prisoner was actually called to the bar. Oh yes! he had plenty of time, now that he was sure of victory.

The girl wandered mechanically towards the door, her trembling hand sought the latch, but was too weak to turn it. She glued her ear to the lock and perchance heard a word or two, for even the Cardinal caught the sound of a loud voice reading the deadly indictment.

"The prisoner hath confessed ...

"This most heinous crime ...

"For which sentence of death ...

"Return his precept and bring forth the prisoner."

Ursula straightened out her girlish figure; with a firm hand now she smoothed her veil over her hair, and rearranged the disordered folds of her kerchief. She crossed the room with an unfaltering step, and once more took a seat on the low stool opposite to His Eminence the Cardinal.

She seemed to have reassumed the same icy calm which she had worn earlier in the interview; she was quite pale again, and all traces of tears had disappeared from her eyes.

Quite instinctively, certainly against his will, the Cardinal failed to return the steady gaze which she now fixed upon him. As she sat there close to him, her great lustrous eyes trying to search his very soul, he knew that at last she had guessed.

She knew that he was fully aware of the fact that she was not the woman for whose sake the Duke of Wessex was suffering condemnation at this very moment. All the meshes of the base intrigue which had landed the man she loved in a felon's dock escaped her utterly, but this much she realized, that the Cardinal had worked for the Duke's undoing, that he knew who her rival was, that he was wilfully shielding that woman, whilst callously sacrificing her—Ursula Glynde—to the success of some further scheme.

She knew all that, yet she did not hesitate. Her love for Wessex had filled all her life—first as a child, then as an ignorant girl worshipping an ideal. When she saw him, and in him saw the embodiment of all her most romantic beliefs, she loved him with all the passionate ardour of her newly awakened woman's heart. From the moment that his touch had thrilled her, that his voice had set her temples throbbing, that her pure lips had met his own, she had given him her whole love, given herself to him body and soul for his happiness and her own.

So great was her love that jealousy had not killed it; it had changed her joy into sorrow, her happiness into bitterness, but the

156

heart which she gave to him she was powerless to take away. He had fooled her, led her to believe in his love for her, but his life was as precious to her now as it had been that afternoon—which seemed so long ago—when she first raised her eyes to his and met his ardent gaze.

She was face to face with the most cruel problem ever set before a human heart, for she firmly believed that if through her self-sacrifice she saved him from death and dishonour, he would nevertheless inevitably turn to the other woman, for whose sake he was suffering now; yet she was ready with the sacrifice, because of the selflessness of her love.

How well the Cardinal had managed the tragedy which had parted two noble hearts! Each believed the other treacherous and guilty, yet each was prepared to lay down life, honour, happiness for the sake of the loved one.

"Your Eminence," said Ursula very quietly after a little while, "you said just now that I could save His Grace of Wessex from unmerited disgrace and death. Tell me now, what must I do?"

"It is simple enough, my daughter," he replied, still avoiding her clear, steadfast gaze; "you have but to speak the truth."

"The truth, they say, oft lies hidden in a well, my lord," she rejoined. "I pray Your Eminence to guide me to its depths."

"I can but guide your memory, my daughter, to the events of the fateful night when Don Miguel was murdered."

"Yes?"

"You were there, in the Audience Chamber, were you not?"

"I was there," she repeated mechanically.

"With Don Miguel de Suarez, who, taking advantage of the late hour and the loneliness of this part of the Palace ... insulted you ... or..."

"Let us say that he insulted me ...."

"His Grace then came upon the scene?"

"Just as Your Eminence describes it."

"And 'twas to defend your honour that the Duke of Wessex killed Don Miguel."

"To defend mine honour the Duke of Wessex killed Don Miguel."

"This you will swear to be true?"

"Without hope of absolution."

"And you will make this tardy confession, my daughter, to His Grace's judges freely?"

"Whenever it is deemed necessary I will make the confession to His Grace's judges freely."

She swayed as if her senses were leaving her. Instinctively the Cardinal put out his arm to support her, but with a mighty effort she drew herself together, and looked down upon him with all the regal majesty of her own sublime self-sacrifice.

But, flushed with victory, His Eminence cared nothing for the contempt of the vanquished. It had been a hard-fought battle. His

Grace was saved from death and Queen Mary Tudor could not help but keep her word. It was a triumph indeed!

He touched a hand-bell, a servant appeared. A few whispered instructions and the end was accomplished at last.

But, God in Heaven, at what terrible cost!

CHAPTER XXXIV

WESTMINSTER HALL

A surging, seething crowd! heads upon heads in a dense, compact mass—a double row of men, women, boys, and girls, held back with difficulty by the Serjeant-at-Arms and his men, armed with halberds and tipstaves!

A crowd come to gape and grin, some to sympathize—but only a very few of these. All come to see how the proudest gentleman in England would bear himself in a felon's dock.

The dull grey light of an early November day came in ghostly streaks through the huge window of the Hall, throwing into bold relief the scarlet-clad figures of the twenty-four noble lords who were to be the Duke's triers, the gorgeous robes of the judges, and the dull black gowns of the attorneys and the minor dignitaries.

Quick, excited whispers passed from mouth to mouth as now and then a familiar face detached itself from the crowd of all these awesome personages and was recognized by the people.

"That's my lord Huntingdon," said an elderly merchant, pointing to a grey-bearded lord who had just taken his seat. "I mind him well when first he bought a pair of spurs in my father's shop."

"Aye! and there's Lord Northampton," commented another, "and mightily thankful he should be not to be standing at the bar himself for high treason."

"That's Mr. Gilbert Gerard, the Attorney-General," quoth one who knew.

"Sh! sh! sh!" came in excited whispers all around, "here comes the Lord High Steward himself and all the judges."

The procession awed the populace, for every new-comer—gorgeously apparelled though he was—wore a grave face and a saddened mien. The crowd, who had come for a day's pageant, a frolic not unlike the happy doings at East Molesey Fair, felt suddenly silenced and oppressed. Some of the women shivered beneath their thin kerchiefs; the devout ones made a quick sign of the cross, as if prayers were about to begin.

It was all so solemn and so grand, in this dim winter's light, wherein shadows seemed to hover all around, hiding the remote corners of the Hall and dwelling mysteriously on that tall scaffold, whereon one by one these reverend personages took their allotted seats.

The Queen's Serjeant carried the white rod, and escorted my Lord High Steward to the great chair, covered with a gorgeous cloth, which dominated the entire hall. To the right and left of him sat the twenty-four peers with their ermine-decked cloaks over their shoulders.

Below them sat the Lord Chief Justice of England, the Lord Chief Justice of Common Pleas, and the Lord Chief Baron of the Exchequer, and also the rest of the minor judges. The Clerk of the Crown, in black gown and yellow hose, had been busy some time conversing with his secondary. Next to the judges sat several gentlemen of the Queen's household, their silken doublets of rich though sombre hues adding a crisp note of contrasting colour to the harmonies in scarlet and dull oak, which filled in the background of the picture.

Sir Walter Mildmay, Chancellor of the Exchequer, sat close by with six of the Queen's Privy Councillors, also on their left the Master of Requests and other persons of note. Immediately facing the bar was the Queen's Serjeant, the Attorney-General, the Solicitor-General, and the Attorney-General of the Court of Wards. The Recorder of London had been given a special seat, also Mr. Thomas Norton, the Queen's printer, who wrote out the historical account of the trial, which has been preserved amongst the State papers.

Then my Lord High Steward stood up bareheaded, holding the white rod in his hand, and the Serjeant-at-Arms stepped forward into the immediate centre of the Hall facing the crowd, and read out the proclamation as follows:—

"My Lord's Grace, the Queen's Majesty's Commissioner, High Steward of England, commandeth every man to keep silence on pain of imprisonment and to hear the Queen's Commission read."

This was followed by the reading of the Queen's Commission by the Clerk of the Crown, after which—still standing—he read the indictment in a loud voice, so that all might hear.

"Whereas Robert d'Esclade, fifth Duke of Wessex, did on the night of the fourteenth of October of this year of our Lord one thousand five hundred and fifty-three, unlawfully kill Don Miguel, Marquis de Suarez, grandee of Spain ..."

The voice of the Clerk went droning on, the people amazed, horrified, tried not to lose one single word of this strange document which so loudly proclaimed the fact that a dastardly crime, unparalleled in its cowardice and ferocity, had been committed by one

159

who until now had stood above all Englishmen as a model of honour, loyalty, and truth.

With every fresh charge, skilfully woven together and intertwined with sundry depositions obtained from my lord Cardinal and his retinue, the crowd of spectators realized more and more that they were face to face with a weird and mysterious tragedy, not a pageant, but an appalling drama, the prologue of which was being enacted before them now.

It seemed, as the Clerk pursued his reading, that he was slowly unfolding mesh by mesh a hideous web, in the midst of which the presence of a death-dealing and loathsome spider could as yet only be dimly guessed.

A close, clinging web from which no man, be he the premier peer of England or the humblest commoner, could ever hope to escape.

The web of a rough and misguided justice, of a law of the talion, retributive and blind, distributing with an impartial hand condemnations and punishments to guilty and innocent alike, to the martyr and to the felon, to the coward and the deceived.

This was not a decadent, puny century, peopled with neurotics and feeble-minded weaklings, it was a century of men!—men who were giants alike in their virtues and their passions, their vices and their atrocities, narrow in their views, but staunch in their beliefs, savage in their creeds and prejudices—but MEN for all that.

"The more heinous the offence the less chance shall the prisoner have of justifying his conduct." That was the dictate of the law.

"For truly," said Sir Robert Catline, Lord Chief Justice of England, in the course of the trial of Sir Nicholas Throckmorton for high treason, "justice must not be confused by sundry arguments in the prisoner's cause, which might lead to his acquittal and the non-punishment of so grave a fault."

Witnesses were seldom, if ever, examined in the presence of the accused. Depositions were extorted—often by torture, always by threats—from persons who happened to be friends or associates of the prisoner.

An acquittal?—perish the thought! Let the citizen look to himself ere he fell in the clutches of his country's justice; once there he had little or no chance of proving his innocence.

Lest the guilty escape!

Always that awful possibility! Rough justice demanded punishment—always punishment—lest the guilty escape!

And the people as they listened knew that they had come to see a man's last day upon earth.

Proud, rich, fastidious Wessex! this is the end of all things! Pomp and ceremony, gorgeous robes and costly apparels! these to speed thee on thy way; but as inevitably as the dull winter's night must follow this grey November morning, so will pomp and circumstance fade away

160

into the past and leave thee with but one red-clad figure by thy side—that of the headsman with the axe.

Justice to-day could make short work of her duties.

Robert d'Esclade, fifth Duke of Wessex, had confessed to his crime, why should Justice trouble herself to prove that which was already admitted? She had merely to think out the form and severity of the punishment for this man of high degree, who had sunk and stooped so low.

For form's sake a few depositions had been taken, for this was an unusual event—a specially atrocious crime! the murder of a foreign envoy at the Court of the Queen of England, and at the hand of the premier peer of the realm!

The Cardinal de Moreno, envoy in chief of His Majesty the King of Spain, had given the matter a political significance. In the name of his royal master he had demanded judgment on that most monstrous felony, and the exercise of the full rigour of the law. The Duke of Wessex had been a rival suitor for the hand of the Queen of England, and he had—presumably—wilfully removed a successful diplomatist who threatened to thwart his projects.

And thus Wessex was arraigned for treason as well as for murder, and the indictment set forth the depositions of my lord Cardinal and those of his servant Pasquale, all of which His Grace had declined to peruse. He knew that these statements were lies, guessed well enough how his enemies would heap proof upon proof to bolster up his own brief confession.

His Eminence had made a sworn statement that he heard angry voices 'twixt Don Miguel and His Grace some little time before the Marquis was found dead. Well, that was true enough! There had been a deadly quarrel, and though this did not aggravate the case, it helped to establish the facts, if public opinion was like to sway the judges or if disbelief in Wessex' guilt was too firmly rooted in the minds of his peers.

The indictment was a masterpiece, well could the Solicitor-General pride himself on the perfection of the document.

A dull, oppressive silence had fallen upon this vast concourse of people. Interest, which was at fever-pitch, had forcibly to be kept in check, but now, as the Clerk's final words echoed feebly through the vast hall, a great sigh of eager excitement rose from the entire multitude.

Everything so far had been but preliminary, the somewhat dull, lengthy prologue of the coming palpitating drama. But at last the curtain was about to rise on the first act, and the chief actor was ready to step upon the stage.

Already from afar loud murmurs and excited cries proclaimed the approach of the prisoner.

"He hath arrived from the Tower," whispered the 'prentices to one another.

The distant murmurs grew in volume, then came nearer and nearer. All necks were craned to see the Duke arrive, and even the repeated calls of the Serjeant-at-Arms demanding silence were now left unheeded.

Whispers passed from lip to ear. Comments and conjectures flew through the crowd. Was not this the most interesting moment of this interesting day?

"How would he carry himself?"

"How would he look?"

"How doth a nobleman look when he becomes a felon?"

"Silence! Here they come!"

The Serjeant-at-Arms once more stood up before the people and loudly read a proclamation, calling upon the Lieutenant of the Tower of London to return his precept and bring forth his prisoner.

This was responded to by a call of "Present!" from outside, followed by a loud tumult. The next moment the great doors of the Hall were thrown open, six armed men entered and walked straight up the centre aisle towards the bar.

Behind them appeared the Lieutenant of the Tower of London, with Lord Rich, and between them was Robert d'Esclade, fifth Duke of Wessex, the prisoner.

Dressed all in black, he looked distinctly older than the crowd had remembrance of him. A sigh of excited anticipation went all along the line, a regular bousculade ensued; the people behind trying to catch a nearer glimpse of the Duke and pushing those who were in front. The 'prentices, who were squatting in the foremost rank on the ground, were violently jerked forward, some fell on their faces right up against the Lieutenant and my lord Rich, seeing which and the general excited confusion the Duke was observed to smile.

A woman in the crowd murmured—

"The Lord bless his handsome face!"

"Heaven ward Your Grace!" added another.

The women's pity—and that only momentarily. And the awful publicity of it all! Among the men wagers were offered and taken in his hearing as he passed, whether sentence of death would be passed on him or not.

"Will they hang him, think you?"

"No, no, 'tis always the axe for noble lords; but they'll have him drawn and quartered for sure."

"God help Your Grace!" sighed the women.

Indeed, if pride was a deadly sin, how deadly was its punishment now.

The crowd was not hostile, only indifferent, curious, eager to see;

162

and every remark made by these stolid gapers must have cut the prisoner like a blow.

They watched him cross the entire length of the hall, commenting on his appearance, his clothes, his past life, a coarse jest even came to his ears now and again, a laugh of derision or an exclamation of satisfied envy.

Fallen Wessex indeed!

He tried with all his might not to show what he felt, and evidently he succeeded over well, for Mr. Thomas Norton, in his comments on the trial, states placidly:—

"The prisoner seemeth not to understand the gravity of his position and careth naught for the heinousness of his crime. Truly this indifference marketh a godless soul or else the supreme conceit of wealth and high rank, he having many friends among his peers and being confident of an acquittal."

Lord Rich alone, who walked by the side of the Duke, and stood close to him throughout the awful ordeal, has noted in his interesting memoirs how deeply the accused was moved when he realized that he would have to stand at the bar on a raised dais, in full view of all the crowd.

"Meseemed that his hand trembled when first he rested it on the bar," adds his lordship in his chronicles. "He being passing tall he could be seen by all and sundry, which was trying to his pride. But anon His Grace caught my eye, and I doubt not but that he read therein all the sympathy which I felt for him, for he then threw back his head and scanned the crowd right fearlessly, and more like a king ready to read a proclamation than a felon awaiting his trial. Then, as he looked all around him, his eyes lighted on my lord the Cardinal de Moreno and on a veiled female figure who sat close to the Spanish envoy. He then became deathly pale, and I, fearing that he might swoon, caught him by the arm. But he pressed my hand and thanked me, saying only that the heat of the room was oppressive."

It is evident that my lord Rich was a hot partisan of the accused. He and the Lieutenant of the Tower stood close beside the Duke throughout the trial, the Tower guard forming a semicircle round the bar, and the Chamberlain of the Tower holding the axe with its edge from the prisoner and towards Lord Rich.

Mr. Thomas Norton tells us that at this point of the proceedings the excitement was intense. Lord Chandois himself seemed unable to keep up the rigid dignity of his office. The peers who were the triers were eagerly whispering to one another. The Clerk seemed unable to clear his throat before calling on the accused.

The crowd too felt this acute tension. The people had already noticed the veiled female figure, clad in sombre kirtle and black paniers, who had entered the Hall a little while ago, accompanied by His Eminence the Cardinal, and had since then sat, dull and rigid,

163

beside him, seemingly taking no notice of the proceedings. A hurried6 conversation carried on in whispers between His Eminence and my lord High Steward had been noted by everybody—yet no one dared to ask a question.

It seemed as if an invisible presence had suddenly made itself felt, a spirit from the land of shadows, that awesome precursor of death which is called "Retribution," and that from his ghostly lips there had fallen—unheard yet felt by every heart—the mighty dictate of an almighty will: "Thou shalt do no murder!"

Had the spirit really passed? Who can tell? But the soul of every man and woman there was left quivering. There was not a hand that now did not slightly tremble, not one lid that failed to move, for the supreme moment had come for the accomplishment of an irreparable wrong.

The spectators had before them the picture of that solemn Court, the Lord High Steward with chain and sword of gold, the judges in their red robes, the peers with their ermine, and here and there quaint patches of6 unexpected colour as the wintry sun struck full through the coloured facets of the huge window beyond and alighted on a black gown or the leather jerkins of the guard.

They saw the halberds of the men-at-arms faintly gleaming in the wan, grey light, the Cardinal's purple robes, a brilliant note amidst the dull mass of browns and blacks; the blue doublet of Sir Henry Beddingfield, a jarring bit of discord between the sable-hued garb of the other gentlemen there.

And there, amongst them all, the tall, erect figure, the one quiet, impassive face in this surging sea of excitement—the prisoner at the bar!

CHAPTER XXXV

THE TRIAL

The excitement, great as it was, had perforce to be kept in check.

The Clerk of the Crown had collected his papers: he now stood up and called upon the accused:

"Robert, Duke of Wessex and of Dorchester, Earl of Launceston, Wexford and Bridthorpe, Baron of Greystone, Ullesthorpe and Edbrooke, Premier Peer of England, hold up thy right hand."

The prisoner having done so, Mr. Barham, the Queen's Sergeant, opened the contents of the indictment.

"Whereas it is said that on the fourteenth day of October thou didst unlawfully kill Don Miguel, Marquis de Suarez, grandee of Spain and envoy extraordinary of His Most Catholic Majesty the King of Spain, thou art therefore to make answer to this charge of murder. I therefore charge thee once again: art thou guilty of this crime, whereof thou art indicted, yea or nay?"

"I am guilty," replied Wessex firmly, "and I have confessed."

"By whom wilt thou be tried?"

"By God and by my peers."

"Before we proceed," continued the Sergeant, "what sayest thou, Robert, Duke of Wessex, is that which thou hast confessed true?"

"It is true."

"And didst thou confess it willingly and freely of thyself, or was there any extortion or unfair means to draw it from thee?"

"Surely I made that confession freely," replied the prisoner, "without any constraint, and that is all true."

"And hast thou read the depositions of those who were witness of thy crime, and who have added their testimony to that which thine accusers, the Queen's Commissioners, already know?"

"I have not read those depositions, as there was no one present when Don Miguel died save I—his murderer—and God!"

As Wessex made this last bold declaration, the Queen's Serjeant turned towards His Eminence as if expecting guidance from that direction, but as nothing came he continued—

"I would have thee weigh well what thou sayest. Thine answers and confessions, if spoken truthfully, will do much to mitigate the severity of the punishment which thy crime hath called forth."

"I will make mine own confession," retorted Wessex, with a sudden quick return to his own haughty manner. "I pray you teach me not how to answer or confess. But because I was not cognizant whether my peers did know it all or not, I have made a short declaration of my doings with Don Miguel. That is the truth, my lords," he added, addressing his triers and judges on the bench, "everything else which hath been added contrary to mine own confession is a lie and a perjury, as God here is my witness."

"Thy confession is but a brief record of the fact, as the Clerk of the Crown will presently read. There is neither circumstance nor detail."

"And is it for circumstance or detail that I am being tried?" rejoined Wessex, "or for the murder of Don Miguel de Suarez, to which I hereby plead guilty?"

The Queen's Serjeant looked to Sir Robert Catline for guidance. The Lord Chief Justice, however, was of opinion that the prisoner's confession must be read first, before any further argument about it could be allowed.

The Clerk of the Crown then rose and began to read:—

"The voluntary confession of Robert Duke of Wessex, now a prisoner in the Tower, and accused of murder, treason, and felony: made at the Tower of London on the fifteenth day of October, 1553. I hereby acknowledge and confess that on the fourteenth day of October I did unlawfully kill Don Miguel, Marquis de Suarez, by stabbing him in the back with my dagger. For this murder I plead neither excuse nor justification, and submit myself to a trial by my peers and to the justice of this realm. So help me God."

The bench, the entire hall, was crowded with the Duke's friends; with the exception of a very small faction, who for reasons they deemed good and adequate desired the Spanish alliance; and the death of the man at the bar, not a single man or woman present believed that that confession was an exposé of the truth. The Serjeant himself, the Clerk of the Crown, the Attorney and Solicitor-General who represented the prosecution, knew that some mystery lurked behind that monstrous self-accusation. But it was so straightforward, so categorical, that unless some extraordinary event occurred, unless Wessex himself recanted that confession, nothing could save him from its dire consequences.

Oh! if Wessex would but recant! No one would have disbelieved him then—not that fickle, motley crowd surely, who with its own characteristic inconsequence had suddenly taken the accused to its heart.

"'Tis not true, Wessex!" shouted a manly voice from the body of the hall.

"Deny it! deny it!" came in a regular hubbub from the compact mass of throats in the rear.

The Duke smiled, but did not move. Lord Rich, in his memoirs, here points out that "His Grace seemed all unconscious of his surroundings and like unto a wanderer in the land of dreams."

But the confession had aroused the opposition of the crowd, it was truly past honest men's belief. Every one murmured, and some chroniclers aver that there was a regular tumult, more than encouraged by the Duke's friends, and not checked even by the Lord High Steward himself.

In the turn of a hand public opinion had veered round. Forgetting that a while ago they were ready to hoot and mock the prisoner, the men now were equally prepared to make a rush for the bar and drag him away from that ignominious place, which they suddenly understood that he never should have occupied.

The Serjeant-at-Arms had much ado to make himself heard. The guard had literally to make an onslaught on the crowd. It was fully five or ten minutes before the noise subsided; then only did murmurs die down like the roar of the sea when the surf recedes from the shore.

It was a brief lull, and Mr. Barham, the Queen's Serjeant, having once more enjoined silence on behalf of Her Majesty's Commissioner, and on pain of imprisonment, was at last able to continue his duties.

"It appeareth before you, my lords," he resumed in a loud, clear voice, "that this man hath been indicted and arraigned of a most heinous crime, and hath confessed it before you, which is of record. Wherefore there resteth no more to be done but for the Court to give judgment accordingly, which here I require in the behalf of the Queen's Majesty."

The Lord High Steward rose and a gentleman usher took the white wand from him. He stood bareheaded, and every one in the Hall could see him.

"Robert, Duke of Wessex," he said, and his voice trembled as he spoke, "Duke of Dorchester, Earl of Launceston, Wexford, and Bridthorpe, Baron of Greystone, Ullesthorpe, and Edbrooke, premier peer of England, what have you to say why I may not proceed to judgment?"

The last words almost sounded like an appeal, of friend to friend, comrade to comrade. Lord Chandois' kindly eyes were fixed in deep sorrow on the man whom he had loved and honoured sufficiently to wish to see him on the throne of England.

There was an awed hush in the vast hall, and then a voice, clear and distinct—a woman's voice—broke the momentous silence.

"The Duke of Wessex is innocent of the charge brought against him, as I hereby bear witness on his behalf."

Even as the last bell-like tones echoed through the great chamber a young girl stepped forward, sable-clad and fragile-looking, but unabashed by the hundreds of eyes fixed eagerly upon her.

In the centre of the room she paused, and, throwing back the dark veil which enveloped her face, she looked straight up at my Lord High Steward.

"Who speaks?" he asked in astonishment.

"I, Ursula Glynde," she replied firmly, "daughter of the Earl of Truro."

At sound of her voice Wessex had started. His face became deathly pale and his hand gripped the massive bar of wood before him, until every muscle and sinew in his arm creaked with the intensity of the effort. It was only after she had spoken her own name that he seemed to pull himself together, for he said—

"I pray your lordships not to listen. I desire no witnesses on my behalf."

His temples had begun to throb, a wild horror seized him at

167

thought of what she might do. And her appearance, too, had set his heart beating in a veritable turmoil of emotions. For she stood now before him, before them all, as the vision of purity and innocence which he had first learnt to worship: that other self of hers, that mysterious, half-crazed being who had fooled and mocked him and then committed the awful crime for which he stood self-convicted, that had vanished, leaving only this delicate, ethereal being, the one whom he had clasped in his arms, whose blue eyes had gazed lovingly into his, whose lips had met his in that one mad, passionate embrace.

When he interposed thus coldly, impassively, she shuddered slightly but she did not turn towards him, and he could only see the dainty outline of her fine profile, cut clear against a dark background of moving figures beyond. From the table at which she herself had been sitting and waiting all this while, and which was now in full view of the spectators, two advocates rose and joined the bench of judges. One of them, after a brief consultation with the Clerk of the Crown, turned respectfully towards the Lord High Steward.

"I humbly beseech your lordship," he said firmly, "and you, my lords, to hear the evidence of the Lady Ursula Glynde. There has been no time to obtain a written deposition from her, for God at the eleventh hour hath thought fit to move her to speak that which she knows, so that a dreadful error may not be committed."

"This is a great breach of customary procedure," said Mr. Thomas Bromley, the Solicitor-General, with a dubious shake of the head.

"Not so great as you would have us think, sir," commented Sir Robert Catline, "for e'en in the trial of the late-lamented Queen Catherine of blessed memory, my lord of Uppingham, whose depositions could not be taken previously, was nevertheless allowed to bear witness on behalf of the accused."

But the opinion of the most learned lawyer in England would not now have been listened to, if it had been adverse to the present situation. Lords and judges, noblemen and spectators clamoured with every means at their command, short of absolute contempt of Court, that this new witness should be heard.

"How say you, my lords?" said the Lord High Steward eagerly, "bearing in mind the opinion of our learned colleague, ought we to hear this lady or no?"

"Aye! aye!" came from every voice on the bench.

"By Our Lady! I protest!" said Wessex loudly.

"We will hear this lady," pronounced the Lord High Steward. "Let her step forward and be made to swear the truth of her assertions."

Ursula came forward a step or two. Mr. Thomas Wilbraham, Attorney-General of the Court of Wards, who was sitting close by, held out a small wooden crucifix towards her. She took it and kissed it reverently.

"You are the Lady Ursula Glynde," queried Lord Chandois, "maid-of-honour to the Queen's Majesty?"

"I am."

"Then do I charge you to speak the truth, the whole truth, and naught but the truth, so help you God."

"My lords," protested Wessex hotly, for his brain was in a whirl. He could not allow her to speak and accuse herself of her crime—she, the angel side of her, taking upon herself the evil committed by that mysterious second self over which she had no control. It was too horrible! And all these people gaping at her made his blood tingle with shame. What he had readily borne himself, the disgrace, the staring crowd, the pity and inquisitiveness of the multitude, that he felt he could not endure for her.

Already, as he saw her now, his heart had forgiven her everything; gladly, joyously would he die now, since he had seen her once more as she really was, pure and undefiled by contact with the ignoble wretch whom, in a moment of madness, she had sent to his death.

He protested with all his might. But it was his own past life, his friends, his popularity, which now literally conspired against him, and caused his judges to turn a deaf ear to his entreaties.

"My lord of Wessex," said the High Steward sternly, "in the name of justice and for the dignity of this court, I charge you to be silent."

Then he once more addressed the Lady Ursula.

"Say on, lady. This court will hear you."

She waited a few moments, whilst every spectator there seemed to hear his own heart beat with the intensity of his excitement. Then she began speaking in a firm and even voice, somewhat low at first, but gaining in strength and volume as she proceeded.

"I would have you know, my lords," she said, "that at midnight on the fourteenth day of October, being in the Audience Chamber at Hampton Court Palace, in the company of Don Miguel de Suarez ..."

She paused suddenly and seemed to sway. Mr. Thomas Wilbraham ran to her, offering her a chair, which she declined with a quick wave of the hand.

"My lords," said Wessex, quietly and earnestly, during the brief lull caused by this interruption, "I entreat you in the name of justice, do not hear this lady; she is excited and overwrought and knows not the purport of what she is saying.... You see for yourselves she is scarce conscious of her actions.... I have made full confession ... there rests nothing to be done ...."

"Prisoner at the bar," said the Lord High Steward, "I charge you to be silent. Lady Ursula, continue."

And Wessex perforce had to hold his peace, whilst Ursula resumed her tale more calmly.

"Being in company of Don Miguel, who spoke words of love to

169

me ... and anon did hold me in his arms ... when I tried to escape ... but ... but ... he would not let me go ... he ... he ... your lordships, have patience with me, I pray you ..." she added in tones of intense pathos as the monstrous lie she was so sublimely forcing herself to utter seemed suddenly to be choking her. Then she continued speaking quickly, lest perhaps she might waver before the end.

"His Grace of Wessex did come upon us, and seeing me held with violence, I, who was his betrothed, to save mine honour, the Duke did strike Don Miguel down."

There was dead silence as the young girl had finished speaking. Wessex was staring at her, and Mr. Thomas Norton assures us that he burst out laughing, a laugh which the Queen's printer stigmatizes as "heartless and unworthy a high-born gentleman! for truly," he continues, "the Lady Ursula Glynde was moved by the spirit of God in thus making a tardy confession, and His Grace, methinks, should have shown a proper spirit of reverence before this manifestation of God."

But if Wessex laughed at this supreme and palpitating moment, surely his laugh must have come from the very bitterness of his soul. As far as he knew Ursula had told nothing but a strangely concocted lie. To him, who had—as he thought—seen her with the blood of Don Miguel still warm upon her hands, this extraordinary tale of threatened honour and timely interference was but a tangled tissue of wanton falsehoods—another in the long series which she had told to him.

And purposeless too!

He had no idea of any sacrifice on her part, and merely looked upon her present action as a weak attempt to save him from the gallows and no more.

She just liked him well enough apparently not to wish to see him hang, but that was all. And this suddenly struck him as ridiculous, paltry, and childish, a silly bravado which caused him to laugh. Perhaps she desired to save him publicly at slight cost to herself, in order that she might yet occupy one day the position which she had so avowedly coveted since her childhood—that of Duchess of Wessex!

It was indeed more than ridiculous.

The stain of murder, which was really on her hands, she was full willing that it should rest on him, only slightly palliated by the lie which she had told.

Strange, strange perversion of a girlish soul!

With dulled ears and brain in a turmoil Wessex only partly heard the questions and cross-questions which his judges now put to her. She never wavered from her original story, but repeated it again and again, circumstantially and without hesitation. Never once did she look towards the bar.

"Lady Ursula Glynde," said Lord Chandois finally and with solemn earnestness, "do you swear upon your honour and conscience that you have spoken the truth?"

170

And she replied equally solemnly—

"I swear it upon mine honour and conscience."

"'Tis false from beginning to end," protested Wessex loudly.

Ursula made a low obeisance before my Lord High Steward. The crucifix was once more held up to her and she kissed it reverently. With that pious kiss she reached at that moment the highest pinnacle of her sacrifice—she gave up to the man she loved the very spotlessness of her soul. For his sake she had lied and spoken a false oath—she had sinned in order that he might be saved.

And even now she also reached the greatest depth of her own misery, for, as she told her tale before his judges and before him, she half expected that he would exonerate her from the odious accusations which she was bringing against herself.

The story which she had told had been in accordance with the Cardinal's suggestions, but she herself was quite convinced that Don Miguel had fallen by a woman's hand. Wessex would never have hit another man in the back—that was woman's work, and she who had done it was so dear to him, that he was sacrificing life and honour in order to shield her.

Aye! more than that! for was he not acting a coward's part by allowing Ursula Glynde to sacrifice her fair name for the sake of a wanton?

And thus these two people who loved one another more than life, honour, and happiness, were face to face now with that terrible misunderstanding between them:—still further apart from each other than they had ever been, both suffering acutely in heart and mind for the supposed cowardice and wantonness of the other, and the while my Lord High Steward and the other noble lords were concluding the ceremonies of that strange, eventful trial.

"My lords," said Lord Chandois, once more rising from his seat, "you have heard the evidence of this lady, and Robert Duke of Wessex having put himself upon the trial of God and you his peers, I charge you to consider if it appeareth that he is guilty of this murder or whether he had justification, and thereupon say your minds upon your honour and consciences."

We have Mr. Thomas Norton's authority for stating that my lords, the triers, never left their seats, nor did they deliberate. Hardly were the words out of my Lord High Steward's lips than with one accord four-and-twenty voices were raised saying—

"Not guilty!"

"Then," adds Mr. Norton, "there was a cheer raised from the people inside the Hall which was quite deafening to the ears. Sundry tossed their caps into the air, and many of the women began to cry. My Lord High Steward could not make himself heard for a long while, at which he became very wrathful, and, calling to the Serjeant-at-Arms, he bade him clear the Court of all these noise-makers."

171

There seems to have been considerable difficulty in doing this, for Mr. Thomas Norton continuously refers to "riotous conduct," and even to "contempt of the Queen's Commissioner." Cheers of "God save Wessex!" alternated with the loyal cry of "God save the Queen." The men-at-arms had to use their halberds, and did so very effectually, one or two of the more excited "noise-makers" getting wounded about the face and hands. Finally the suggestion came from Mr. Barham, the Queen's Serjeant, that His Grace of Wessex should be concealed from the view of the populace, and, acting upon this advice, the Lieutenant of the Tower ordered his guard to close around the bar, whilst a low seat was provided for His Grace. The object of this mad enthusiasm being thus placed out of sight, the people became gradually more calm, and the noise subsided sufficiently for the Queen's Serjeant to give forth his final dictum.

"My Lord's Grace, the Queen's Commissioner, High Steward of England, chargeth all persons to depart in God's peace and the Queen's, and hath dissolved this Commission!"

"God save the Queen!" was shouted lustily, and then the great door was opened and the people began quietly to file out.

The pale November sun had struggled out of its misty coverings, and touched the pinnacles and towers of the old Abbey with delicate gleams of golden grey. Slowly the crowd moved on, some of the more venturesome or more enthusiastic townsfolk, the 'prentices, and younger men, lingered round the precincts to see the great personages come out and to give a final cheer for His Grace of Wessex.

The Hall itself seemed lonely now that the people had gone. The Lord High Steward once more called on the prisoner, who had already risen as soon as his noisy partisans had departed.

As he had been impassive throughout the terrible ordeal of this trial for his life, so he remained now that on every face before him he read the inevitable acquittal. He had watched Ursula Glynde's graceful figure as, accompanied by the Cardinal de Moreno, she had finally made an obeisance before the judges, then had retired through the doors of the Lord Chancellor's Court.

A great and awful disgust filled his whole heart. It was he now who was conscious of the loathsome web, which had enveloped him more completely than he had ever anticipated.

He saw his acquittal hovering on the lips of his peers. Lord Chandois' kindly face was beaming with delight, Sir Robert Catline and Mr. Gilbert Gerard were conversing quite excitedly: his own friends, Sir Henry Beddingfield and Lord Mordaunt, Lord Huntingdon and Sir John Williams, were openly expressing their intense satisfaction.

But for him, what did it all mean? An acquittal based on a lie, and that lie told by a woman to save him!

But a lie for all that, and one which he could not refute, without telling the whole truth to his judges and branding her publicly as a murderess and worse.

He, who had ever held his own honour, his pride, the cleanness of his whole existence as a fetish to be worshipped, now saw himself forced to barter all that which he held so sacred and gain his own life in exchange. How much more gladly would he have heard his death-sentence pronounced now by his friend's kind lips. Death—however ignominious—would have purified and exalted honour.

Mechanically he listened to Lord Chandois' speech, and mechanically he protested. The web was tightly woven around him, and he was powerless to tear it asunder.

"Robert Duke of Wessex and of Dorchester," said the Lord High Steward, "Earl of Launceston, Wexford, and Bridthorpe, Baron of Greystone, Ullesthorpe and Edbrooke, premier peer of England, the lords, your peers, have found you not guilty of this crime of murder."

"My lords," said Wessex in a final appeal, which he himself felt was a hopeless one, "I thank you from my heart, but I cannot accept this decision; it is based on a falsehood, the hysterical outpourings of a misguided heart, and ..."

But already the Lord High Steward had interrupted him.

"My lord Duke," he said, "the tale this lady hath at last spoken in open Court was one guessed at by all your friends; she hath not only followed the dictates of her conscience, but hath taken a heavy burden from the hearts of your triers, and one which would have saddened many of us, even to our graves. Had it been my terrible duty to pass death-sentence upon you, which had the lady not spoken I should have been bound to do, I myself would have felt akin to a murderer. We cannot but thank heaven that Lady Ursula's heart was touched at the eleventh hour, and that you were not allowed to sacrifice your honour and your life in so worthless a cause."

"But I cannot allow you to believe, nor you, my lords ..." further protested the Duke.

"Nay, my lord, we only believe one thing, and that is that Your Grace leaves this Court this day with the respect and admiration of all men in the land, with unsullied honour, and with stainless name. All else we are content shall remain a mystery betwixt Lady Ursula Glynde and her conscience."

"God save the Queen," added the Lord High Steward as he broke the white wand.

"And," adds Mr. Thomas Norton, "thus ended the trial of His Grace of Wessex and of Dorchester, on a charge of murder, treason, and felony. Surrounded by his friends, cheered by the mob, the Duke left Westminster Hall a free man, but as I watched his face, meseemed that I saw thereon such strange melancholy and a hue like that of death. He smiled to my lord Huntingdon and spoke long and earnestly with my lord Rich. He had mighty cause to be thankful to God and to

173

his friends for his acquittal, yet meseemed almost as if he rebelled against his happy fate, and I hereby bear witness that the blood of the Spanish envoy must still have clung to His Grace's hands. In just cause or in unjust no man shall take another's life wantonly, and I doubt not but His Grace's conscience will trouble him unto his death."

CHAPTER XXXVI

AFTERWARDS

Escorted throughout the journey home by His Eminence, Ursula had not uttered one word. She sat in the barge, gazing out along the river, her veil closely drawn over her head, lest prying eyes noted the expression on her face.

She was as one who had seen all that she held most dear dying before her eyes. She had made her sacrifice willingly, had offered up her fair name, her every feminine instinct of honour and modesty upon the altar of her love. She had by that sublime holocaust offered up to God a thanksgiving for two brief hours of happiness which she had enjoyed.

How far, far away those transient moments seemed now to be. That half-hour in the park of old Hampton Court, with the nightingale singing its sweet song as an accompaniment to the great hosanna which filled her heart. She closed her eyes, for her heart ached nigh to bursting when she remembered that first touch of his hand upon hers, the gay, merry words which fell from his lips, the passionate ardour which gleamed in his eyes.

Oh God! she had worshipped one of Thy creatures and found him less than human after all. The murmur of the river as the boat glided along recalled to her those few moments among the rushes, when a golden October sun was sinking slowly in the west, and the water-fowl were calling to their mates, while she leant back in a boat, lulled by the peace of that exquisite hour, rocked to blissful rest by the gentle motion of the river, and dreaming of heaven, for he sat opposite to her, and every look of his told her that he thought her fair.

Oh God! she had worshipped one of Thy creatures! How great is Thy vengeance now!

He was false to love! false to her!

All jealousy had died from her heart. Her pain now was because he was false. She had forgotten the other woman, she only remembered

174

him—that he did not love her, that he had accepted her sacrifice, and laughed bitterly, cruelly, when first she told her sublime lie for his sake.

At the Water Gate of the Palace the barge drew up and Ursula prepared to alight. She had spent the short moments of the transit between Westminster and Hampton Court in these heart-breaking daydreams. She hardly realized where she was and what she was doing. Once only, when first the cupolas of the Palace detached themselves from out the mist, she had felt such a desperate pain in her heart, that for a moment the wild hope came to her that God would be merciful and would allow her to die.

But when she alighted she suddenly became conscious that the Cardinal de Moreno was standing before her, his delicate white hand outstretched to help her to step ashore. She shrank away from him as from a viper who had stung her and might sting her again. Not understanding his attitude, nor the motives which had led him to suggest to her the lie that had saved Wessex, she yet knew by instinct that this purple-clad, benevolent person, this kindly and courteous diplomatist was a thing of evil which had first polluted and then killed her love.

His Eminence smiled—a kind, indulgent smile—when he saw the quick look of horror in the young girl's face, and he said very gently—

"Will you not allow me, my daughter, to accompany you to your apartments? The Queen, remember, hath confided you to my charge; I would wish to see you safely in Her Grace of Lincoln's care."

"Your Eminence does me too much honour," she said coldly. "I can find my way alone through the Water Gallery."

"Yet Her Majesty, meseems, will not allow her maids-of-honour to walk unattended in this part of the grounds," he added, with a slight touch of benevolent sarcasm.

"My comings and goings have ceased to interest Her Majesty," rejoined Ursula quietly, "and I am no longer of sufficient importance to require watching or to demand an escort."

"Well, as you will, my daughter. It is not for me to force my presence upon you, though, believe me, I would have wished to serve you."

He was about to beckon to his retinue, who had stood respectfully aside during this brief colloquy, when with a quick, wholly unexpected movement, the young girl placed her hand upon his arm and forced him once more to turn and face her.

"Your Eminence would wish to serve me?" she said, speaking rapidly and with a strange, peremptory ring in her voice.

"Can you doubt it, my child?" he replied urbanely.

"No," she said firmly, "for there is that between Your Eminence and me which, if known to the Queen of England, would for ever ruin your position in any court of Europe."

"You would find it difficult ..." he began, whilst a slight look—oh, a mere shade!—of fear seemed to creep into his eyes.

"Nay! I was not thinking of betraying Your Eminence, nor the trap which you set for me, into which I was full willing to fall. I merely mentioned the existence of this secret for the awakening of your own conscience and because I have need of a service from you."

"I will endeavour to fulfil your behests, my child."

"I desire three words with His Grace of Wessex this afternoon."

"My child ... !" he ejaculated, with still a tone of nervousness perceptible in his voice, and a trace of that newly awakened fear lurking in the anxious look which he cast upon her.

But she seemed quite self-possessed, and almost commanding as one who had the right to demand obedience. The Cardinal did not quite know how to read her character at this moment. There was no doubt that if she chose to betray the part which he had played in her voluntary self-immolation, there would be plenty of people at the English Court only too ready to believe her, or at any rate to seem to do so. The Queen of England herself would lend a willing ear to any tale which would release her from her promise, with a semblance of honour to herself. His Grace of Wessex stood fully exonerated now, and in the face of so much humiliation the Cardinal would find it impossible to demand a fresh trial, whilst Mary Tudor had probably already repented of her pledge to marry King Philip of Spain.

On the other hand, was it not dangerous to allow an interview to take place between Wessex and Ursula? In a flash the Cardinal reviewed the situation, and weighed all the consequences of the two courses thus opened before him—acquiescence and negation, and with his usual quickness of intellect he decided that acquiescence would be least dangerous. All he wanted was the time in which he could obtain the Queen's actual signature to her pledge. Once that was done, Mary Tudor would never go back on her royal sign-manual. In any case not much harm could be done in a brief interview. Both Wessex and Ursula were so far from guessing the truth, so ignorant of the tangled meshes of the intrigue in which they were still being held, that it would undoubtedly require the testimony of a third person at least, to bring daylight into the black shadows of the mystery.

Therefore His Eminence, after these few seconds of serious thought, resumed his kind, suave manner and, dismissing all fears from his mind, placed his services with alacrity at Lady Ursula's disposal.

"But I fear me," he added reflectively, "that you place too much reliance upon my humble powers. His Grace of Wessex is not like to listen to me, and meseems that you could more easily obtain an interview with him through your own influence, which just now should be boundless, if the Duke has any gratitude in his heart."

"Your Eminence seems to be the prime mover in this drama of puppets," rejoined Ursula drily, "and the Queen will put every obstacle in my way unless Your Eminence interferes."

"Your confidence honours me, my daughter; I will do my humble best beside Her Majesty, and you can do the rest. But this, on one condition."

"Name it."

"That you will have patience until to-morrow. His Grace arrives at the Palace to-night, Her Majesty will no doubt honour him specially; there may be festivities to-morrow afternoon. I think I can so contrive it that you have ten minutes alone then with His Grace."

She bent her head in acquiescence, and then stepped back so as to intimate to him that this interview was at an end.

"Be prudent, my daughter," he added, as he finally turned to go, "and remember that a sin is best atoned for by humility and silence."

"At what hour can I rely on Your Eminence's promise to-morrow?" she rejoined, calmly ignoring his urbane speech.

"In the early part of the afternoon, if God will grant me power."

"Your Eminence had best pray for that power then," she added finally.

The Cardinal took leave of her with his usual dignified benevolence. It did not suit him at present to appear to be taking notice of her thinly veiled threats. He did not think that she would actually betray him, even if she did talk to His Grace for a few moments, for to betray the lie would mean also to acknowledge her love and her jealousy, and proud Ursula Glynde would never suffer that humiliation.

The situation was delicate and difficult, more so perhaps than it had ever been, but the next few hours should see the Queen of England's signature at the bottom of a bond.

Thoughtfully His Eminence began walking along the Water Gallery, whilst Ursula quietly watched his purple robes gliding along the flagged corridor.

She too had gained her wish—to see and speak to Wessex. What would she say? and how would he reply? Vaguely she wondered if she would have the strength to show him the contempt which she felt for his cowardice, and inwardly prayed for the strength not to let him see how much she loved him still.

CHAPTER XXXVII

THE CARDINAL'S PUPPETS

His Eminence the Cardinal de Moreno knew well how to gauge the moods and tempers of the English people of his time. He had rightly guessed that the Duke of Wessex, whom but a few hours ago his countrymen were ready to condemn to a shameful death, would remain the hero of the hour, until the enthusiasm of his friends had once more cooled down to a more normal pitch.

Mary Tudor was deeply grateful to the Cardinal, for what she truly believed was a wonderful triumph of persuasion over the obstinacy of a guilty conscience. If in her innermost heart she bitterly resented the fact that Wessex owed his acquittal to outside influences rather than to the will of his Queen, she nevertheless was ready enough to acknowledge how completely His Eminence had succeeded, and how little ground she had for not keeping her share of the momentous compact which she had made with him.

"If Your Eminence is instrumental in saving His Grace from the block I will marry King Philip of Spain!"

That was her bond, and already the Cardinal had claimed its fulfilment. The Queen of England stood definitely pledged to give her hand to Philip II, King of Spain.

The Spanish alliance, so much dreaded by the patriotic faction of England, was all but an accomplished fact. Bitter disappointment reigned in the hearts of all those who had hoped to see an English peer upon the English throne. Yet all Wessex' friends were bound to admit that from the very moment when the Duke's acquittal suddenly roused all their dormant hopes, one look at his face had sufficed to tell them that those same hopes had been born but to die again. There stood a man, broken in health and spirits, tired of life, without buoyancy or youth, or that delightful vigour which had made the name of Wessex sound a note of gladness throughout the land.

Even as he stepped down from the bar and his adherents showered good wishes upon him, he looked twenty years older than he had done on that bright happy day a fortnight ago when, the cynosure of all eyes, the most brilliant ornament of that gorgeous court, he seemed to stand smiling on the steps of the throne, gently dallying with a crown.

Yet Mary Tudor, wilfully forgetting for the moment her pledge to the Spaniards, longing to enjoy these last few hours when she was still free, had showered smiles, fêtes, honours upon the man she loved, happy to feel his lips pressed upon her hand in loyalty and gratitude.

She had never inquired of him how much real truth there was in the story which Ursula Glynde had told in open court. Perhaps she did not care to know. She was weak enough—woman enough—to rejoice at the thought of her rival's complete humiliation. She was content to let the events of that fateful night remain completely wrapped in mystery. Vaguely she felt that in some sort of way the elucidation of it would not be altogether detrimental to Ursula Glynde, at the same time she knew that never now could the young girl, who had come between her and the man she loved, aspire to become Duchess of Wessex.

The scandal had been too great, and unless some unexpected and wonderful thing happened, which would signally clear Ursula's maiden fame, she would for ever remain under the ban of this mystery which had besmirched her good name.

Ursula had been quite right when she asserted with bitter sarcasm that His Eminence the Cardinal de Moreno seemed to be the prime mover in the game of puppets, which was now proceeding within the precincts of the Palace. With the royal signature appended to his bond, he felt that his position was now impregnable, and he moved about among the English lords and courtiers as a vice-regent would in the absence of a king.

The fact that a messenger from Scotland had arrived in the morning with news of the ambassadors to the Queen Regent, without any mention of either Lord Pembroke's or Lord Everingham's sudden departure from thence, had completely calmed any fears he still might have of the latter's too sudden reappearance at Hampton Court. In any case now he had still some days before him during which he could consolidate his success, by establishing direct intercourse between King Philip and the Queen of England. He hoped before many hours had elapsed to obtain from Mary Tudor an actual letter, writ in her own hand to her royal betrothed.

Thus secure in his invulnerable position, the Cardinal had thought it prudent as well as expedient to accede to Ursula's wishes, which seemed very like commands, and he had used his diplomatic skill to good purpose in persuading Mary Tudor to allow the interview between the young girl and His Grace.

At the same time His Eminence was sufficiently wary so to manipulate his puppets that the interview should be of the briefest, and in this he was like enough to succeed.

It was in order to celebrate the happy return of His Grace to Court that the Queen had, at his request, granted a free pardon to all those who were to be brought for trial on the same day as the Duke. Two o'clock in the afternoon of the day following this great event, had been fixed when all these poor people, vagrants and beggars mostly, one or two political prisoners, perhaps, were to thank His Grace for their freedom publicly in the grounds of the Palace.

The Cardinal, well aware of this, skilfully working too on the Queen's still restive jealousy, had suggested to Mary that Ursula Glynde should await the Duke of Wessex in the hall at fifteen minutes before the hour.

"A quarter of an hour, Your Majesty," he said insinuatingly, when first on that same morning he had broached the subject, "fifteen short minutes, during which the breach 'twixt His Grace and a disgraced maiden can but be irretrievably widened."

"Your Eminence seems to think that I desire a breach," retorted Mary with Tudor-like haughtiness.

"Far from me even to think such a thought," rejoined the Cardinal blandly; "but as a faithful servant of Your Majesty, soon to become a loyal subject when Your Grace is Queen of Spain, I hold the welfare of all those whom you deign to honour very much at heart.... And I was thinking of His Grace of Wessex."

"What of him, my lord?"

"The Duke is proud, Your Majesty; would it be well, think you, if a girl of Lady Ursula Glynde's reputation were to become Duchess of Wessex?"

"Think you she hath the desire?"

"Quien sabe?" he replied guardedly, "but an Your Majesty will trust my judgment, a brief interview with His Grace would soon scatter her hopes to the winds."

Thus did this astute diplomatist play upon every fibre of a woman's emotions. His calculations were made to a nicety—only the interview which Ursula had demanded and no more! This to pacify the young girl in case she became defiant, but the meeting itself just short enough to avoid any harm.

At twenty minutes before two, Ursula was bidden to the Great Hall by command of Her Majesty. The Duchess of Lincoln—tearful and kind—received her in the great window embrasure. Her motherly heart ached to see the bitter sorrow of the beautiful girl, who had been so full of vitality and merriment a brief fortnight ago.

With a strange instinct, which she herself could not have explained, Ursula had dressed herself all in white. A rich brocaded kirtle and shimmery silken paniers seemed to accentuate the dull pallor of her cheeks. Only her golden hair gave a brilliant note of colour and of life to this marble statue, who seemed only to exist through its blue magnetic eyes.

"The page has gone to bid His Grace of Wessex attend upon you here, my child," said the good old Duchess, as she took Ursula's cold hands in hers, and mechanically stroked them with her own kind, wrinkled palms.

"Think you he will come?" asked Ursula dully.

"I doubt not but he will, my dear. His Grace owes you his life."

"Yes?"

"But before he comes, my treasure," murmured the dear old soul, "I would have you know that I'll never believe aught, save that you are good and pure. Some day, perhaps, you will love me well enough to tell me the secret which is gnawing at your heart."

She paused, quite frightened at the expression of intense soul-agony which was suddenly apparent in every line of the wan young face.

Ursula bent her tall, graceful figure, and raising the gentle motherly hands to her hot lips she kissed them with passionate tenderness.

"In God's name, my dear, kind Duchess," she murmured, "do not speak soft words to me. The Holy Virgin has helped me to keep calm; I must not break down ... not now ... that he is coming."

Now there was the sound of firm footsteps crossing the chamber beyond. Ursula drew herself up, and for a moment a strange, scared expression came into her face, then one of intense, yet inexpressible tenderness.

Mutely she beckoned to the old Duchess, who, understanding this earnest appeal, withdrew without uttering another word.

The next moment the door at the further end of the hall was opened. A page loudly announced—

"His Grace the Duke of Wessex!"

And for the first time since the awful moment when alien intrigues had parted them, these two, who had so fondly loved, so deeply suffered, were alone, face to face at last.

CHAPTER XXXVIII

THE LAST FAREWELL

She saw in a moment how much older he looked, and quaintly wondered whether the black doublet and cloak caused him to seem so. Harry Plantagenet—happiest of dogs now that his master roamed about with him once more—walked with a proud step beside him.

She looked such a dainty picture, framed in the rich embrasure of the great window, her graceful figure with its crown of gold looking majestic and noble on the raised dais, ethereal and almost ghostlike, with its rich white draperies.

Just for one moment as Wessex entered the room the events of the last fortnight suddenly vanished from his memory. She was there before him, in that same soft gown of white, as she had stood that day, with a sheaf of roses in her arms—or were they marguerites?—and once more, as he had done then, he vaguely wondered what colour were her eyes. On his lips he seemed to feel again the savour of her passionate kiss, and once again to smell the perfume of her golden hair as for that one brief, heavenly minute she had lain next to his heart.

But reality—wanton, crude, and cruel—chased this brief, happy vision away with one cut of her swishing lash, and then brought before his eyes that same face and form, but with wild, restless eyes, bare neck and bosom, and with the Spaniard's hand resting masterfully on her shoulder. And Ursula, who had watched him keenly, saw the cold, contemptuous look in his eyes, the shudder which shook his powerful frame as he approached her, and she even seemed actually to be touching that stony barrier of wilful self-control, which he interposed between himself and her.

But the obeisance which he made to her was profound and full of cold respect.

"You desired to speak with me, lady?" he said. "My life, which you have deigned to save, is entirely at your service."

She had stepped down from the dais as he approached, calling upon every fibre within her, upon every power granted to a woman who loves to touch the heart of the loved one. Though she knew that for ever after, he and she would henceforth be parted, her heart had so yearned for him that vaguely she had begun to delude herself with the hope that after all only a great misunderstanding existed between him and her, and that before they spoke the last words of farewell their hands would meet just once again—only as friends—only as comrades perhaps—but closely, trustfully for all that.

It was solely in this hope that she had begged for an interview.

His coldness chilled her. Now that he was near her again, she once more became conscious of that bitter feeling of awful jealousy which had caused her the most exquisite heart-ache which a human being could be called upon to endure. Memory brought back to her the vision of another woman—an unknown creature whom he loved, to the destruction of his own soul and honour.

And with the advent of this memory the tender appeal died upon her lips, and she only said in a hard, callous voice—

"Is that all that Your Grace would say to me?"

"Nay, indeed," he replied with the same icy calm, "there is much I ought to say, is there not? I should tell you how grateful I am for my life, which I owe to you. And yet I cannot even find it in my heart to say 'thank you' for so worthless a gift."

"Does life then seem so bitter now that the woman you love has proved a wanton and a coward?" she retorted vehemently.

He looked at her, a little puzzled by her tone, then said quietly—

"Nay! the woman I loved has proved neither a wanton nor a coward ... only an illusion, a sweet dream of youth and innocence, which I, poor fool, mistook for reality."

There was such an infinity of sadness, of deception, and of life-enduring sorrow in his voice as he spoke that every motherly instinct, never far absent from a true woman's heart, was aroused in hers in an instant. She forgot her bitterness in the intensity of her desire to comfort him, and she said quite gently—

"You loved her very dearly, then?"

"I worshipped my dream, but 'tis gone."

"Already?" she asked, not understanding.

And he, not comprehending, replied—

"Nothing flies so quickly as an illusion when it is on the wing."

Then he added more lightly—

"But I pray you, do not think of that. I am grateful to you—very grateful. Your ladyship hath deigned to send for me. What do you desire of me? My name and protection are now at your service, and I am ready—whenever you wish it—to fulfil the promise our fathers made on our behalf."

She drew back as if a poisoned adder had stung her.

At first she had not realized what he meant to say; then the intention dawned upon her and the insult nearly knocked her down like a blow. She could hardly speak, her own words seemed to choke her; her rich young blood flew to her pallid cheeks and dyed them with the crimson hue of shame.

"You would ...?" she murmured faintly. "You thought that I ...? Oh! ..." she gasped in the infinity of her pain.

But like the wounded beast when first it sees its own hurt, so did this man now—gentle, artistic, fastidious though he was—suddenly feel every cruel instinct of the primitive savage rise within him at the thought of the great wrong which he believed this woman had done him. All the latent tenderness in his heart was crushed. Manlike, he only longed now to make her suffer one tithe of the agony which he had endured because of her treachery. He thought that she had played with him and fooled him in sheer wantonness, and he wished to crush her pride, her youth, her gaiety as she had broken his life and his honour.

He despised her for what she had done, and longed to let her see the full measure of his contempt. Glad that he had succeeded in hurting her, he tried to turn the blade within the wound.

"Nay, you need have no fear, lady," he said, "the wars in France will soon claim my presence, and the world will be quite ready to forgive to the Duchess of Wessex the sins of Lady Ursula Glynde, especially after a chance French arrow had made her free again."

But it was the very magnitude of the insult which restored to Ursula her self-possession, nor would she let him see now how deeply she was wounded. With her self-control, her dignity also returned to her, and she said with a coldness at least equal to his own—

"The world has naught to forgive me, as you know best, my lord."

"Nay! but I know that I must be grateful. By the mass! the story was well concocted, and I must congratulate you, fair Bacchante!" He laughed bitterly, ironically. "Your honour threatened! ... my timely interference! ... and I who feared for the moment you might make full confession."

"Confession of what? ... you are mad, my lord."

She had drawn nearer to him, and for the first time since the commencement of this terrible tragedy of errors, one corner of that veil of impenetrable mystery was lifted from before her eyes. She did not make even a remote guess at the truth as yet, but vaguely she became aware that she and this man whom she loved were at some deadly cross-purposes, were playing at some horrible hide-and-seek, wherein they were staking their life and happiness. There was something in his look which suddenly revealed to that unerring feminine instinct in her that his bitterness, his cruelty, his insults, had their rise in a heart overburdened with a hopeless passion. He, the most perfect gentleman, most elegant courtier of his time, did not even try to curb his tongue, when speaking to her, who had never wronged him, and who had nobly saved his life, when he must know that she had done it out of disinterested self-sacrifice.

Did he know that?

The question struck at her heart with sudden, overwhelming power. The look of him, his whole attitude, told her in a vague, undefinable, ununderstandable way that it was herself whom he loved, that he despised her for something she had not done, and yet that he spoke of her when he sighed after an illusion.

"Confession of what? You are mad, my lord!" she repeated wildly.

"Aye! mad!" he said bitterly, "mad when I feel the magic of your eyes stealing my honour away! ... mad, indeed! for with a fellow-creature's blood still warm upon that dainty hand, I long to fall on my knees and cover it with kisses."

His voice broke almost in a sob now that at last he had given utterance to that which had weighed on his soul all these days. He loathed her crime, yet loved her more passionately than before. Oh! eternal mystery of the heart of man!

"Blood on my hands?" she retorted violently. "You are mad, my lord ... mad, I say! A man's blood? ... Did you not then kill Don Miguel to save her whom you loved? ... did you not suffer disgrace, prepare for death, all because of her? ... Did I not lie for you, give up mine honour ... mine all for you? ... Is it I who am mad, my lord, or you?"

"Nay! an you will have it so, fair one," he replied, trying to steady his voice, which still was trembling, "'tis I am mad! I'll believe anything, doubt everything, mine eyes, mine ears ... the memory of you ... as I saw you that night.... I'll try to remember only that I owe you my life ... such as it is ... and let my senses be gladdened at the thought that you are beautiful."

Ursula watched him with wild, burning eyes. Was the truth

184

dawning at last? She, as the woman, was bent on knowing what lay hidden beneath the expression of this debasing passion. He, as the man, had fought a battle and lost; he loved her too madly, too completely to tear her out of his life. His passion had become base; he despised himself now more than he had ever despised her, but he could no longer battle against that overpowering desire to fold her once more to his heart, to forgive and forget all save her beauty and the magic of her presence.

But she, though loving as ardently as he, wanted the truth above all. Never would she have accepted this degrading passion, which would have left her for ever bruised and ashamed. She mustered up all her energy, all her presence of mind; it was her turn now to fight for happiness and for honour.

Who knows what destiny fate would have meted out to these two young people if only she had been left a free hand? Would she have brought them together or parted them finally and for ever? The fickle jade smiled upon them for a moment or two, then allowed a stronger hand to lead her away into bondage.

So accurately had the Cardinal de Moreno calculated his chance of final success that he himself was able to lead the Queen of England to the Great Hall for the approaching ceremony, at the very moment when Wessex and Ursula were on the point of understanding one another.

Ursula had just uttered an energetic and momentous—
"My lord! ..."

She had stepped away from him and was looking him fearlessly in the face, resolved to question and cross-question until she understood everything, when the door was suddenly opened and Mary Tudor appeared, escorted by some of her ladies, and accompanied by His Eminence the Spanish envoy.

It was the stroke of a relentless sword across the Gordian knot which she had sought to unravel. She had only just made up her mind to stake her all upon a final throw of the dice—an explanation with Wessex. He was still completely deceived. She could see that what she already more than guessed he had not even begun to suspect. The idea of a gigantic misunderstanding had not yet entered his brain; she would have brought it before him, made him understand.... And fate suddenly said, No!

Fate, or that cruel hand which pulled the strings that brought all puppets forward on this momentous stage? The Cardinal had darted a quick, anxious look on Wessex and then had smiled with satisfaction. Ursula caught both look and smile, and also that sudden hardening of the Cardinal's clever face, and knew that her last chance had gone.

Wessex had seemed relieved when the Queen entered, and Ursula knew that never again would she be allowed to see him alone, never again would she be able to speak to him undisturbed.

"Nothing flies more quickly than an illusion when it is on the wing!"

Nothing! ... save happiness ... when it begins to slip slowly away, and tired hands are too weak to retain it.

CHAPTER XXXIX

A FORLORN HOPE

The Great Hall had quickly filled with ladies and gentlemen. Mary Tudor had rapidly approached the dais, holding out one gracious hand to Wessex and vouchsafing but a cold, callous look to Ursula Glynde, who, like some young, wounded fawn, seemed to be standing at bay, facing this crowd of indifferent spectators who had literally come between her and her happiness.

It seemed as if Mary felt a cruel delight in bringing before the young girl's notice the hopelessness of her position, the irreparability of the breach which existed now between her and His Grace of Wessex.

The Queen's jealous eyes had already noted the cold salutation with which Wessex so readily left Ursula's side, in order to turn to the new-comers. His Grace was evidently glad to see the end of a painful interview, and Mary was too weak a woman not to rejoice at sight of the heartache which was expressed in Ursula's pallid face, and not to try to enhance the pain of the wound.

Therefore when Wessex respectfully kissed her hand she kept him close beside her, whispering tender words which she hoped her rival might hear.

"It seems like a beautiful dream, my lord," she said gently, "to see you once more at our Court. The ugly nightmare is over, and I am almost happy."

"I humbly thank Your Majesty," replied the Duke. "My whole life can henceforth be spent in expressing my gratitude for a graciousness, which I so little deserve."

"Nay! I pray you to put us to the test, my dear lord. My heart aches with the desire to grant your every whim."

"Then I beg of Your Majesty a command in France."

"You wish to leave me?" said Mary with tender reproach.

"I hope to save Calais for Your Majesty's crown."

"Ah, my lord! I have more need of friends just now than cities! Whilst you go to France your Queen will wed King Philip of Spain."

"I hope not, Your Majesty," he rejoined earnestly.

"The letter of acceptance for my royal master already bears Her Majesty's signature," here interposed the Cardinal blandly.

"Aye! I have pledged my royal word," added the Queen with a short sigh. "His Eminence hath served us well and ..."

She made an effort to steady her voice, and avoided meeting the anxious look which Wessex had cast upon her.

"But we will not mar the happiness of this joyous day," she continued after a while, speaking with enforced cheerfulness. "My Lord High Steward here would desire our confirmation of the free pardon granted in honour of it, to all who were awaiting trial."

"If Your Majesty will deign to append the royal signature," said Lord Chandois, who was fingering a large document.

"With pleasure, my lord. Are there many awaiting trial?"

Lord Chandois spread the document out on the table, and Mary Tudor prepared to sign it.

"A dozen or so, Your Majesty," explained the Lord High Steward; "men and women accused of roguery, witchcraft, and vagabondage."

With a bold stroke of her pen Mary added her royal name to the declaration of a free pardon.

"Let them be set free," she said, while Lord Chandois once more took possession of the paper. "It is our royal desire that these poor louts should thank His Grace of Wessex for their liberty, which they owe to him."

Once more she turned with her usual affectionate gentleness towards the Duke. Throughout this brief, seemingly indifferent scene, Ursula had stood by, like an image carved in stone.

Etiquette forbade her retirement until the Queen granted her leave, and Mary seemed desirous to keep her close at hand, as a contrast, perhaps, to the exuberant joy which prevailed among the other ladies and gentlemen there.

In the midst of all this merriment and gaiety, the hubbub of many voices, the pleasant laughter and lively banter, two silent figures stood out in strange contrast. Ursula, rigid, ghostlike in her white draperies, her young face expressive of hopeless despair and of deadly sorrow kept in check, lest indifferent eyes read its miserable tale; and Wessex, moving like an automaton among his friends, answering at random, trying with all his might to keep his thoughts from straying, his eyes from wandering, towards that beautiful statue, which now seemed like an exquisite carven monument of his own vanished happiness.

No one took much notice of Ursula Glynde, she was the disgraced maid-of-honour, the fallen star, scarce worth beholding, and she was glad of this isolation, which the selfishness of her former friends created around her. She looked for the last time upon the pomp and pageant of this glittering Court life; her very soul yearned for the peace and seclusion of austere convent walls. For the last time too she looked upon the man on whom she had lavished all the tenderness of her romantic temperament, whom she had set up on a pedestal of chivalry from which she felt loath even now to dethrone him.

She could see that he suffered and that he did not understand. The misunderstanding, which nothing could clear up now, still made a veil of darkness before his eyes. Her tender heart ached for him, her soul went out to him amidst all these people who laughed and chatted around her. For one brief moment their eyes met across a sea of indifferent faces—his lighted up with all the ardour of a never-fading passionate love, and hers spoke to him an eternal farewell.

CHAPTER XL

POOR MIRRAB

A few moments later the whole gay and giddy throng, like a flight of brilliantly hued butterflies, had fluttered out into the garden.

The wintry sun was bestowing its last cold kiss on the terraces and bosquets of the park. Beyond, the landscape—wrapped in a delicate haze of purple—was gently swooning in the arms of this November afternoon. All bird-song was silent, save the harsh chirrup of aggressive sparrows and the occasional brisk note of an irrepressible robin.

Close by the fountain a strange, dull group moved about somewhat listlessly—men and women, a dozen or so, in faded or ragged worsted mantles, shoes through which the flesh appeared, and mud-stained, bedraggled hose. Truly a wondrous spectacle on the delicately gravelled paths of the regal residence! a remarkable picture against the majestic background of carefully trimmed hedges, or conventional, well-cared-for shrubberies.

They looked indifferently round them, these poor shreds of society—the happy recipients of unlooked-for royal bounty. There were all sorts and conditions of men and women here, from the wrinkly-visaged hag who plied a precarious trade in illicit goods, to the hardened, sullen lout who made of Her Majesty's prisons an habitual home. A vagrant too here and there—one boy, barely in his teens, with pinched, haggard features, on which starvation had already scribbled her ugly name; a young girl, with bold, dark eyes, and coarse face masked with glaring cosmetics; and, far in the remote background, a huddled-up figure of a woman in tawdry finery, with a torn, bedraggled white dress ill concealing her naked shoulders, a few scraps of faded ivy-leaves still clinging to her bright-hued, matted hair.

They were astonished to find themselves here: made curious, senseless jokes about the marble basin, the trimmed shrubs, the fish in the ponds. The whole thing was a puzzle, and poverty and hunger had dulled all joy in them. They had been told that by the Queen's desire and at His Grace of Wessex' prayer, they were to be immune from punishment for their present offences, and a vague, dull wonder as to the meaning of this unexpected clemency filled their benighted souls. They were at liberty, inasmuch as no man-at-arms actually dogged their footsteps, but they felt the eyes of stern guardians, court lackeys, or park-keepers fixed unrelentingly upon them.

So they did not take special advantage of this so-called freedom, nor of the permission to roam about at will in Her Majesty's own garden. They clung together in one compact group, feeling a certain strength in this union of their common misery, and stared open-mouthed at what was nearest to them and required least effort of the brain to understand.

When at a given moment they saw a number of rich lords and ladies emerge upon the distant terrace, they felt wholly terrified, and would have beaten a quick and general retreat had not one of the royal servitors suddenly called upon them severally to listen.

"His Grace the Duke of Wessex is coming to speak with ye!" said this gorgeously apparelled personage, addressing the massed group of miserable humanity. "Stay ye all here, until His Grace arrives. Your good behaviour may prove for your own good."

And silently, dully, they obeyed. They ceased their aimless wanderings and concentrated their attention after a while upon a tall figure, dressed in rich black, which had detached itself from the brilliant groups on the terrace and was walking rapidly towards them.

So that was His Grace the Duke of Wessex. A serious-minded gentleman, surely, but lately accused of murder, and proved to be innocent. They could not yet see his face, only his tall, robust figure moving swiftly towards them. Strange that a noble duke, a rich and great lord, should wish to speak with them. The women, as if half ashamed of their ragged kirtles, had retreated behind the men. The latter had doffed their caps and were mechanically passing their thin fingers through their tangled hair.

Quite in the rear the female figure in the bedraggled white gown cowered against the edge of the marble basin.

Then gradually His Grace came nearer, the women ventured to peep at him over the shoulders of the men. His face looked kind, though very sad. The poor people gathered up their courage to face him bravely since he came all unattended amongst them. One or two of the younger lads ventured as he approached to utter an humble—

"God save His Grace of Wessex!"

"I thank you all," he said graciously. "And now, my friends, I'd have you believe that 'twas not idle curiosity which hath brought me here beside you. But yesterday I stood like you, accused of offence against the law of the land. I have known the sorrows and humiliations of a public trial. By Her Majesty's grace you have escaped that trouble this time, and I have it at heart that all of you who, like myself, have passed through prison doors should not again be tempted to break the dictates of your lawgivers. Hunger and sorrow are evil councillors. Though I know naught of the one I'd have you think sometimes of me as one who has tasted of the bitter cup of sorrow, and thus thinking, I'd have you pray to God for mercy on my soul and on that of one who is more sinful, more misguided than yourselves."

It was a strange little homily, thus delivered without any affectation by this high-born gentleman to his fellows in sorrow. They did not perhaps altogether understand him, but in his own quaint way he had appealed to a comradeship of misery, and the hearts of his hearers went out to him in a vague feeling of pity and reverence.

They had no need to call for "largesse," for with his own hand he was already distributing gold to those from whom he had asked prayers.

"God save Your Grace!" muttered men and women, as one by one their rough palms closed over the munificent donations.

The ladies and gentlemen on the terrace had all watched this little scene from afar. After a while the curiosity of all these gay idlers was still further aroused. Some of them wished to watch it a little more closely, and began slowly strolling down the terrace steps, towards the quaint group made up of all these miserable vagrants surrounding the imposing, sable-clad figure of the Duke.

The Queen herself, attracted by the novelty of the spectacle, and her heart ever yearning for the near presence of the man she still loved so dearly, turned her steps towards the marble basin, with His Eminence the Cardinal—ever a faithful attendant—by her side.

When Mary Tudor, closely followed by some of her ladies and courtiers, thus reached the scene where the little drama was being enacted, they saw His Grace standing somewhat irresolutely beside the huddled figure of a woman, whose tawdry drapings and matted, brilliant hair presented a strange contrast to the dull greys and browns of the other people around her.

"Wilt thou not hold thy hand out to me, wench," His Grace was saying somewhat impatiently. "I would fain help thee, as it hath pleased Heaven I should help thy companions in misfortune."

The servitor who had stood close by all this while, lest the people prove too importunate or troublesome, now came up to the woman, and, less benevolently inclined than His Grace, he caught hold of her, somewhat rudely, by the shoulder.

"Come, wench, wake up!" he said roughly, "think thou His Grace hath more time to waste on thee? She seems somewhat daft, so please Your Grace," added the man with a shrug of the shoulders, "and hath not spoken since her arrest."

"Who is she?"

"Some vagrant or worse, so please Your Grace. She was arrested a fortnight ago, and hath never been heard to utter one word."

"Wilt look up, wench?" said Wessex gently.

"I dare not," murmured the woman under her breath.

"Dare not? Why? I'll not harm thee."

"'Tis I have wronged thee so."

Wessex laughed lightly. Clearly the poor wretch was demented, but he would have liked to have put some money into her own hand, lest some unscrupulous person should rob her of his gift. Therefore he said as kindly as he could—

"I forgive thee gladly any wrong thou mayst have done me, and now wilt look at me in token that thou'rt no more afraid?"

There was silence for a few moments. The poor people, happy with the rich gifts in their hands, scared too by the presence of so many lords and ladies, among whom they, however, had not yet recognized the Queen, all retreated into the background, leaving Wessex and the strange woman alone and isolated from their own groups, his rich black doublet and fine mantle and plumes contrasting strangely against the dank, mud-bespattered white dress of the unfortunate vagrant.

What a quaint picture did they present—these two, whose destinies had been so closely knit. No one spoke, for every one felt that curious, unexplainable awe which falls upon the spirit of every man and woman when in the presence of an unfathomable mystery. And that mystery, every one felt it. The woman's voice had such a solemn ring in it when she said, "'Tis I have wronged thee so."

In the very midst of this awed silence the woman suddenly threw back her head, brushed the hair back from her face, and looked straight into the eyes of the Duke.

She was wan and pale with hunger, smears of mud spoilt the beauty of her features, but there was a look even now in that face which made Wessex recoil with horror. He did not utter a word, but gazed on as if a ghostly vision had suddenly appeared before him and was mocking him with its terrifying aspects.

Grinning monsters seemed to surround that girlish figure before him, pointing with claw-like fingers at the golden hair, the delicate straight nose, the childish mouth. As in a hellish panorama he suddenly saw the whole hideousness of the mistake which had wrecked his life's happiness, and half dazed, helpless, he gazed on as upon the risen spectre of his past.

A murmur close behind him broke the spell of this magic moment.

"So like the Lady Ursula," whispered one lady to her gallant.

But the name seemed to have reached the woman's dulled ears, and to have struck upon a sensitive fibre of her intellect.

"Ursula again!" she said vehemently, turning now to face the group of the elegant ladies who stood staring at her. "Why do you all plague me with that name? ... I am Mirrab, the soothsayer ... I've been taught to read the secrets of the stars, of the waters, the air, and the winds; I foretell the future and brew the elixir of life. Wessex saved my life! 'tis his!—I read in the stars that he was in great danger and came to warn him!"

Her apathy had totally deserted her now. She was gradually working herself up to a fever of excitement, talking more and more wildly, and letting her eyes roam restlessly on the brilliant groups before her—the ladies, the courtiers ... the Queen ....

Then they alighted upon the Cardinal de Moreno, who, pale to the lips, strove in vain to smother the growing agitation which had mastered him from the moment when he too first recognized Mirrab. Her passion at sight of him now turned to fury, and, pointing a vengeful finger at him, she shouted wildly—

"'Twas he who tricked and fooled me ... with smooth and lying tongue he cajoled me! ... he and his friend ... then they threatened to have me whipped ... if I did not depart in peace!"

Awed, horrified, every one listened. Mary Tudor herself hung upon the girl's lips. The Cardinal made a final effort to preserve his outward composure.

"A madwoman!" he murmured with a shrug of the shoulders. "Your Majesty would do well to retire; there's danger in the creature's eyes."

But Wessex was slowly coming to himself. His horror had vanished, leaving him calm before this terrible revelation. With the privilege ever accorded to him by the fond Queen, he now placed a firm hand upon her arm.

"In the name of Your Majesty's ever-present graciousness to me, I entreat you to listen to this woman," he said quietly. "Meseems that some dastardly trick hath been played upon us all."

The Cardinal tried to protest, but already Mary had acquiesced in Wessex' wish, with a nod of the head.

"I have naught to refuse you, my dear lord," she said sadly.

Vaguely she too had begun to guess the appalling riddle which had puzzled her for so long, and though her heart dimly felt that she was even now losing for ever the man whom she so ardently loved, she was too fearless a Queen, too much of a proud Tudor, not to see justice done in the face of so much treachery.

Then Wessex once more turned to Mirrab.

"Tell me, girl," he said with utmost calm and gentleness, lest he should scare again her poor, wandering wits, "tell me without any fear.... I am the Duke of Wessex and I saved thy life ... then thou hadst

192

the wish to warn me of some danger ... and came to the Palace here ... and my lord Cardinal tricked thee.... How?"

"I do not know," she said piteously, turning appealing, dog-like eyes upon him. "They dressed me up in fine clothes ... and then ... then ... when I saw thee ... and wished to speak with thee ... he ... the dark foreigner barred the way ... and I know not how it happened ..." she added, as a trembling suddenly seized her whole body, "he jeered at me ... and ... and I killed him!"

"'Twas thou, wench, who killed Don Miguel?" ejaculated the Queen, horrified. "Oh! ..."

But Wessex only bent his head and murmured in the intensity of his misery—

"Heaven above me! ... that I should have been so blind!"

"I killed him ..." repeated Mirrab with strange persistence, "I killed him ... he would not let me go to thee."

"A madwoman and a wanton," here protested the Cardinal with all the vigour at his command. "Surely Your Majesty will not believe this miserable creature's calumnies."

"No, my lord," replied Mary with quiet dignity, "we'll believe nothing until we have heard what Lady Ursula Glynde has to say. Lady Alicia," she added, turning to one of her maids-of-honour, "I pray you find the Lady Ursula. Tell her what has happened and bid her come to us."

In the meanwhile, however, Mirrab seemed to have become aware of the consequences of her vehement confession. Her wandering wits came slowly back to her. Terrified, she looked from one to the other of the grave faces which were fixed upon her.

"What will they do to me?" she murmured, turning appealing eyes on the one man whom she dared to trust.

"Nay, Mirrab, have no fear," said Wessex kindly, as he took her rough hands in his and tried to soothe her scared spirits with a gentle touch. "Once by chance I saved thy life ... but thou in return hast now restored to me that which is far dearer than life itself. I am eternally thy debtor, Mirrab, and I pledge thee the honour of Wessex that no harm shall come to thee ... for I myself will beg for thy pardon of Her Majesty on my knees."

"Nay, my lord," rejoined Mary Tudor earnestly, for he had turned to the Queen, prepared to proffer his request on his knees, "meseems a grievous wrong has been done to you—if unwittingly—by your Queen and country. Let the wench be free to pray to the Holy Virgin for her great sin. I myself will care for her, and she shall enter any convent she may choose, and be honoured there as if she had brought with her the richest dowry in the land. But," she added, turning to Lord Chandois, "I desire her to make full confession once more before you, my lord, in writing, and to swear to it and sign it with her name. You may go, wench," she said finally, turning to Mirrab, "your Queen has pardoned

193

you. May you be happy in the peace of the convent. We will never forget you, and ever see that joy shall always be in your life."

Slowly, as the Queen spoke, Mirrab sank upon her knees. It seemed to the poor girl as if God's angels were whispering words of comfort in her ear. Two servitors now came close to her, ready to lead her back to the Palace, there to place her under the charge of waiting-women until her confession had been duly written and sworn to.

But before she finally allowed herself to be led away she once more turned to Wessex.

"May I kiss thy hand?" she murmured gently.

He gave her his hand, and she covered it with kisses, and then she passed out of his life, ever remembered by him, ever comforted, happy in the peaceful and silent home which the Queen had so royally provided for her.

But this little interlude had roused the Cardinal's feverish impatience to boiling point. Already he had tortured his astute brain for some sort of issue out of this tangled web. He would not own a defeat so readily, certainly not before he made a final struggle to reassert the dignity of his position. He forced his face to express nothing but delicate irony, his eyes not to betray the slightest hint of fear.

"Truly, this is somewhat curious justice," he said, as Mirrab's strange figure disappeared behind a turn of the tall yew hedge, "surely Your Majesty will not condemn unheard? ..."

"No, my lord Cardinal, not unheard," retorted Mary Tudor haughtily. "We have seen strange things to-day, and can only guess at the terrible tangle which caused the first gentleman in England to take upon himself the burden of a heinous crime."

"And no doubt," added Wessex, "that His Eminence can solve the riddle of how a pure and noble girl was led into sacrificing her honour."

"Nay!" retorted the Cardinal bitingly, "His Grace of Wessex is more competent than I to solve the riddle of a woman's heart. The Lady Ursula has confessed; this trick of trying to disprove her tale," he added with cutting sarcasm, "was well thought on by the most chivalrous gentleman in England.... An it satisfies His Grace," he continued with a careless shrug of the shoulders, "surely I could never wish to dispel so pleasant an illusion."

Perhaps the Duke would have retorted in angry words, despite the unutterable contempt which he felt for this final poisoned shaft aimed at him by the Cardinal; but just then the groups which surrounded him, the Queen and His Eminence, parted, and Ursula Glynde stood before them all.

She still wore the white robes which became her so well, but now they only helped to enhance the brilliancy of her hair, the clear blue of her eyes, and a certain rosy flush, which lent to her delicate face a delicious air of childishness and innocence. She looked at no one,

194

though her eyes were actually fixed respectfully on the Queen, but her spirit seemed to have wandered off into a land of dreams.

"Your Majesty sent for me?" she said.

"Lady Alicia has told you?" rejoined the Queen.

Ursula closed her glorious eyes. A ray of intense joy seemed to illumine her whole face, lighting it with a radiance which surely had its origin in heaven. Then she slowly turned her head towards Wessex, and in one little word told him all that her soul contained.

"Everything!" she said.

Everything! that is to say, his sin, his mistrust of her, his great passionate love, and self-sacrifice for her. Everything! which meant her own love, her own devotion, her joy to find him true and chivalrous, her happiness and her hope.

Mary Tudor saw the look and its response from Wessex' eyes. She saw the end of the one dream which had filled her dull, rigid life and rendered it hopeful and bright. But she was above all a Tudor. She accepted the dictate of Fate, she bent the neck to a greater will than her own, and closed the book of her illusions, never to peruse its pages again. One last look at the man who had had the one passion of which her strange hard heart was capable, one short farewell to the vague hope, which until now would not be gainsaid.

From now and to the end of her days she would be Queen alone— the woman lay buried amongst the autumn leaves which strewed the walks of old Hampton Court Palace.

As Queen now she once more turned to Ursula. Justice in her demanded that every wrong should be righted, every misdoer punished.

"Child," she said quietly, "it was not you then who was with Don Miguel?"

"No, Your Majesty," replied Ursula, returning to earth at sound of the Queen's kindly voice, "Lady Alicia tells me that a girl ... a poor, sad girl, was in face so like to me ... that His Grace must have been mistaken ... and ..."

"But, child ... then why have told a lie? ..."

"His Eminence told me what to say before the Court, and promised His Grace would be saved by it."

Her voice dropped to so low a murmur that no one heard it but the Queen ... and Wessex.

"I did it to save him!"

"A lie, Your Majesty," protested the Cardinal.

"The truth!" protested Ursula loudly. "I pray Your Majesty to look on me and him and see on whose face is writ the word—fear."

Almost as if in obedience to Ursula's words Mary Tudor turned and faced the Spanish Cardinal. He tried to meet her look boldly. Even in defeat there was a certain grandeur in this man.

He had staked and lost his own position, his future career, his hopes of a greater destiny, but he had succeeded in his schemes. He knew Mary Tudor well enough to rejoice in this—that she would never now break her word to Philip, even though she let the flood of her royal wrath fall full heavily upon him.

"Go back, my lord, to your royal master," said Queen Mary with lofty contempt. "My word is my bond, and my pledge to him is sacred; but tell him, an he wishes to win the heart of the Queen of England, he must send an honest man to woo her."

Then without another glance at him, without looking to see if he followed her or not, she beckoned to her ladies and gentlemen, her attendants and her courtiers, and, without once turning her royal head towards the spot where had died her happiness, she walked firmly in the direction of her Palace.

CHAPTER XLI

THE END

And now every one had gone.

The wintry sun was already sinking towards the west, faint purple shadows wrapped the alleys and bosquets of the park in dim and ghostly arms.

The last call of a belated robin broke the silence of the gathering dusk, then it too was silenced, and only the "hush—sh—sh—sh" of fallen leaves on the gravelled path murmured a soft accompaniment to the music of the night.

A man and a woman were alone beside the marble basin, face to face, eye to eye, yet finding not one word to say. Both had so much to atone for, so much to forgive, that mere words were but the poor expression of all that filled their hearts.

The moments sped on—a few brief seconds or an eternity, who can say which?

The shadows merged one in the other. Far away the river murmured gently.

Now Wessex had sunk on his knees, and she bent down to him.

All the birds had gone to rest; one by one, pale winter stars peeped down upon the gorgeous Palace, the majestic pile which had seen so many glories, hidden so many miseries, one by one they peeped down on the silent park, the mysterious river, the ghostly outlines of walls and cupolas.

But beside the marble basin two human hearts had found one another, soul had gone out to soul at last, and Ursula lay once more in the arms of her future lord.